THE BEST LAID PLANS

BIRTH OF THE STARCLAN

Starclan Book II

by

James Warren McAllister

Cover design: James Warren McAllister

Titles and Lettering: Robyn Dickson

For Joel Wayne McAllister

"In space, things can happen very quickly, or very, very slowly. Either way, they can happen despite our best efforts to alter or avoid them."
Jock MacAlister

"It is by no means enough that an officer should be capable. He should be as well a gentleman of liberal education, refined manners, punctilious courtesy, and the nicest sense of personal honor. No meritorious act of a subordinate should escape his attention, even if the reward be only one word of approval. Conversely, he should not be blind to a single fault in any subordinate."
Attributed to John Paul Jones, 1775

Table Of Contents

Prologue

Prologue

Large Survey Vessel USF Sagan,
Star System 44G92216
Standard Earth Date July 21 3803

"Captain, I have an anomaly!" Senior Sensor Officer Ellie Joslyn exclaimed as obnoxious alarms fulfilled their purpose by agitating everyone on the bridge.

The Large Survey Vessel USF Sagan was following standard approach procedure for entering unexplored star systems, running in Stealth Mode Alpha. The four kilometer long exploration vessel emitted no energy, and moved with silent invisibility through the outer reaches of the star system designated 44G92216. The ship was traveling under momentum built up well outside the system. Now fourteen Astronomical Units, or AUs, out from the bright yellow star, the dull charcoal colored Sagan coasted at 0.3 effective light-speed.

The primary exploration vessel class of the USF, the Sagan was a Magellan class vessel based upon the Excalibur Heavy Cruiser design. While the streamlined dumbbell shaped, starship shared all the stealth and defensive capabilities of her military cousin, the Sagan was modestly armed with only four twin heavy rail gun turrets and two GravTorp Tubes as offensive firepower, along with two hangers for the one Wildcat fighter squadron and several transport and utility vessels used for exploration. Military presence was limited to one company of Marines. The extra space and power was used for an increased scientific crew along with an extensive sensor and communications array.

"Let's have it, Miss Joslyn!" Captain Howard Sloan prodded, successfully hiding his nervous apprehension from his crew. No USF exploration vessel had ever contacted any evidence of an alien life form, let alone an actual live alien.

"Only visual, sir. And that is, well, weird!" The young blonde Sensor Officer could not keep the excitement and nervous tension she felt out of her voice. This could only mean one thing, she thought; Contact!

"On screen."

"Aye-aye, sir"

The huge viscreen display at the front of the bridge had been displaying a real-scale view of the star system before them. Now it quickly zoomed in to the third planet from the star. The advanced gravity optics bent the available light to give a miraculous view of incredible detail.

"Opinion, Miss Joslyn?"

"It's twelve AUs away sir. It's moving towards us, and fast. And, it's big. REAL big." Joslyn excitedly reported.

"Crew; this is the Captain: Execute Contact Protocol Alpha" Sloan announced throughout the ship. "How big is it, Johnson?" Immediately wishing he had phrased that differently when he heard Joslyn's combination giggle/whisper, "Told you that size matters!" directed at Sensor Chief Barry Johnson, seated at the adjacent station. Johnson rolled his eyes and nodded towards the Captain. A slight grin had crept onto the Captain's face as he relaxed just a little.

"Estimated diameter is……180 Kilometers, sir." Joslyn's awed voice nearly a whisper at the thought of those intimidating dimensions.

"ETA?" Before Joslyn could answer, the Captain Sloan added, "Can we get a better picture on it?"

"That is a true rendering, sir; it really does shimmer like that! ETA, is, um, now, sir. It's *here*!" she gasped.

The object stopped 200 Km from the Sagan, perfectly matching her speed and vector. A light grey sphere, it shimmered as if seen through very hot air rising off of sun-baked asphalt.

"Part of the ship has come into focus, sir. Like something underwater breaking the surface!"

"Energy emissions; it's scanning us, sir!" Sensor Officer Passives Johnson exclaimed.

"Capta…." Joslyn's shout began and died as a very bright, red light flashed from the surface of the object.

The standard procedure for exploring an uncharted system was to drop a Stealth Comm Recon Drone outside the system. And Captain Sloan always followed procedure; the Mk 12 SCRD he had dropped dutifully recorded the huge ship and its 1,200-member crew evaporate into an expanding cloud of glowing plasma.

After six weeks of quiet sensors, the probe left for home.

Chapter One

USF Excalibur
Between Perseus and Orion
Standard Earth Date December 6 3811

Big, fat, and happy.

That was the attitude of USF Excalibur as she cruised home. The five kilometer long, pearl grey starship was officially designated a Heavy Cruiser, but the implication in that type was that there existed larger ships in the fleet. The reality was that the thirty kilometer long Battleships and twenty kilometer long Battle Cruisers had been mothballed near Alpha Centauri shortly after Excalibur's launch over 225 years ago.

Homeward bound, the glistening fleet flagship had every reason to cruise big, fat, and happy; accompanied by sister ships Enterprise and Edinburgh, as well the light cruisers Brooklyn, Prince Eugen, Constellation, Tiger, Sheffield, Bonhomme Richard, Richelieu, Nagaya, and Olympia; the frigates John Paul Jones, The Sullivans, De Gaul, Odysseus, Hawk, Tiger, Monitor, Suvorov, Ural, Shinano, Hiru, Littorio, and Sao Paulo; the destroyers Erie, Columbus, Hudson, Sommers, Lehigh, Onondaga, Casco, Havoc, Hull, Daring, Tribal, Fubuki, Titan, Phobos, Luna, and Argos; and the fleet support vessels Mars, Venus, Jupiter, and Saturn, Excalibur was the Flag Ship of the most powerful fleet man had ever seen assembled in this quarter of the galaxy.

Old as the Excalibur was, she was really just a teenager; she had been built to serve for over a thousand years. Strange to look at, the huge ship gleamed in a gloss pearl grey finish that could instantly allow the ship to become effectively transparent to any type of known energy. She had no obvious bow or stern, looking most like a streamlined dumbbell. One kilometer from each "end" of the ship were the propulsion modules; circling the ship, each had three huge Gravitic Drive Units, which could rotate around the hull as well as swivel on their mountings. The result was that the Excalibur could push all of its main thrust in any direction nearly instantly, giving the huge ship unsurpassed maneuverability for a spacecraft of any size.

Formed gravity screens kept out any radiation or interstellar particles when the ship traveled at high velocity, as well as any projectile weapons, from ionized particle beams, plasma blasts, missiles and torpedoes to the largest Kinetic Energy Projectiles. The Photon Screen that made the ship disappear also protects the ship from energy weapons of every known type. Small close in kinetic projectile, focused energy beams, and missile batteries defend against anything penetrating the outer defensive layers. And the hull is covered with composite gravity-compressed armor over twenty meters thick.

Excalibur is also a sharp edged sword. On each end of the ship, outboard of the two propulsion modules, heavy railgun turrets ring the hull.

Heavy Phase Adjustable Beam turrets and Heavy Pulse Laser Grids supplement the heavy rail guns.

On each of the "ends" of the ship, Multi Launch Missile Grids alternate around the hull with GravTorp Tubes. In between the propulsion modules, the hull carried more MLM Grids and GT Tubes.

Each end of Excalibur carries her main punch; the muzzles of triple two-kilometer long Ultra-Velocity Heavy Rail Cannon, each firing a 60,000-ton solid, gravity-compressed projectile the size of a locomotive engine at near light speeds.   Sensors and communication arrays dotted the hull, giving a redundancy measured in the dozens.

In the center of the ship are the huge flight decks, two on each side. The Excalibur carries three hundred Wildcat class fighters, ninety-six Devastator class attack plus, three marine transport Wings, six patrol craft/gunboats, and assorted ship's boats.

Between the ship's crew, 5,000 marines, and the Combined Air Force's pilots and support, the Excalibur carried nearly 14,000 souls on board.

No wars had been fought over the last 350 years, only sporadic police actions against pirates and a few would-be despots; humanity had only had two encounters with other space faring species in the last four centuries.

The first encounter had nearly wiped out mankind. Barely able to reach the outer edge of their own solar system, the settlements of humanity were invaded by an alien race of bird-like terrors. Four feet tall, covered with a light, downy coat of feathers, the unnamed invaders managed to conquer Mars, Moon Base Armstrong, Australia, North and South America before the various factions of humanity managed to work together and destroy the invaders, but not until most of Brazil was under the Atlantic Ocean. While the invasion and the loss of billions had provided the urgency to unite the race under the United Space States of Man, the expected follow up attack never came. In the centuries that followed, man never found any other sign of the Birds as he settled over a quarter of the Milky Way.

The second encounter of a space faring species came nearly a century after the invasion of the birds. The newly formed Space Force was dismantling the defenses placed after the invasion as a cost cutting measure. The Bugs came when only one Turret was left, waiting to be decommissioned. That Turret saved man from extinction.

The Bugs were not insects, but one could think of little else to describe them if you saw one. Looking like a nerdy adolescent's idea for a homemade cockroach Halloween costume, the Bugs were centuries ahead of man in technological development, except for the two areas of stealth and gravity. Man had learned to control gravity in many ways, and through this to nearly control the fabric of physical space itself.

Asteroid Defense Station 1437 was the last active ADS, and was scheduled to stand down in two months when the Bugs arrived. Known as 'Turrets", an ADS was actually an effectively invisible, stealthy system of hollowed out asteroids forming a powerful sensor and weapons array, covering a huge volume of space. The Turrets were placed at strategically important gravitational points around the solar system. The purpose of the ADS was to alert Earth of any extraterrestrial contacts, and to delay the progress of those contacts as long as possible to give the United Space Force adequate time to respond. Using the gravity fields and beams in ways never thought of, the young commander of the ADS, lieutenant Jock MacAlister, managed to capture a Bug scout ship and discover many of technological secrets it held. When the Bugs invaded 40 years later, Space Force was ready.

Using the gravity-driven faster than light drive invented by Jock MacAlister, and adapting Bug technology, Earth created a force armed specifically to defeat the Bugs. The re-commissioned Turrets and a powerful United Space Force Fleet wiped out The Bugs invasion armada. The Fleet then raced back to the home world of The Bugs, and wiped them out.

Every last one of them.

Research into what was left speculated, on very shaky evidence, that the Bugs had wiped out the Birds at the same time as the Birds invaded Earth. No other evidence of any intelligent life or any civilization has been found in the three centuries of exploration since.

In the centuries that followed the defeat of the Bugs, the lack of external threats eroded the sense of purpose for the men in Space Force. Constant threats of budget cuts, stemmed only by occasional outbreaks of pirating and the rare would-be dictator, gradually changed the Space Force into a bureaucratic organization which focused more on keeping its budget intact than maintaining readiness for conflict. It remained this way for a very long time.

This trip was much more than the usual end of a scheduled 3-year patrol cruise deployment. The unprecedented assemblage of half of the fleet of mankind for the homeward bound leg of the trip was a tribute to just one man, Admiral Angus MacAlister.

Over the last twenty-five years, the admiral had remade the Space Force, transforming a stagnant swamp of slogging, apathetic and disinterested star sailors into a proud, professional, and deadly efficient fighting force. Space Force had been a joke, populated by officers thinking more like grimy, grafting bureaucrats than leaders of warriors until Angus MacAlister, descendant of Jock, became the youngest Admiral of the Fleet in history. The technical refurbishment of the ships had been the easy part. Even the lobbying for funds was nothing compared to the remaking of the Space Force culture. His refinements to the ancient military practice of inspection had been the key to this transformation, as his methods and frequency of inspections not only monitored the performance of his crew but also taught and reinforced the expectations he placed upon that performance. That had taken a lot of energy, a lot of persistence, and had tested his convictions to the core.

Now 55, The Admiral had seemingly instantaneously and singlehandedly transformed Space Force into The United Star Force, the proud professional force respected throughout human space. He would often tell anyone who would listen that he just pointed out the direction; that the officers and sailors drove The United Star Force back through respectability and onto an unprecedented level of military professionalism. Pirate uprisings that had taken years to quell in the past were dealt with in days or weeks; the profession of "pirate" had become dangerous to one's health.

Regular patrols of The Colonies that once were dreaded by worlds as bringing a plague of drunken, vandalizing hoodlums in uniform, now were anticipated civic events cherished by every world. The mere presence of a United Star Force Sailor walking down the street was said to drop a city's crime rate by 90%; a USF ship was said to do the same for the entire star system. Political organizations clamored for The Admiral's attention, begging him to run for Senator under their banner, some even offering a run for Chancellor. The Admiral politely declined all offers. He had no interest in political maneuvering. He had fulfilled his mission of service to his Fleet, now it was time for another, more important assignment.

In two weeks, when the Fleet arrived at Earth, the man known to a quarter of the galaxy simply as "The Admiral" would officially retire at a great party at the Lunar Grand Ballroom Among The Stars. And then his second career would begin.

Such were the plans they had made.

Chapter Two

Frontlines
The Battle of Skunk City
North America
Standard Earth Date July 14 3764

The bright July sun relentlessly beat down on the two soldiers squinting through deadly serious expressions as they crouched behind their makeshift barricade, pointing their bright yellow and orange M-87 pulse rifles in the general direction of The Enemy. They had known each other most of their young lives, and each knew he could depend on the other no matter what.

"Do you see any Birds or Bugs?" Vance Anderson asked, squinting out over the battlefield.

"Nah, they're hiding. Sneaking up on us. Waiting for the right time to rush our position, I'll bet! Who would have thought they had survived in secret, building up their forces so they could join together against us!"

A projectile flew into their foxhole from an unexpected direction, glancing off of the side of Vance's plastic helmet. "Ow!" the smaller soldier yelled as he began crying from the shock and pain.

"Hey, dammit, what are you doing? You could have hurt him!" eight-year-old Angus MacAlister screamed as his friend cried next to him.

"So what!" the much bigger bully laughed as his friend fired another rock at the boys.

"This is what!" Angus yelled as he ran at the rock thrower and hit him twice with balled up fists, then pushed him to the ground. Turning to the second bully, Angus shoved him down also as he yelled, "He's a bleeder! You could have killed him". Under the assault from the determined eight year old, the two ten year olds took off like roaches in a spotlight.

"Wow, you beat up two ten year olds by your self!" Vance exclaimed excitedly as he wiped away his tears.

"It's not right to throw rocks at people!" Angus growled as only a very angry eight year old can.

****

Onondaga Hill
Overlooking Syracuse, New York

"Mom, we need more chips and drinks!"

"Enjoying your graduation party, sweetie? A shame Bob couldn't be here."

"Yeah, well…thanks for letting me have it, mom!" Cindy said as she gave her mother a quick peck on the cheek.

"Hi, Mrs. Grabelle! Hey, Cindy, do you need help bringing the stuff out?"

"No, I've got it, Angus. Thanks for asking, though" Cindy replied through batting eyelashes.

"Cindy, are you flirting with the MacAlister boy?"

"Um, no……" Her red face betrayed her fib.

"Then why are you blushing? Oh, well, never mind, he *is* a handsome one!"

"Mom, he's going out with Gina, he's going into Space Force soon, and I'm going out with Bob and I'm going into politics or music."

"Well, none of those things last forever, dear. Things change some times."

"MOM!" a blushing Cindy exclaimed as she turned and carried the drinks outside.

Mrs. Grabelle shot a grin to her husband. "What?" he answered.

As she leaned in and kissed her husband's cheek, she whispered, "She'll marry that boy someday."

"Women!" her husband muttered, shaking his head as he muttered to himself under his breath, "I'd better start saving for a wedding; she is *never* wrong when she gets *that* look!" shaking his head.

****

Luigi's Restaurante
The Valley, Syracuse, NY
Standard Earth Date August 1 3774

The pretty young woman's jet-black hair made a striking vision against the bright red vinyl upholstery of the small booth. A large, athletic young man knelt beside her seat.

"Gina Fonteyn, will you, um, m-m,….uh…"

"Oh, Angus, don't! STOP! I'm sorry. I can't!" Gina's eyes were wide with fear. "I mean, I love you, Angus. You are the most decent, kind, honest person I've ever known. But I've always wanted to write, to be a journalist. This is a big break, a full journalism scholarship. And, you're going off into space and,... stuff......" her voice trailed of as she fought back the sobs boiling within her.

"Gina, please! I can't think of being without you! I'll apply to State, we can go together. I can be there next year"

"You know that won't work. Angus, you need the stars as much as I need to write. I, Oh, GOD! I, I have to go. Good bye, Angus."

The heartbroken olive-skinned beauty ran, tears streaming down her face, out of the restaurant, leaving the young man with his head in his hands, sobbing on one knee in the aisle.

"Gina. Oh. God. Gina"

****

USF Excalibur
Between Perseus and Orion
Standard Earth Date December 6 3811

Admiral Angus MacAlister walked through Reactor Station 6, a half step behind Commodore Will Gridley, who was a half step behind Fleet Chief Martin Wells. Commodore Gridley was the Excalibur's Captain, and also the highest-ranking officer besides The Admiral in the fleet. In just a few days, shortly after The Admiral retired, Gridley would most likely become the next Admiral of The Fleet. Wells was the highest-ranking non-com ever to serve in The United Star Force.

The group stopped by a huge sailor squeezing his six-foot, ten-inch frame around the containment wall. The sailor pulled his mop up straight against his side and came to attention as he spotted the group, snapping a salute that seemed too perfect for his rough, scarred face.

"At ease, Dave." The Admiral said as he returned the salute.

"Aye-aye, Admiral."

"Mr. Ellis, these hallways; are they your doing?" Captain Gridley barked.

"Yes, sir! Clean enough for my Mama to eat from, as you taught me, sir!"

"Good job, Dave. As usual. Keep it up."

"Aye, Captain! Will do. Oh, and Admiral, sir?"

"Yes, Dave?"

"Best wishes on your retirement, sir. We'll all miss you."

"I'll miss the crew as well. And you, too, Dave. Are you OK, Sailor?" the Admiral asked, noticing the sailor rubbing his right shoulder. Angus noticed a few small bloodstains on the sailor's tee shirt, in a roughly circular pattern.

8

"Just a little sore, sir. We all, well, a bunch of us got new tattoos last night, Admiral."

"Suitable for mixed company, I hope, Dave?"

Dave looked at the Chief, who was subtly shaking his head 'no'.

"Don't worry, sir, we will always keep you proud of Excalibur and her crew!"

"Keep Captain Gridley proud, Dave. You've already made me the proudest of all sailors to have been able to serve this crew, this fleet. Carry on, Sailor!" the Admiral grinned as he saluted.

"Aye-aye, Sir!" Dave said as he snapped off a very sharp salute in response.

The Admiral had been grooming Gridley for this for 2 years. This inspection tour of Gravity Warp Generator Six was a repeat of thousands of inspections The Admiral had used to change the culture of the fleet, even though it had been some time since he had conducted one himself. The Admiral, and the Captain as well, knew the names of every sailor on the ship. He used them to train new captains, lieutenants, ensigns, and chiefs. If fact, every moment The Admiral spent near any United Star Force Sailor he naturally thought of as a mentoring moment. These inspections had been the keystone to his methods. And, it had worked; *every* Sailor in this fleet *knew* he had The Admiral as a personal mentor.

Normally, he would mention every detail on his list, and he had a list for every section of every ship in the fleet, cheerfully complimenting the appropriate sailor for every single item that was correct, right down to the shine on his shoes and the direction he hung his dog tags. Each item requiring improvement had the correct behavior clearly identified along with the reason for its importance. It made for a rather long inspection sometimes, but the repeat inspections always got shorter. The lists he used were made available to the crew and officers. When mentoring new command staff, he told them three things only: always do your homework, what gets watched gets done, and what you mention becomes important. The rest of his mentoring was learning by observing, then doing.

****

Yankee Stadium
The Bronx, New York
Standard Earth Date November 12 3778

"Damn, damn, DAMN!"

"Crap call! That receiver pushed off! CRAP!"

"STOW IT!" The huge baritone voice immediately silenced the whiners. "Huddle-up." The team gathered around as the shadow of their Captain, a huge fullback, number 44, seemed to cover half of Yankee Stadium.

The coach's eyes met his Captain's. They held for exactly three seconds, and then the coach gave one nod as he pulled his staff back.

"I do NOT like to lose. Ready?!" the Captain growled. *What had Coach told him? Oh, yeah; sometimes, the right spark can make despair erupt into determination.*

"FORTITER!" the shouted response rolled across the stadium. A stadium that had been suddenly draped in silence after the score.

"OK. So we're down by four with three minutes left. This is the last game any of us are ever gonna play, right here, right now. I will NOT allow us to lose it. First, we need a good return. Clark, you WILL get that ball out past the 35."

"Aye-aye, consider it done, Cap!"

"Charlie, We need you to get open."

"I hear ya, Cap, but I just can't shake that guy. I've done every trick I know, but he's so damn fast I can't get any daylight."

Angus grabbed the slim wide receiver's jersey and pulled him so close their helmets clanged. "Charlie, we do thirty-five fifty-yard sprints after every practice. Has anyone EVER been able to finish with you?"

"Now, Cap, you know, after about a dozen, anyone trying to stay with me just seems ta fall down!"

"THAT'S how we're gonna win this game!"

Angus released Charlie and called the offense together; OK, you guys. You wanna be undefeated?"

"Ooh-RAH!" came a shout from one of the Marine linemen, and was instantly echoed by the team.

"You remember how we beat Army?"

"Runs. Right up the middle. Eight, ten, twelve yards a play, no huddles, no stopping. sixty yards in three minutes, Harlow kicks the winning field goal. But, these guys KNOW that, they'll be expecting it!"

"Well, here's our plan for THAT."

The kickoff came to Clark seven yards deep in the end zone. The small but fast return man exploded to his left, bouncing off one would-be tackler, spinning out of the grasp of one after another, not stopping until six defenders dragged him down just over the fifty-yard line.

USFA's offense was on the line without huddling, pressuring the officials to spot the ball quickly. The first play ran the fullback left for eight yards, despite the three linebackers assigned to shadow him. From there on out, yards became tougher and tougher as the clock ran down. The big fullback seemed to TRY to run time off the clock by dragging multiple defenders for extra inches, rather than go down to preserve precious seconds. The defenders, tired from the pace, trying themselves to speed the end of the game, took longer and longer to get back up. On every play Charlie would sprint straight down field as fast as he could, dragging the cornerback thirty yards or more downfield, then sprint back at the whistle so the cornerback had to keep up. Now, with twenty-two seconds left and the ball on the twenty-yard line, Charlie listened as he busted it back to line up again; when he heard the faint groan, and a lot of huffing behind him, he thought, "Now, you're mine, sucka."

Charlie looked over at Kowalski. Turning his helmet so only his team could see, Charlie winked. Kowalski's head nodded ever so slightly. Stepping under center, Kowalski turned to look at his fullback, gave him the wink.

"My god!" Flashed through the quarterback's mind as he saw the blood flowing down from the fullback's broken nose, the six-inch long crack running across the front of his helmet, the way the steel facemask was caved in on the right side. Jerry watched his Captain's left arm hanging with an unnatural limpness as the big fullback took his stance. For a moment he thought of calling an injury time-out, but then he caught the glare from those eyes.

"I do NOT like to lose." The big fullback's grunt roared across the field. The slight grin on his face came from seeing the tip of Kowalski's tongue hanging out of the right corner of his mouth. He'll bite that off some day, Angus thought. He knew Jerry would make the play; he *never* failed when that tongue came out.

"Fortiter!" signaled the Kowalski from under center.

"FORTITER!" echoed the rest of the team.

Kowalski felt the hairs on the back of his neck rise as he turned back and faced the defense; *This. WILL. Work!* he thought. He heard it then; a faint murmur he couldn't quite hear, then building as the entire stadium rocked under the explosive chants from the crowd; "ANGUS! ANGUS! ANGUS!"

A confident grin crept onto Kowalski's face as he moved under center.

"HUT-HUT!"

Adamy snapped the ball on the anticipation of the second 'hut', giving his line that split-second's advantage. Kowalski took the ball and turned to offer it to 44 as he had on each of the last eleven plays. Charlie

11

took four hard steps as if he was going to sprint straight ahead yet one more time, then stopped and turned to face Kowalski. The cornerback, fatigued muscles operating more on the conditioned responses from the last eleven plays, screamed as he tried to make them stop and change direction as he scrambled, slipping once at the unexpected move, recovered and ran up to cover Charlie. Except, Charlie wasn't there. He had sprinted again and was on a post to the center of the end zone, the area vacated by the safety who had rushed up to stop that tank of a fullback, number 44. Charlie heard him cry "damn!" and thought, *I got this, just catch the damn ball!*

Jerry Kowalski pulled the ball back from 44 at the last second and spun to his left, running away from the sound of nineteen sets of shoulder pads and helmets crashing into each other, but mostly into the big fullback. After two steps he stopped and floated the ball out to the goal line. As the scene in front of him began to sink in, he raised both arms as Charlie Sims caught the ball while crossing the goal line. The game was over.

"Gentlemen!" The Coach Constantino bellowed into the raucous locker room. Players quieted down. This was to be the last such speech many would hear from their coach, their big brother here. The last speech. Ever.

"Gentlemen, that was *some* performance. You have proven that you understand what the word '*TEAM*' truly means. I'm proud to have known you men. Thirteen and *ZERO*! No USFA team has ever done this before. Never. I've coached for 33 years, and I've had more talented players, but I've *never* seen a more tenacious, determined group. 62 leaders. Each and, um….each and every one of you will be, no, scratch that, you ARE, leaders of men. Men. Um, uh. Eh-hem. Here, I have this season's last……. game ball……." The coach tried to finish his speech, but gave up as the words came out harder and harder while the locker room erupted in the chants of team mates for their Captain; "Angus! Angus! Angus!…….."

****

USF Drake
High Mars orbit
Standard Earth Date July 12 3779

Lieutenant Angus MacAlister landed in the cramped shuttle bay of the Martian Patrol Cutter USF Drake. Assigned right out of the Academy as First Officer, he had planned that his first act as XO would be an inspection of the engine and power plant section. After reporting to the ship's Captain, the tall, muscular lieutenant JG made aft and passed the pudgy and pockmarked lieutenant he was replacing. Briggs was retiring, having managed to serve long enough in what many considered safe, backwater assignments to qualify for a life time pension. He seemed in quite the hurry to leave to the young MacAlister, not even pausing long enough to return his salute.

"Attention!" Chief Petty Office Alvarez announced in a rather worn out, tired voice as Angus entered the engineering section.

"At ease. Chief, is your area ready for an inspection?" Angus boomed in what he considered his most intimidating baritone.

"Ah, well, sir, we sorta are. You see, Lt. Briggs just inspected us, sir."

"Then I trust everything will be in order, Chief."

"Well, it is, sir", Alvarez muttered sheepishly. "Ya see, we can't give you any 'appreciation', sir, 'cause the men are, well, we're tapped out sir. Every one of us.."

"Excuse me, Chief?"

"We're broke, Sir."

"Broken, Chief?

"No Sir. Broke, tapped out. No cash, Sir.

"I thought the crew was just paid this morning. And, what the hell does that have to do with inspection, sailor?" Something's not right here. What the hell did they send me into?

"Um, Sir, it's kind of, well…"

"Out with it Chief! Fortiter!"

"For who, Sir?"

"Fortiter; Bravely and boldly, Chief. Now, tell me what is going on, Mister!"

"Um, well, Lt Briggs made us give him everything sir, as 'appreciation' for him passing us on his inspections."

"Chief, are you telling me that Lt. Briggs took all of the month's pay from twelve sailors as 'appreciation'?"

"Sorta, sir; we were out for two months, so we missed the last payday. He took all of it, sir."

"How much, Chief?" Angus asked, somewhere between a growl and a whisper.

"That would be 2,847 dexi-creds, sir. He made me count it out to him."

"As you were, I'll be back shortly, Chief. Have your section ready for inspection. Tell your crew the only 'appreciation' that I will *ever* expect from them is a clean inspection. By the book. Clear?"

"Aye-aye, sir!" the wide-eyed Chief snapped with a perfect salute in response.

Angus walked briskly from engineering, and as soon as he was out of sight, he broke into a trot and hit his comm: "Security; MacAlister. Has Briggs left yet?"

"Jackson here, sir. Lieutenant Briggs is in the shuttle bay, sir. His shuttle has been delayed".

"Anyone else near there?"

"No, sir. He's the only scheduled departure, sir. The shuttle pilot and bay crew just went to mess. I expect they'd be there for the next half hour, Sir."

"I need you to run a level four diagnostic on the security cams in the shuttle bay, Jackson."

"Sir, that will shut down camera feeds for at least twenty minutes, sir."

"Understood. You have your orders, Jackson. Fortiter"

"Sir?"

"Bravely and boldly, Jackson."

"Aye-aye, sir."

Fifteen minutes later, Lieutenant MacAlister hit his comm as he walked away from the shuttle bay. Counting bills as he walked back towards engineering, he barked into his comm, "Jackson, I hear the security cams are down in the shuttle bay! Explain."

"We're running a level four diagnostic, Sir, as you ordered!"

"Jackson, I ordered a level one diagnostic. Please get those cameras back on line!"

"Aye-aye, Sir."

Angus stopped when he finished counting, turning momentarily back towards the shuttle bay, then shook his head as he pulled a smaller roll of bills from his pocket and added all of them to the larger roll. He stopped, and with a sigh reached into his back pocket and pulled out his wallet; he removed several bills from a hidden slot, replaced his wallet, and smiled a little as he continued on his way. He straightened his tie and his cap, grinned, shook his head and whispered, "Fortiter, yeah." as he resumed his way to his first inspection.

"Ready for inspection, Chief?"

"Aye-aye, Mr. MacAlister!" Snapped an energetic reply from Alvarez as he passed out the last of the bills to his crew. He had a hard time keeping a smile from his face and not staring at the reddened and bloodied knuckles on the right hand of his new XO. "Fortiter", he whispered to himself. "I'll have to remember that one."

Red City
Mars
Standard Earth Date September 12 3779

"C'mon, sir! The men really want you to come with us. Ya know, to show their 'appreciation' for real, sir. It just wouldn't be *right* for ya not to come!"

"OK, Este. I'll meet you there at 20:00. Let me call home first."

"Aye-aye Mr. Angus!" a chorus of voices snapped loud and clear from the hallway behind him.

The Martian Mess was a modest looking nightclub, typical of many well-run bars near military bases and spaceports. The sign above Angus' head read, "TONIGHT ONLY! CINDY GRABELLE". His face erupted into a big grin as he went in.

The engineering crew had been watching for him; they all stood up and called him over. Angus couldn't help but wear an embarrassed grin as he sat down amidst his crew. Before saying anything to them, the round of drinks he had ordered when he came in arrived; half the crew downed the twelve-year-old Glenfiddich single malt Scotch before Angus could warn them. After much discussion, those drinks were replaced, and the crew, slightly disappointed at the less than anticipated volume of consumables the evening was promising, began sipping the honey like whiskey as the show began.

From the moment she walked on stage, Angus lost track of everything else. Her voice was angelic as she sang one popular song after another. The tall, raven haired, freckle-faced beauty with the button nose, the figure of Venus, and eyes that sparkled as if they held the entire universe, was all he could see or hear. Was she THAT gorgeous in high school?

He remembered all the teasing he had given her, that first year in high school, and how his friend had announced going steady with her the day Angus had planned to ask her to the Fall Dance. He had never heard her sing; listening to her slow, sultry rendition of "Wouldn't It Be Loverly" was like being in the presence of an angel; a very sultry, very personal, just-for-him angel. Her voice made everything else in the room fade away. Angus just grinned and stared at her, resting his chin in his hand. He was in heaven.

That is, until the drunken heckling broke into his rapture.

Four tables of space dockworkers that had way too much to drink began rather loud, unflattering comments about the performer. As Cindy finished singing an old favorite, Angus stretched his two-hundred and fifty pounds up to its six-foot, six-inch height, walked over to the loudest table, and politely requested they "refrain from interrupting the nice lass' songs" in an amazingly booming, yet quietly powerful baritone that seemed to vibrate the entire nightclub.

The four tables stared quietly, and then mumbled something close enough to agreement for Angus to sit back down.

The show resumed, but soon the heckling returned. Angus again went over, feeling his rage growing as he simply stared at them.

The four tables responded as one by standing and glaring at the young officer. Then they noticed the engineering crew of the Drake had moved to stand around the four tables, while the Chief and the Petty Officer moved next to their XO, Wells on his right, Alvarez on his left. Behind them stood six Marines, five privates and one mean looking young lieutenant.

Twenty minutes later Alvarez was counting out bills for the damaged tables, broken chairs, and general loss of business to the Martian Mess caused by the brawl. Alvarez said something to the owner, gave a few more bills to him, and then followed him out of sight. Alvarez gathered the walking wounded, looked around and shook his head.

An hour later, Alvarez was half-carrying the groggy XO back to their ship.

"I'll be damned. Thirteen of us, forty of them, and all of 'em out cold!"

"Well, thirteen PLUS those six Marines. Wonder why those Jarheads got involved? Damn glad they did, though! From what they did in their fatigues, I'd hate to run up against one in his combat armor! What them yarders was sayin' about that cute little girl just weren't right!"

"My dad told me, 'the best way to deal with Marines in a bar is to buy them a drink.' So, when I walked in and saw them, that's what I did" a freshly awakened Angus mumbled.

"Yeah, Mr. A, but they're from the Drake too. You inspect 'em sometimes, like us. Just not as often."

As they carried, limped, and dragged each other back to the ship, Alvarez, slapping his XO's right shoulder, said, "By the way, Mr. Angus, happy birthday", and Alvarez handed a comm number to his XO. "Consider it our 'appreciation', Sir!" he added as he slapped the officer's right shoulder again.

Angus cringed at each slap, "that stings! Dammit." The he squinted through his less swollen eye at the paper while rubbing his shoulder. "What the hell…" looking at his torn sleeve and still bleeding tattoo of an armored fist inside a circle, holding a dirk pointing upward, with the word "FORTITER" above, then looked at his shipmates; each with the same sleeve torn off, each of their shoulders sporting the same tattoo. Almost. The tattoo on Angus alone had a larger word beneath, and the number 44 below that. Turning his attention back to the paper, Angus grinned trough a split lip as he read the paper, just above the comm number, that same word; "Cindy".

****

Captain's Office
USF Drake
High Mars orbit
Standard Earth Date September 13 3779

"CPO Martin Wells, reporting as ordered, Captain!"
"You seem a little stiff, Chief. Are you alright, Mr. Wells?"
"Aye, sir."
"Anything you wish to report, officially?"
"No, sir."
"Anything you wish to 'get off your chest', unofficially, off the record?"
"No, sir. It's just my right shoulder sir. A new tattoo seemed to appear this morning."

****

Captain's Office
USF Drake
High Mars orbit
Standard Earth Date September 12 3780

"You asked to see me, Captain?" Angus managed to squeak out. Somehow, swallowing had just become a significant challenge.
"Sit down, Lieutenant. I have your evaluation completed. We need to review it. Comm, record: present; Captain Richard Alexander, Lieutenant Angus MacAlister. Subject; annual performance review for Mr. MacAlister." Swallowing was now impossible. The serious, stern voice of the Captain only served to increase Angus' anxiety. He didn't think he had screwed up, but the Captain HAD told him several times

that his methods were 'unusual' and 'unorthodox'.

"Mr. MacAlister has been serving as XO on this ship for the past fourteen months. The effects of MacAlister's leadership, including the unusual, but within regulations, manner in which he conducts his inspections have been profound. Interviews of crew members documents that each understands exactly what he expects of them, they know the reasons why even the most nebulous regulations are in place, and they each state how and why their job is important to the safe and efficient operation of this ship." The Captains eyes never left Angus' as he spoke to the recorder while holding the evaluation form in his hands.

"On-duty injuries on this ship over the last six months were zero, a goal the previous XO was never able to achieve. This ship has not experienced an equipment malfunction of any kind in seven months. Recent performance documentation trials showed a 20% gain in acceleration and turning radius." The Captain still wore an almost angry expression as he placed the first page of the report face down on his desk, still holding the young XO's eyes with his own.

"Crew observation by ship's Captain documents one-hundred percent regulation compliance for every crew member observed on duty; footnote one, recorded Captain's observations: note the number is double that required by regulations."

"Mr. MacAlister was given personal responsibility for a transfer to this ship ten months ago who had a less than stellar service record. This sailor encountered some initial, e-hem, 'friction' with the crew, which is not uncommon. My investigation revealed this was due to the crew's perception that the new sailor was not giving one-hundred percent. This 'friction' was very short lived; the transferred sailor has performed well enough to be promoted to Section Head."

The Captain took a slow, large breath in, and let it out just as slowly before continuing, "Mr. MacAlister takes direction extremely well. He has retained what he learned at The Academy, is able to distribute that knowledge effectively, yet he is never reluctant to ask questions. I have found his opinions, when solicited, and, eh-hrmpf!-" the Captain cleared his throat before continuing, "-'otherwise', to be unerringly sound, if occasionally inexperienced."

Captain Alexander then placed the last page of the evaluation he had never looked at face down on his desk.

"It is the opinion of this evaluating officer that Lieutenant Angus MacAlister will one day become an exemplary ships' Captain; he is already an exceptional leader. My recommendation is that he be promoted to the rank of Lieutenant Commander at the Admiralty

Board's earliest convenience.

"Captain Richard Alexander, USF Drake. Com, pause recording."

"At ease, son." The Captain sat back, staring at Angus for three full seconds before he smiled broadly and said, "Well? Your comments, mister? I've never seen you take this long to use an opportunity to express them!"

"Th-thank you sir! I've just tried to do what seemed right, sir, from my training, the best I can, sir." Angus had no idea what to say, or feel; he wanted to jump around, feel ecstatic, but still, this was The Captain's office, and the anxiety that came with that kept him numb. For now.

"The crew did everything, sir. They are really on top of everything."

"They are on top of everything because you made them WANT to be on top of it. Angus, just keep doing that. You're a natural leader, you have good instincts, and you've learned everything The Academy could teach anyone. You've learned all I could teach you. You will get the promotion; I'm putting it on the fast track list. You do understand this will mean you will be transferred off this scow within three months?"

"I never thought of THAT, sir. Thank you. I would miss this ship, the crew, and you a lot."

"One question, off the record. I keep hearing an unusual word all over this ship; 'Fortiter'. I've looked it up. Did this come from you, Mister?"

"The men may have heard me use it once or twice, Sir!" Angus replied.

"I see. First assignment. I'm glad yours was here. Comm, record; Mr. MacAlister will now give his response."

"Um, eh…Yes, Sir!"

****

The Grabelle house
Onondaga Hill
Standard Earth Date September 21 3780

"Mr. Grabelle, Sir, may I have a word with you please?"

"Certainly, Angus. What's on your mind?"

"I am here to ask for your daughter, for Cindy's hand in marriage, Sir. We love each other very much, and we would ask for your permission to get married."

"Young man, are you prepared to take care of my daughter, to provide for her, to protect her?" *This young man has a sense of honor about him, that's for sure, digging up this ancient ritual. I sort of like it, though.*

"I have dedicated my life to do just that, Sir!"

"I would like that very much, young man. Permission granted!"

"That woman is never wrong. Ever! Amazing!" Douglas Grabelle mumbled, as Angus shook his hand, and then ran out to tell his fiancée'.

****

Orion Sector
Chang-Hoi Mission
Standard Earth Date June 21 3785

"Dammit, Sky, we need extraction NOW!" Lieutenant William Marx had lost all patience with the Naval SkyCap controller. His platoon was being overrun, and had minutes before the pirate batbots over ran their position and wiped them out.

Their mission was to evacuate an ill-conceived missionary post/spy base. The 'missionaries' had all been extracted, and now his Marines needed to *LEAVE!*

"LCS 4 was lost to AA, Marine." Damn, that was the last empty landing craft, their ride out. Now they had to wait for one of the other shuttles to unload, refuel, and make the trip back down.

"Another is inbound. It will be cramped. Be ready for a Wham-Bam extraction. AA has picked up quite a lot."

"What boat is coming? The LCSs are an hour out from you!"

"Eyes out for a white and gold skiff. Sky out."

The Captain's skiff? What Navy SOB would bring THAT into a hotfire zone? The Captain will have his hide over this.

"Jenkins, lay down a perimeter barrage with that Mark 12, HE. Platoon, fall back to extraction zone. It'll be cramped, so be ready to dump all extraneous & expendable equipment."

"Aye-aye, Sir!"

Jenkins set his Mark 12 60mm Multi-grenade launcher on 200 meters, primed the chamber, and set it for 200 meters. With a 200 round magazine, this should buy them enough time to get out of here. He listened and heard the "thhhhhhh-UMPF!" of the first round, followed two seconds later by the second. Time to go.

Lt. Marx scanned the perimeter, and saw the six foot long black and silver combat robots closing in on their tank-like treads. Then the first grenades hit, and several were destroyed; the rest kept coming. Behind them rose a hell-wall of fire, smoke and dirt, as small, twelve kilogram railgun rounds, traveling at extreme velocity, hit the enemy's position with a devastating covering bombardment.

"Finally! 'bout damn time!" Marx muttered at the wall of destruction raining down from orbit.

"Recon One this is Clan One. Ten seconds from touchdown. Please be ready for *im*-mediate *de*-parture!" a passionless voice came over his com. *Damn! Angus is flying in here? That silly somuvabitch sounds like he's enjoying this,* Marx thought, wondering if it had anything to do with a little altercation in a Martian bar five, no, six years ago. Something about a cute dark haired singer and some damned rude dockworkers. *I woke up with busted knuckles and a solar hangover the next day!*

"Roger that, sir!"

"Marines, perimeter formation Devil Dogs! Expand out over the LZ, you lazy Sons of Bitches!"

Lt. Marx watched his men move with almost mechanical efficiency, but at a speed driven by human desperation. Then he stared as the gleaming white and gold Captain's Skiff rocketed down at seeming light speed, slowing at *THE* last instant to make a landing instead of a crater.

"OK, Marines! Move it! EVAC! Jenkins, with me, lay down a cover fire here."

Lt. Marx laid down covering fire with Jenkins as the Marines ran onto the Skiff. "OK, Jenkins, go, go, go!" Marx shouted as he took off right behind Jenkins. Marx had to jump the last step, as the skiff was already rising up and was speeding through the sky before the hatch had closed. The Lieutenant made his way up to the cockpit amidst the shudders from AA near misses, tapped the pilot on his shoulder, and said, "Glenfiddich, on the rocks, if I remember correctly, Sir?"

****

United Space Force Academy
USFA Stars Stadium
Cape Canaveral, Florida
Standard Earth Date June 21 3802

There were 62 of them, "The Unbeatens". 59 had made it. Three were lost to the cold embrace of space. Dress uniforms for all of those in attendance, of course. Each of the 4,350 plus had taken particular care to see that their dress whites were perfect, to every last detail. Over 4,350 active and retired USF sailors, now everything from business men, politicians, lawyers, doctors, to dockworkers and welders;

everyone a leader in his field, all former USFA football players, had come. They stood together, slightly apart from the other sailors; the entire Academy complement, cadets and faculty, past and current, as well as local community leaders, filled the 70,000-seat stadium to overflowing. Thousands more, alumni and fans, gathered in the parking lots around the stadium, watching on the giant vid-screens erected last night. Untold thousands more tuned in to the broadcast. All stood in silence as the Chaplin began to speak of the influence of a good man's life had had on them all. Today, four days after the Academy Graduation Ceremony, they all laid Coach Victor Constantino to rest.

****

Mars Orbital Transit Station
Inner Sol System
Standard Earth Date June 23 3802

Your new skiff is in bay 7, Admiral!" The Marine offered with a sharp salute.

"Thank you, Corporal." Angus said as he returned the salute.

The trip in for the funeral was also used to replace the Admiral's skiff with a new model. The new boat would be faster, more comfortable, with better communications and a longer range. It would also have a new ECM suite, but still be unarmed. Angus was not sure he liked that part. Budgets for the Fleet and planetary defenses were difficult to maintain without larger threats than pirates and an occasional would-be colonial dictator.

The trip had also been a homecoming for his long time pilot who had unexpectedly elected retirement due to a family illness. Angus had a younger pilot tagged for his replacement when he returned to the Excalibur, but he had no pilot to get him there now. Fleet promised to send the best available pilot; the one they sent had a year to go before her graduation!

As he turned the corner coming up on bay 7, Angus noticed a tiny young Ensign in a very sharp uniform standing at attention outside the door. Looking very closely, the Admiral saw that she had managed to disguise her very nice figure in her uniform some how; Angus doubted that ninety percent of the Fleet would be able to pick that up. Interesting.

"Ensign, at ease!"

"Admiral! Ensign Jenitka Kowalski, SIR!"

"You are my pilot, Kowalski?"

"Sir, yes, Sir!"

"Isn't it a little unusual to be piloting the Admiral's skiff a year before graduation, Ensign?"

"My orders, Sir!" Jen reached inside her uniform jacket and offered the papers she withdrew to the Admiral, wondering just how he knew she had not yet graduated. Did she look *that* green?

"Your impression of this boat, Ensign?"

"A fine craft, sir. Very responsive."

Angus noticed this Ensign was not nervous at all. He remembered that name from the service report; top of her class, number one in pilot ratings, turned down offers each year of school for Fighter Command Training.

"Lets go then, Ensign." Angus smiled.

So, he didn't know! She had been hoping that the Admiral would not recognize the last name of his old Academy quarterback. She wanted to make her way on her own merits. But, the stories her dad had told her about this man, his kindness, brains, raw determination, loyalty, and courage! She only half believed them.

"Aye-aye, Admiral."

Take off and cruise was uneventful. They had a long trip back to Excalibur, and the shuttle would almost fly itself to Way Station Alpha, where it would dock with a gravitic drive FTL module and continue on to the Excalibur. Angus passed the time grilling the young Ensign on her background; her studies, her future career and family plans. Leaving Alpha was where the excitement began.

"Twelve bogies coming in fast sir!" Jen excitedly announced to the Admiral almost concurrently with multiple alarms. "Alpha Control, Four Star One, I have twelve bogies hot inbound. Zero IFF", Jen reported to Alpha Control in a clear, calm and almost computer-like voice.

How did she calm that voice down so fast? Angus wondered to himself.

"Roger, Four Star One. Fighters scrambling. Suggest you take evasive action and route back into base defense sphere." Angus noted the Alpha Control voice showed much more stress than the Ensign flying his skiff did.

"Affirmative, course changes already executed, Alpha Control. ETA twelve minutes plus evasives." That cold, computer voice again.

The dozen sleek, dark shapes split into three groups, trying to outflank the unarmed skiff. Angus made a mental note to get this boat some teeth, politicians be damned, *if* they survived. The Admiral was well known everywhere man had settled; he was very popular with most for bringing law and order to outlying regions where pirates had prospered. He was not so well thought of among the pirates and certain Space Force types of less than stellar ethics. This was likely another attempt to kidnap or kill him.

Angus slid into the co-pilot's seat. "Your boat, Ensign. Tell me if you need help."

"Aye-aye, Sir. Strap in and hold on" Jen's voice was again bright-eyed with excitement.

It seems like she's enjoying this, almost relishing it! The Admiral thought.

"Four Star One, this is Alpha Station Fighter Force Leader. ETA nine minutes to interception."

"Roger that, FFL" droned on Jen's 'computer' voice. It must be the new comm system training, Angus figured.

Violently turning the small boat into the closest attackers, Jen flew straight at them, and then sent the ship into a maneuver the Admiral had never heard of, and did not think he could ever describe. Three of the pirates trying to follow and target them collided and exploded.

"Warning: missiles fired. Two targets inbound. Four inbound. Deploy Countermeasures?" The skiff's computer asked.

"Negative on 'deploy countermeasures'!" Jen ordered the computer calmly, the tip of her tongue visible peeking out of the right hand corner of her mouth as she jerked the controls around violently.

Angus looked at the young pilot with slightly widening eyes. *She definitely seems to be enjoying this; cool under pressure, tongue hanging out, she reminds me of our QB…hmm… Kowalski! Angus, ya damn fool! She HAS to be Jerry's girl! I sure hope she's as good as I've heard,* he thought.

When, eleven minutes later, the sixteen SF-9 Space Hawk fighters arrived and blasted the six remaining pirate fighters trailing the Admiral's skiff, Jen felt a wave of exhaustion wash over her as her adrenalin rush faded with the end of the crisis.

"Four Star One, I thought you said there were twelve bogies?"

"FFL, this is Admiral MacAlister. There *were* twelve bogies. Ensign Kowalski managed to, well, *'reduce'* their combat effectiveness."

"Your skiff is unarmed, sir. How the hell, pardon, Admiral, but how did she do *that?*"

"You'd have had to have seen it, Flight Leader. I could never explain it to you."

"I can't wait to see those flight recordings, Sir!"

"They should just be thankful they didn't piss me off. Um, Sir." Jen was still riding the 'high' of her first combat.

"Yes, I believe they should be, Ensign." The Admiral grinned at his young pilot. *She's got Jerry's spunk. I like that!*

Jen allowed a self-satisfied grin to emerge through the exhaustion on her freckled face. But only for a moment.

****

United Space Force Academy Hilton
Cape Canaveral, Florida
Standard Earth Date July 6 3804

"Permission to enter, SIR!" Lieutenant Jenitka Kowalski's sharp voice signaled that something had upset the Admiral's Pilot as she stood outside his hotel room.

"Lieutenant, is that wise? I have a reputation to uphold!" Angus droned.

"Computer, engage HR recording. Permission to enter, SIR!"

"Come in, Lieutenant. What's on your mind?" Admiral Angus MacAlister replied in a flat voice while he scanned his speech for errors.

"Permission to speak freely, SIR!"

"Lieutenant, IF I had given you the impression that you *ever* need *permission* to speak freely to me, I apologize. Now, what has you so on edge?"

"My career, Sir!"

"Damn it, Jen, am I going to have to drag this out of you one word at a time? You are the Admiral's Pilot, and have been since *before* your graduation. You completed your final year's studies in three months while fulfilling your duties as such. You are the best pilot I've ever seen, hell, that I've ever *heard* of! For a young officer less than two years out of the academy, I'd say your career is going pretty damn well!"

"I……uh,…Sir! I have much more to offer you than being just a damn good pilot, Sir!"

"You want a crack at editing this crap Fleet wrote for me? It's yours!" Angus had a twinkle in his eye as he slid the datatab across the table and leaned back in his chair. "And, SIT DOWN!" The Admiral pointed to the other chair in the room. *She's actually nervous! There is a first time for everything.*

Jen looked a little shaky as she took the chair at the corner of the desk. *You've planned and rehearsed this a million times!* "Sir, I need more responsibility. I can't grow as an officer, as a *person* without it."

"Do you want a release? A transfer? Say the word, and it's yours. You would most likely have a squadron of fighters or freighters, or anything in between, under your command within three months. Your choice"

"No, Sir, I want to take more responsibility with the Admiral, Sir!"

"And you think you have the knowledge and experience to do, what, exactly?"

"You need a Chief of Staff, Sir! No one knows you better than I do, Sir. I am a meticulous organizer, Sir. I am an expert at managing schedules, Sir. I have completed my Master's in Diplomatic Communications, Sir. I am an expert on the etiquettes and protocols of every major culture, and most minor ones, Sir. I am the perfect choice, the only *right* choice. SIR!"

"Cindy may argue the point about you knowing me that well, Lieutenant Commander. Just what makes you think you have what the job takes?"

"Sir, the Admiral's wife is the one who told me that I know the Admiral better than anyone else, Sir! And, I've been studying battle tactics and strategic deployments as well as running simms with Captain Gridley, Sir. I…….." Jen stood up with wide eyes, slapped both of her hands on the desk as she leaned towards Angus. "LIEUTENANT COMMANDER?"

"Will tells me you are a gifted tactician, and that you've taken on almost twice the study load we had planned for you. The only thing holding you back was wanting the job enough, Lieutenant Commander Kowalski. I told you, I have a reputation to uphold. How would I look with a Lieutenant as my COS? Now, Lieutenant Commander, is there anything else?"

"I… Sir! Um, I, uh, no, Sir. I….Thank you, Sir!"

"Here are your oak leafs. They used to be mine. You've earned 'em Jen. Your second duty as my COS is to fly me to Syracuse after the speech and join Cindy and me for dinner tonight. We're having Haggis, in honor of Alex being home on leave. You should meet him; you're going to help keep him out of my Chain of Command." Angus flashed a satisfied smile as he leaned back in his chair, clasping his hands behind his head. "Now, for your first Chief Of Staff assignment; make me proud, and fix this damn speech! You've got four hours."

****

USF Excalibur
Between Perseus and Orion
Standard Earth Date December 6 3811

Today The Admiral was not consciously teaching the men he had mentored. This inspection was like sitting in an old, comfortable chair;

it was as much about the memories of inspections past as it was about teaching, and yet one more time to gaze at the standard pale yellow-green walls of a USF Starship corridor. Yet he had another motive as well; to be sure he had done everything possible to prepare this fleet for what he knew was ahead. He wouldn't be there to guide them through it, of that he was sure; he had no idea when it would come, but he was sure it would come; and he could not tell them any of what he knew. Not yet. Still, he did seem to enjoy keeping to areas of the ship off limits to the gaggle of reporters assigned to his last cruise.

"You have a real all-star crew here, Will. You know how to keep them on the ball. They're that good because you expect them to be that good, and taught them to want to be that good. Or better."

"You taught me that, Angus. And, you taught them as well. There is literally not a soul aboard a ship in this fleet that you have spent less than four hours of personal time mentoring on something. They see you every day, and they know you would be likely to inspect them at some time; they know this is your last cruise, and everyone of them has been pulling extra duty to make your last inspection perfect. Admiral, they all have a very personal connection with you. They will not let you down, sir."

"They won't let themselves down, Will. You gave them that pride. I pretty much just watched this past year. Don't underestimate yourself, Will. You are a very good leader. Don't get too cocky, but always remember that."

"Thank you, sir. I won't let you down. I have to get to the bridge, Admiral."

"You just do *not* want me to have to un-retire, Commodore." The Admiral smiled, "Seriously, Will, great job. Your crew is ready for, well, for anything. They need to be. See you soon on the bridge." *Damn, almost. Stay focused*, Angus thought. *Don't give everything away just yet.*

"Trying to avoid those reporters a little while longer, sir?"

The Admiral responded with a slight nod of his head and a raised eyebrow. "There is a special inspection I need to perform."

The Commodore saluted and walked briskly away, a sly grin creeping onto his face when he was sure the Admiral couldn't see.

"Well, sir, did we pass inspection?" grinned the Chief.

"You don't have to ask me, Marty. You could have told me that when I stepped into the section!" Angus grinned back to his old friend.

"Have you heard from Alvarez lately?"

"He's still with Gravitas Propulsion, working out the kinks from their new drive designs. He tells me the next generation is really spectacular. He tells me to say hello, and to give you hell for not retiring and joining him."

"Hrumpf! I may just take him up on that. That man could find out any secret....You get that place on the lake all set up? You really gonna fish off the back porch all the time, Angus? I can't see that. Pity the poor fish that don't meet your standards, sir."

"We'll do some ground based traveling, Marty. I've got a lot of years to make up to her, you know. I've seen a quarter of the galaxy, but never been sight seeing on Earth!" How he hated lying to his old friend. *Soon, he will know, when I ask him to volunteer and come with me,* Angus thought.

"Well, with all due respect sir, jus' give the poor lass some time to catch her breath once in a while!"

"Ha! Only when you drop by!"

Both men chuckled as they walked through the section. The Chief reached inside his immaculate uniform top and removed a thin silver flask. "Glenfiddich. 25 years old. To ya health, Angus!"

"Marty, promise me you'll take care of yourself. I mean, keep your standards high. Don't let up. They need that, they deserve it."

"Angus, why so damn serious all of a sudden? You're givin' me the willies!"

"Just want to be sure they'll be ready for anything. The galaxy's an unpredictable and dangerous place."

"Aye, Boss, that she be!"

For the next ninety minutes, the Admiral and the Chief were no where to be found; Angus MacAlister and Marty Wells walked slowly, down the deserted Heavy Rail Cannon maintenance corridor, the two friends looking at everything, seeing nothing, and talking about nothing in particular, as old friends will do when about to part ways.

A too-short hour and a half later, The Admiral returned to his quarters. A sense of, something-sadness?-melancholy?-nostalgia? All three? Or was it the apprehension over fooling so many good Sailors with this fake retirement act? Do not think of THAT now. Nothing you can do about it, it has to be this way. It's the only retirement party he'll ever get. Was he angry about not being able to retire? Well, sort of. Still, it added itself to the ever-growing feeling of impending disaster building on top of the gentle warmth of the fine single malt Scotch inside him.

Marty Wells walked briskly to his quarters, wiping a never seen in public tear from his scarred and grizzled cheek, his brow furrowed by his friend's strange warnings. As he walked, his concerned expression was slowly being replaced by a sly grin spreading across his face.

Chrysler Building
55th Floor
New York City
Standard Earth Date December 4 3811

"Our man is in place then? How reliable is this, this, *person*?"

"He is well motivated; jealousy, revenge, perceived inferiority. He is well known to the Admiral, and will have access to make the 'delivery'. He should have little problem delivering our 'message'. Of course, his expected payment will never have to be delivered."

"Spare me the details; you always plan these things very well, Senator. Just get it done; we know something big is in the works, and it's bad enough we have to deal with his wife; we can not afford to have this self-appointed do-gooder war-hero campaigning for his wife or otherwise mucking around in politics after he retires".

****

USF Excalibur
Between Perseus and Orion
Standard Earth Date December 6 3811

"Good job, people! Better than I had asked for, better than I had expected! And I expect *a lot* from you all! Excellent!" Lieutenant Commander Chester Jones exclaimed. The Groups' performance in the recent drill *was* very good; they had put in extra effort that could save lives in combat, and he knew they needed to hear his appreciation of the effort for them to continue performing at such a high level.

"Boss, does this mean we get leave once we get to Earth?"

"Huckleberry, keep it in your pants! You've all earned leave!"

"Oooh-RAH!" chorused throughout the hangar bay.

"AFTER The Admiral's retirement party! Is that clear?"

"AYE-AYE, SIR!" echoed off the walls.

"Now, are there any other issues?" CJ always asked, and his Group *knew* two things; first, if they had a personal problem they had better bring it up here and now; second, if they did it was treated as a "Group" problem, never to be disclosed or discussed outside the Group. These rules, that CJ had put into effect almost a year ago, resulted in the most cohesive and close knit group of fighter pilots anywhere. It was so good, The CAG, Commander Singh, had asked

Admiral MacAlister for permission to expand the system throughout the Fleet.

"Sir! I, um need some advice, SIR!" Lieutenant Doug Coon stepped forward.

"What has you in knots, Doug?" CJ used the informal address as a signal to all; this was private, within the group only; the only mentions were to be helpful, no heavy ribbing on this subject.

"Sir, I..."

"Doug, for this topic, it's CJ or Chester."

"Sorry, CJ. I have this problem, Sir, um, CJ. It's Alice; I want to ask her to marry me, but I don't have any money for it. Her enlistment ends when we get to Earth, Sir, eh, CJ, and, I'm afraid, I'll, she'll...."

"She's smarter than that, Doug. I've seen her files, her picture; she's too good-looking for you, so you'll need a *big* ring." CJ knew the answer before he asked, "Do you have a ring?" CJ knew Doug had a problem hanging on to cash. Heck, the entire group knew that. CJ also knew that Ensign Alice Hanson, RN, was deeply, hopelessly in love with Doug. A good CO checked out such things about his pilots, at least, Chester Jones did.

"No, Boss. And I don't have a dime to get one from the Commissary."

CJ stood silent. After ten seconds, pilots began walking up and stuffing credits into Doug's shirt pocket, shaking his hand, congratulating him and wishing him happiness. When Doug started tearing up, every pilot silently turned away from him. After a minute, when Doug had regained his composure, CJ coughed, and the pilots resumed their congratulations. After every pilot had contributed what they felt was appropriate, CJ dismissed the group.

"Doug, hang a minute."

"Yes, Sir."

"Doug, you and Alice have a chance at something special. Something really special. That is important to everyone in this Group, as you have seen."

"Yes, Boss. I, I can't...."

"Doug, you're with family here." CJ reached into his pocket and took out a huge wad of credits. "Doug, take care of her. What you two have is why we are here." Chester put the wad in Doug's pocket. "You get that girl the ring of her dreams, pilot!"

"Aye....Aye-aye, sir." Doug managed to say through misty eyes.

Chapter Three

Cygnus 78
'The Graveyard'
Standard Earth Date December 3 3811

Commander Alex MacAlister paced his broad shouldered six-foot, eight-inch frame slowly down the broad, ecru colored corridor. The pale yellow color was nearly constant throughout the ship, having been chosen because it quickly faded from notice, yet gave a light, open feeling to the spaces it was applied to. Unlike smaller ships, here the wide passage was unencumbered by pipes, tubing, or wires. These items were routed under floor on each side near the walls, allowing quick emergency repair access while maintaining the passage throughout the ship. This project was nearly finished. He had been four years in near exile at the Cygnus 78 Fleet Vessel Storage Area, grimly known as The Graveyard. Cygnus 78 was the most remote area under USF control, hidden among the sparse star fields at the very rim of the galaxy. Isolated in position, with a neutron star at its center, the system was cloaked by the star's radiation as well as the latest stealth technology; the maintenance and repair facilities, as well as the 342 Fleet ships there, while mothballed, were too powerful to chance falling into the hands of rebels or pirates.

As an officer in the R & D Command, Alex was removed from the direct chain of command that ended with his father. Here he could make his own way, and knowing that he had earned every inch of it by himself was very important to him.

Besides, R & D was somewhat of a family vocation, having been founded by his ancestor, Jock MacAlister. And this case was a very unusual project. Alex was assigned to the near total gutting and refitting of the battleship USF Victory, BB-44. The thirty-kilometer long, five-kilometer wide vessel was the largest spaceship ever built, nearly twice the size of her predecessors, and one of only three in the class that shared her name. The entire interior, power plants, engines, everything was removed from inside the 100-meter thick gravity-compressed diamond armored hull. The hull was formed of the strongest material even produced by man, a super-dense carbon crystallization compressed to extreme density in a gravity forge; it could stay inside a star for six months, keeping it's crew alive without any other shielding. The exterior had been made over as well, with experimental stealth covering for the armor and shielding for the new power plants and gravity drives. The weapons systems upgrades made to the ship included replacing of most of the standard USF battleship armament mix with experimental directed energy, plasma, and particle beam projectors of unrivaled power. On the defensive side, gravity screens and, his personal contribution, the new energy force screens. Alex had described them in his Doctoral Thesis, and the engineers here had made them work. All this was made possible by a power system generating outputs equaling 120 Sol type stars. Where the standard power plants generated power by holding the protons and electrons of hydrogen atoms in close proximity while not allowing the electrons to orbit the protons, this new design used anti-matter atoms opposite 'normal' atoms to generate power on an order of magnitude trillions of times higher. The power generated was so great that only a ship built as heavily as the Victory was could absorb it. And Alex wasn't completely sure about that.

While the Near Ship Defense guns and missiles had been increased in number and effectiveness, gone were mechanically trained turrets for heavy rail guns and cannon; the new energy weapons were aimed electronically. The only remnants of the original armament were the GravTorp tubes and the central Heavy Rail Gun installation. Each of the three barrels of this weapon had originally fired 80,000-ton projectiles at .75C. The Victory Class had one installed on each end of the huge dreadnought. With the huge increase in available power, the muzzle velocity of these projectiles now topped out at .98C, and the size of the projectiles had doubled, allowing a Grav-drive to be installed in certain models; these projectiles had extra-light speed capability. Victory was now the single most powerful force in the known galaxy. Crew requirements, the reason these huge ships were mothballed, were reduced from 38,000 ship and flight crew, plus 20,000 Marines, to a crew of 9,000 and a capacity of 40,000 Marines.

3,000 of those 9,000 were the flight crew, comprising pilots and support staff. The huge size of the Victory meant that she could carry huge numbers of fighters, bombers, and gunboats. There was even room for four destroyers and their crews without cramping the hangers too much.

Even the fighters were of an entirely new design,

The Victory had another survival trick. The ship was the most undetectable item larger than toothpick ever built. The hull material was zero-reflective, and massive generators made use of the huge power reserves available to add to the capability; even the null-shimmer of the stealth fields was reduced to nearly unnoticeable levels.

And the computer system was nothing short of revolutionary. While previous systems had run on a simple "yes-no" binary system, modern computers had advanced in flexibility and predictive capabilities by introducing "maybe" into the mix; the trinary system was also known as the "+ 0 –" system. Alex had pioneered a quantum leap with his "quatinary" data system, which allowed each data bit to change from +, -, or 0 over time. In short, his system allowed a data bit to be + for a set time then change to 0 or – and back at the appropriate time during the calculation, each bit expressed as a derivative over time. The fourth dimensional advancement held unbelievable promise for Artificial Intelligence applications as well as a leap in standard processing speed several orders of magnitude higher than had ever been dreamed of. The Victory was the first large ship to carry this system, after it's successful deployment on the newest fighters in the fleet.

Provided it all actually worked. Testing that was the next step, and Alex was excited and just a bit nervous at the thought of running trials tomorrow. Adding to his anxiety was the fact that no one in Fleet seemed to know why this was being done. Even his father had told him that he only knew that a really big R & D project that could lead to fleet wide upgrades was in the early stages, without any details.

Why go through the expense of testing this on such a scale? Fleet usually tested these types of innovations on mothballed corvettes or frigates. Sure, some of these components needed a lot of room, but they could easily be scaled to the size of a frigate, or a light cruiser at least. To do this to a battleship must have taken half the fleet budget for the last six years. Testing, refining, re-testing. Setting up facilities for mass production. Why?

Alex walked slowly thinking hard as he headed to the mess. A slight frown showed the seriousness of his contemplations. It was late in the day, and some how lunch had escaped his attention again. It seemed that every second not dedicated to training the crew, checking the systems, planning the procedures for new equipment, he was daydreaming of her; gorgeous, smart, funny, kind, and pledged to him forever. A full, face-wide grin faded onto his face without him noticing as he thought of her. His fiancé filled every spare moment in his thoughts, for Alex was helplessly, deeply in love with her. Much to his surprise she had said yes when he finally conjured up the courage and had asked her to marry him; it had taken him almost two months to actually ask her after he had decided. He never thought she would, due to her commitment to serve and her love of space as well as his commitment to serve; but nothing had ever given him more joy than her answer. Alex simply considered himself the luckiest man in the creation.

Throughout his Academy studies Alex had fought to distance himself from his father's shadow; being engaged to his father's aide did not help. Sometimes the expectations were unreasonable. Sometimes there were assumptions of nepotism. Mostly there was an awe that arose like the battlements of a fortress to isolate Alex from those around him. Requesting R & D Command assignment had removed much of that from his life, but it had also isolated him from his academy friends and from HER. And the secrecy! His dad knew not to ask about the project, but when he did get leave twice each year, his friends outside of USF service bugged him unrelentingly.

BEEP-beep-DING! His comm alert sounded. "MacAlister. Go."

"Perry, Sir. A new comm came in from JC, sir."

"The Joint Chiefs?" Alex stopped. "Read it, Pete."

"Sir! 'URGENT! Directive from The Joint Chiefs USF Combined Command. USF Victory BB-44 hereby ordered by the Chancellor and unanimous consent of the combined legislature to be renamed. Christening to be at 1700 local time. Ultra VIP arriving 16:55 local time aboard USF Farragut. New commission carried by Ultra VIP, to announced upon Christening. That is all."

Alex just stood there for ten seconds until his comm snapped him back, "Sir?"

"Peter, contact the appropriate departments. Have them ready everything from ship's stationary to tablecloths and silverware for immediate application of the ship's new name." *Whatever the hell that is gonna be! I just hope it won't be 'Pansy' or some such PC nonsense.* Ultra VIP. That meant an official somewhere in line of succession for Chancellor.

"Aye, Commander."

"Just pray it's not 'Pansy'" Alex muttered.

"Roger that, sir!" his comm replied softly.

"MacAlister out." Alex frowned. Damn new comms. Why did they take the 'auto off' out of the new comms?

At least tomorrow they would begin shakedown, and he could fill his head with the ship, he thought as he looked around the empty mess. Then he smiled, whispering, "Hmm. This thing is huge. What a great place for a wedding!"

****

UASC 524th Space Fighter Group
"The Hounds of Heaven"
Griffiths SFB, Rome, NY

"Well, will you look at those birds! Just look at 'em!" Captain Fred Yeager just could not stand at attention once he got sight of the sleek, dull black fighters.

"Put it back in yer pants, pilot!" Major Warren Bong snapped his men back into line. "Are you gonna act like little kids around a Christmas Tree or Aerospace Force pilots! OK, Flight, these are your new birds, as of twelve seconds ago! The General Aerospace SF-12 Mustang. You have thirty minutes to familiarize yourselves with them. The you will report to training room twenty-four for you pilot's manuals and initial training on how to use the simms. Provided you all check out in the simms, you will solo in these birds tomorrow. Atmospheric flight only. Clear?"

"Atmospheric flight only? What do you mean, Major, these are sub-orbital birds?"

"No, son. These are Inter*stellar* birds. Ground based interstellar fighters."

****

USF Excalibur
Between Perseus and Orion
Standard Earth Date December 6 3811

"Well, why not?"

Sure, it was marginally against regulations, but what were they going to do, fire him? They've already 'postponed' his retirement, even if that wasn't for publication just yet. Angus MacAlister had it all laid out on his bunk, the complete full dress military kilt that cost him way too much money. At least, his wife would think so, if she knew. The Scottish made wool MacAlister Clan tartan kilt and fly plaid, MacAlister Clan Crest broach pin, shirt, horsehair sporran, dirk, sigian dubh, hose, belt, Clan Crest buckle, Clan Crest cufflinks, and of course, the Brogues. Fortiter! The Clan motto. He would wear his Fleet Dress jacket and a tartan tie. But, after all, was this one indulgence too much? He chuckled as he thought about what to wear, or not, *under* the kilt. No one knew he had it aboard. He had never mentioned to anyone, had brought it aboard in his luggage, and unpacked it himself from the locked and sealed carton just this morning. But, it *could* be considered a violation. What if I wore it for the test? That may be even better, mock combat in a dress kilt! No, better to save it for the party. There, the reporters were sure to make a galactic event out of it. Well, perhaps that would keep the politicians from bugging him to run for some damned political office. He just wanted time for Cindy and himself, and it looked like they may never get that. Angus sighed, seeing her face before him as he did in that nightclub long ago, and the day of their wedding. All he could remember of that day was the angel, HIS angel, floating down the aisle.......

He was still debating himself when his door chime rang.

"Come" he said as he walked from the bedroom to his office, closing the door to hide the bright MacAlister tartan wool laid on his bed.

"Admiral, one hour to entry point, sir."

"Thanks, Jen. Do I really have to give a speech?" he asked his aide, Lieutenant Commander Jennifer Kowalski. The 5'5" tall, pretty blonde had been his Chief of Staff for almost eight years now. How she always seemed to hide her spectacular figure under regulation uniforms always escaped him. Part secretary, part big sister, part den mother, all about ruthless efficiency, organization, endless energy, with just the right amount of mischief behind her fiery eyes, Angus decided that this freckle-faced little fireplug was the smartest person, besides his son Alex, that he had ever met; being Jerry Kowalski's little girl didn't help or hurt her any, she earned every assignment, honor, and rank herself. As a fresh new cadet, she had piloted his corvette through a pirate ambush almost a decade ago. A year later she was his aide. The only aide he had ever had.

"Now, Admiral, you *know* they all want to hear a few words. It's an emotional time for them, you know", she explained as she straightened his necktie. Turning, she headed for the bedroom. "You aren't wearing *this*, are you? Dress whites would be best. Let me get them out for you", Jen grinned as she started her trademark fast walk towards his bedroom.

"Um, that's OK, I'll get it. It's a mess in there."

She stopped, put her hands on her hips, and shook her head, then cocked her head to the right as she looked up at the barrel-shaped 6'6" Admiral. "Other than declaring politics as out of the question, you've been pretty quiet about your plans. What are you going to do?" she asked in a quieter tone.

"I'm planning on spending the rest of my days giving Cindy the attention she deserves. I hope I can make up for the all time I've been gone. With Alex assigned to R & D, I should be able to see him more often too. Maybe I can talk him into getting serious about starting a family-yeah, right. Ha!" he grinned. "How about you? Are you going to tell me, or keep me guessing forever?"

"You know your wife is *very* happy with the life you've given her. And Alex is a *very* amazing young man. You know, I've heard rumors that say you're retiring because you're afraid to compete with him!"

"Yeah! Right. I'd lose. No doubt. By a landslide! But you may *never* tell him that! Direct order!" boomed his patented 'no doubt' baritone. With a gentler, quieter voice reserved for friends, Angus continued, "so, you're not going to tell me then?" Angus MacAlister flashed his 'puppy dog' look; it seemed to work on his wife, though he had no idea why.

"That look *won't* work on me, Admiral! Your wife told me all about it years ago when you hired me; and that it *only* works on her!" *and then, only because she lets it,* Jen thought. Jen's face broke into a huge smile, and her reddening face revealed the freckles few ever saw. "OK"

She stuck out her left hand, showing off the large, but not obnoxious diamond ring. "My term is up in two weeks. I have, well, I have *plans...*" her smile shining infinitely brighter than her ring.

"Jen, I'm happy as all get out *and* angry as hell." The Admiral's eyebrows pressed down deeply. "Who is this guy? I need to check him out. He had better be on the up-and-up. I'll have InTel check him out...." He said in his best, most serious 'Big Brother' voice.

"You already have." That smile sure was bright, the Admiral thought.

"What are you talking about?" his eyebrows nearly hitting the ceiling.

"You *do* know him pretty well," She grinned. *"Dad."*

The puzzled look hung on the Admiral's face for exactly three seconds. Then his left eyebrow shot up.

"Alex?"

"Yup."

"What did you say, Lt. Commander?" smiled the Admiral.

"Yup, Dad?"

"That's 'yup Dad, *SIR*', Lt. Commander", he grinned as his act faded fast. Then that serious look returned as he gently covered each of her shoulders with his huge hands.

"He could be deployed at any time, Jen. You will be separated for long periods. It's going to get pretty tough."

"What do you think your wife and I talk about all the time? Your favorite cookie recipe?" His expression just got way too serious, Jen thought. What was he not telling me?

"You have never made me cookies!" His serious tone matching the look on his face. Then his smile opened up his face, "Jen, I am so happy for you both". His serious look returned as he said, "Hmmm, I'll have to have a talk with Alex before the party at Fleet."

"Admiral, Dad, *Sir*, don't be mad at Alex, it was my idea not to tell you, Alex wanted to, but I thought…"

"I'll have to tell him it worked perfectly", he said, rubbing his chin and suddenly wearing a 'cat that just ate the canary' look.

"What?" Jen's puzzled look demanded.

"He told me the night before that he was going to propose. We had a long talk. We decided you had to think I didn't know in order for you to keep your sanity. He's in deep for you. Be good to him, Jen. You *will* be my favorite daughter-in-law!" Angus said as he bent forward and softly kissed her forehead.

"You!" Her frown turned into a smile as her fists, ready to hit his shoulders, turned into a quick hug. Angus felt her flinch slightly as he squeezed her shoulders.

"You OK?"

"Just a little sore from fencing practice yesterday", Jen said as she rubbed her right shoulder. Angus noted a few specks of dark red on her uniform there, but accepted her explanation.

"Just promise me, little one, that you'll make the most of each minute, each second together!" The Admiral whispered into her ear as he leaned in a little closer.

Jen stepped back, wondering if this had anything to do with those "retirement planning" trips he had taken without her over the last two years. She pushed those thoughts out of her mind as she stepped back and straightened up.

"You have 40 minutes now, *Admiral*, until you *have* to be on the bridge, *Sir*", she said in her best professional, no-nonsense voice.

"Any way you can lock those reporters up?"

"That would be against regs, Admiral!"

"Have you taken those precautions we discussed?"

"Aye. Sir" Jen stated coldly. Angus knew that look, saw her tongue flash into the right corner of her mouth, and, knowing that whomever it was aimed at was in for a world of hurt, nodded once as his reply.

Lieutenant Commander Jenitka Kowalski turned and walked out of the office, her sly grin hidden from the her boss, mentor, friend, and soon to be father-in-law.

It was a long time after that before the Admirals grin faded, that sort-of sad feeling temporarily forgotten.

"Incoming message. Personal stamp" chimed his desk.

"Connect".

"Hey, Angus! Ready for the Big Day? Less than a week left!?"

"Vance! Good to see you! No, I'll never be ready. But I guess I'll survive it. How're things in the Senate? Is Cindy giving you a hard time?" I can't even tell him, a Senator, and my best friend.

"They'd be better if you'd listen to me and join us. The next election's eight months away, and Barton is retiring. You'd be a cinch, Angus."

"Vance, I've told you before, I hate that bureaucratic crap. I can't understand how you or Cindy can tolerate it. Ha-ha, I just can't. Besides, well, you know……".

"OK, OK. So, what do you have planned after the party? If you need a 'quick exit', I can arrange one."

"Before. I'm doing it before. I just have to ditch the reporters for a day."

****

The Hounds of Heaven
Griffiths SFB
Standard Earth Date December 6 3811

"OK, Gentlemen and Ladies, we are going out for a little *simulated* combat. We will follow our flight plan to Mars orbit and back. Somewhere along the way we just may encounter bogies; a flight of SF-11 Thunderbolts has been given the honor of being our targets today." Major Bong always sounded pissed off at the targets during his briefings.

"Those Jugs are no match for our 'Tangs, Major!" Captain Arleta Simulak boasted.

"They will surprise you knuckleheads; despite being twice your size, Captain, those Jugs can flip faster than a church breakfast pancake. And they've got a lot of power, so do not underestimate your opponent; not ever, not now! Clear!"

"Clear, Sir!"

"Then let's go squeeze some lightnin' out of those Jugs!"

With every pilot eager to test their new mounts, the briefing room cleared in record time.

****

The Graveyard
Standard Earth Date December 6 3811

"Atten-TION!"

The assembled crew, all 4,843 sailors and the 10,000 marines so far assigned, all resplendent in spotless dress uniforms, moved into that designated, ageless posture. The United Senate diplomatic shuttle from the Farragut had just arrived, and the crew was there for a christening ceremony scheduled to begin, well, now.

The shuttle was a big one, designed to make an impression with smooth, aerodynamic lines, the Seal of The United Senate larger than life on each side, and an overall vary ornate trim. Who ever THIS was, they were important.

The shuttle's doors opened, and stepping out was a ravishingly beautiful woman with salt and pepper hair, a freckled face, and a button nose.

"Mom!" Alex gasped under his breath.

Walking over to her son, Chair of The Veteran's Affairs Committee, Senator Cindy MacAlister smiled up at him. Understanding military protocols, she refrained from the big hugs she usually gave her son. Looking up at him with tears in her eyes, she said simply, "Alex, the Joint Chiefs have assigned you to command SBB-44. Effective immediately. This envelope contains the orders. The chain of command issue with your father has been 'set aside'.

"The Space Veteran's Administration is ordering you to make ready all mothballed living quarters for use as retired veteran's living facilities immediately. The mothballed portions of the medical facilities will be reopened and updated to serve that population immediately. Additional quarters and facilities will be constructed to house and support a total of 120 million.

"The Chancellor, with the consent and approval of The Combined Legislature have decreed that the new name of USF SBB-44 is to be...'Fortiter'."

40

Chapter Four

USF Excalibur
Between Perseus and Orion
Standard Earth Date December 6 3811

"Thank you all for being here. Thank you. Thanks. OK, SHUDDUP!" Angus boomed out in his distinctive baritone as he grinned as the crew of the USF Excalibur cheered and whistled at a volume all out of proportion to the numbers on hand.

The eight pool reporters that had joined the Fleet were quartered on the Tiger. They patiently waited in the front row, all taking in the show of support for the 'Old Man' that seemed more at place in a remake of the finale of "White Christmas" than the mess deck of the Fleet's most powerful starship. All of them wore unabashed grins, all except one Robert Arnault. He wore a slight grin as poor makeup covering his displeasure at the affection and loyalty the Admiral had earned. Indeed, Arnault passionately hated everything about the Admiral. Especially the fact that he was married to Gina Fonteyn, the old high school sweetheart of Angus MacAlister.

Every new acclaim, every new honor, every bit of public adoration only served to drive up the hate Arnault felt for the Admiral. He had met Gina when she was an intern at Niles News Network, where he was a midlevel reporter. Her connections to the Admiral kept Arnault interested in her, and he eventually talked her into marriage. Now, after the anticipated advancement from those connections did not happen, Arnault became more and more bitter inside every day. He was married to a woman he didn't like, let alone love, and her famous old boyfriend treated her like a little sister but would have nothing to do with Arnault. And his job would be lost if he left the bitch.

Yes, Arnault hated Angus MacAlister. As he filtered out the frequent laughter and applause from the Admiral's speech, he slipped, letting a sneer hit his face momentarily. Recovering quickly, he clapped energetically at the next opportunity. He had to bide his time for now. But he would have his enjoyment. He had made a deal. Soon, yes, and enough credits so a job and that stupid, complaining cow would no longer be required. Nervously he fingered the tiny device hidden inside his suit as Admiral MacAlister spoke on.

****

The Hounds of Heaven

41

"Major, I've got nothing on sensors. You sure they didn't all get space-sick?"

"Can it, Adamy! Keep 'em peeled, Hounds!"

"Bogies, down forty-five degrees at twelve degrees port, sir! GravDrives!"

"Got 'em! Just like simms, short bursts. No friendlies! Right Alpha-spiral on my mark, MARK!"

The twelve SF-12s broke out into an interlaced spiral 'dive' onto the contacts. "Here we go!" thought Yeager. The targeting computer selected the bogie he would attack, and gave him the best path to a kill marked on his visor. Weapon selection was PPCs only; Plasma Pulse Cannon. These small babies could punch holes in a destroyer; they were deadly against fighter-sized craft. For training, their power settings were reduced to a low-output training laser. But, while he had four of them, each Thunderbolt carried eight! And, while the Mustangs could carry two ship killer Mk 5 Mini-GravTorps, the Thunderbolts could carry three in addition to eight Mk IV 250KT nuke rockets.

As the first pass was made at high C fractions, the targeting computers directed all firing; no pilot could even guess at those speeds. Here the newer Mustangs with their quatinary computers simply did not miss; the Thunderbolts with their older systems only hit with twenty percent of their shots on this opening pass. With all weapons fire simulated, the action soon looked like an old atmospheric 'fur-ball'. Fighters everywhere, every eye and sensor straining to find death before death found them. The Mustangs could turn on a dime, and out accelerate the Jugs, but the Jugs had a slightly faster top-end speed, in atmosphere and in space, and were very hard to knock out; either the pilots of the Jugs had rigged the scoring, or they really were one *very* tough bird.

Fred had a Jug right where he wanted him, in front of his PPCs. Then all hell broke loose as alarms went off and simulated PPC fire flashed past his canopy.

"Break! Break! Break!" Bong shouted as a dozen sleek, tri-hulled birds shot through the dogfight at unbelievable speed, taking out both Mustangs and Thunderbolts. In four seconds all ships were dead in space, computer-enforced 'kills'. The exercise was over.

"What the hell were THOSE?"

"Lightings. SP-15 Lightings, boys. Faster than Thunderbolts, with twice the power of a Mustang. Carrying four One-point five PPCs, one

Four-point-five PPC, four Mini-GravTorps, and ten Mk VII nuke rockets each. Did I or did I NOT tell you to ALWAYS keep you eyes peeled and scanning?"

****

USF Excalibur
Between Perseus and Orion
Standard Earth Date December 6 3811

The crowd seemed to close in on him wherever he moved in the mess area turned reception hall. Angus realized he had to 'make the rounds', but still dreaded the whole thing. Now this, a 'preliminary reception'!

"Admiral! Congratulations on your retirement!" Angus heard the familiar voice spew like a bad smell from a small, greasy looking man in a light grey jacket and black shirt. Arnault was one person he never wanted to spend any time with. The rat had married his first love, but by then Angus had been over Gina for some time. He and Gina had become friends. But he still felt, he *knew* she deserved so much better than this slime. And, when Angus had heard of his abusing her, there had been a *very* personal visit to be sure Arnault understood that would never be tolerated again.

So, now Angus had to talk with this, this *thing*.

"Well, hello, Robert! Thank you, very much. That has a *special* meaning coming from *you*." Angus looked down, squinting through his grin at the mousey little man. "How is Gina these days? So sorry she couldn't come. Will she be at the party at Fleet?" Angus' internal clock started counting down the allotted time he had set for each reporter. He had spoken slowly, so as to use most of it up before Arnault could start pestering him.

Then Arnault reached his hand out, offering it to the Admiral, and said, "She was disappointed she could not be here, Admiral."

Angus caught a glimpse of dark metal hidden in that hand. Instinctively the Admiral moved so fast that only the trained eyes of the military in the room saw it; he lifted his hand to accept Arnault's, then he was behind the reporter, holding the little man's arm up to his throat, the poison needle a scant half-inch from Arnault's carotid artery. Angus quickly turned marched the man out of the reception as every sailor and marine in the room moved to attract attention away from where the Admiral and two marine guards were moving out of the room. Jen covered for the Admiral, explaining that nature calls even among the super-stars. Two minutes later, Angus was back in the reception area as if nothing had happened. The civilian guests never did notice the quite arrival of twenty sailors and a dozen marines, all in full dress uniforms, mingling among the guests, or that there were now four conspicuously armed marine guards at each doorway.

****

The Graveyard
Standard Earth Date December 6 3811

The huge thirty kilometer long ship looked to move in slow motion as it eased out from the dock. That is, it would have if an outside observer could have seen anything except her navigation lights. The black passive stealth pigments had rendered the ship nearly invisible without those lights on. Gone were the six projecting drive pods that mechanically swiveled and rotated to give a USF ship full thrust in any direction; these were replaced with new units which gave one thousand times the thrust in any direction with only six shallow bumps along the now smoothly flowing lines of her hull. The ship was now shaped like a huge, elongated football.

"Status, Miss Holloway?" Captain Alex MacAlister asked from his chair in the center rear of the large command bridge. Unlike the hallways and common rooms, the wedge-shaped bridge was painted a neutral medium grey, with a lighter grey ceiling and charcoal grey flooring.

"Sensors show all clear on projected course and forty degrees peripherally, sir!" Sensor Officer Lieutenant Nancy Holloway replied.

"Ahead ten percent Mr. Shin. Easy, please."

"Aye, Captain." Helmsman Lt. Commander Ito Shin snapped in smart reply.

"Clear of all moorings, Captain", stated Navigator Lt. Commander Susan Harlow.

"Increase to twenty percent Mr. Shin."

"Twenty percent, aye-aye, sir"

"V-rel zero-point-three C, zero-point-four C sir! Inertial dampers on line and nominal." Harlow noted in a very professional tone.

"She is fast, Miss Harlow. Set your course for Cygnus 12. Let's see just how fast."

"Course set, Captain. Ready on command."

"Helm, set Grav-drive at fifty percent. Go."

"Grav-drive, fifty percent, engaged."

"ETA Cygnus 12 system twelve minutes, sir!"

"She is *damn* fast, isn't she!"

****

"Fleet reports dead stop, Admiral"

"Civilian passenger status, Will?"

"Security reports all civilians are touring the Edinburgh, sir, except our 'guest' in the brig. Edinburgh reports all accounted for and appropriate sensor images engaged. Their two day tour of the Perseus Nebulas will begin in two hours"

"Very well. Comm, ship-wide, please."

"Ship-wide ready, Admiral."

"Attention crew; this is Admiral MacAlister. We will be taking a little side trip very shortly. Everything about this trip is classified Top Secret. You will discuss nothing of this trip, including the very existence of it, with anyone. Ever. Section Chiefs, Open your sealed orders."

Throughout the ship, Section Chiefs entered passwords into datatabs to unlock their encrypted orders.

"Crew; your Section Chefs will fill in the details you need to know for this training mission. That is all."

Jen just stared at the Admiral, mouth open. She shot a quick glance with her eyes to Will, who just shrugged and mouthed, "I don't know". The fact that the Admiral had been able to keep a secret from her, no matter how classified, bothered her immensely.

"Will, let's go."

"Sound General Quarters! Battle Stations! Helm, set course for Cygnus 12."

"Course set, sir."

"Go."

"Command Staff briefing in my Ready Room. Now."

****

"I don't care, check it again! If this is some top secret mission, rest assured the Captain or the Admiral WILL inspect us again, and NOT just as a good-bye kiss!"

"Aye, Lieutenant!" Chief of the Flight Deck Edwards saluted and turned to his crew, "All right, ladies, you heard the CAG! I want to be able to eat soup off this deck in ten minutes, off of these fighters in twelve minutes! These bombers and transports in thirteen! Now move it! Move it! Move it!" The Chief always thought that yelling things three times helped get them done; he was the Chief of the Flight Deck on the Fleet's flagship after all, so few ever argued the point.

Lieutenant Commander JG Chester Jones approached his Commander Air Group and asked, "Captain Singh, Sir, do you know what's going on?"

"CJ, you know better than to ask that!" Barked the CAG. He had THE last word on all flight ops on the Excalibur; absolutely nothing moved on or off of this flight deck without his OK. Lt. Singh had been the top rated pilot to have made it out of Fighter Command training alive. Ever. Jones had scored just fractionally below Singh's record due to equipment failure ending the test prematurely.

Singh leaned in close to Jones and said in a low voice, "not a clue, CJ. Keep that quiet. We may not even fly Cap, but suit up anyway. How's your shoulder?"

"Just a little sore, sir, not bad" he whispered in return. Then, for his Fighter Force, a loud and sharp "Sir!" Jones saluted and turned away from his CAG. Singh always had pushed him hard, and at first CJ thought it was because the CAG wanted to reinforce that his score was still the record, but it was Singh who showed CJ the mathematical projection of his score had the simm run as designed; it was Singh who petitioned the Academy to adopt that number as CJ's Score of Record. That score was a two percent improvement on Singh's score. And, CJ knew some one had beaten the 'old man's' score, and his, last fall. By a lot. CJ figured it was anger over that which led the CAG to push him harder than all the other pilots. Way harder. Until the clash with the Orion pirates. A mine damaged CAG's fighter early on. CJ had to command the Wing as they attacked the pirate base. He never thought about it until everything was over, but he was never nervous, never lost focus; it was just like any one of the 'old man's' drills. That's when he knew why he was ridden so hard. Since that time, Singh had given CJ more and more control over the day-to-day operations of his Fighter Force.

As he walked back to tell the wing that CAG was as much in the dark as they were, a small grin hit his boyish good looks. His wing. Yeah. He liked the sound of that.

****

"Contact, captain!" Alex heard the thought through his combat link implant.

"Well, tell me what you have, Miss Holloway."

"Heavy cruiser, Excalibur Class configuration, ten degrees port, five degrees below dead ahead, sir." After weeks of drills and simms, the crew was used to using the links to communicate faster and in more detail than ever thought possible; Alex heard the thought and saw exactly where the contact was.

"Any indication she has seen us?"

"No sir. She's running silent, no active sensors, full stealth sir."

"Mr. Shin, bring us in at One-point-five C, attack vector Alpha, twelve km separation. Let's keep this first run simple."

"Aye, aye, Sir! One-point-five C, twelve km sep. Attack run initiated, now."

"Mr. Vaughn, give the computer weapons control, training levels at zero-point-zero-two percent."

"Computer control, training levels set at zero-point-zero-two percent, Sir."

"Closing, firing in approximately three seconds, Sir."

"All batteries reporting hits, Sir! One-hundred percent!"

"Calm down, Mr. Vaughn. Mr. Shin, come about and match Excalibur's course and speed. Cap her "T" at three million km and maintain."

"3 million km across her bow, aye Sir!"

"The new passives are as good as advertised, I'd say. Weapons?"

"Sir!" Lieutenant Lance Vaughn Jr. replied.

"Zero-point-zero-two percent plasma beam over reactors amidships. Fire when ready."

"Zero-point-zero-two percent plasma beam, aye-aye, sir! Fired!"

****

USF Excalibur
Standard Earth Date December 6 3811

The Excalibur's bridge was a busy place when she was in combat. Each crewman sat at an assigned station; four at sensors, six at weapons, two each at nav and helm, four at defensive systems, two at flight ops, and two at communications. The Captain's armored station sat centered behind and above, with the Admiral's station behind and slightly to the right. Two more comm-techs were behind the Admiral's armored station and were dedicated to fleet coordination. All of the stations faced the main view screen, a four-meter high by ten-meter wide projection of the space outside or inside the ship, from any of the sensor data received by the crew. Each sat in a combination acceleration chair/pressure suit. These chairs would wrap the occupant in a pressure suit automatically should the bridge depressurize. This kept the bridge crew functional in case of severe battle damage. In addition, each station was an escape module, allowing the bridge crew to fight as long as possible. The Captain's station had three retractable walls, which served as armor and communication/information stations as well as part of his escape module. The Admiral's station had a much more sophisticated chair and armored walls, the entire station also becoming an escape module.

"Plasma Training hits! Shields down sir!"

"Where? Where did that shot come from?" Gridley urged. He noticed that his normally calm bridge crew was tense as he scanned their performance.

"Nothing on passives, sir. Not a thing!"

"Actives, all, until you find it!"

"Aye-aye, actives at full search".

"Shields beginning regeneration, ten percent"

"Plasma hits again, forward section." Alarms sounded all over the Excalibur as the plasma beam neutralized the mighty warship's grav-shields and scorched her gravity-compressed hull directly over her gavometron reactors.

A sound like some one dropped a bag of tuning forks spread through the ship for twenty seconds. Alarms blared.

"Sensors see nothing Sir! They tell me we are all alone in empty space!"

"Well, *some one's* ripping us a new garbage port; find them! If you have to open an airlock and stick your head outside to look, find them while we still have a rock to throw at them!""

"Aye, Sir!"

****

"99% hits with plasma cannons, Sir. They still can't find us."

"Bring us around to broadside. Keep us in a spiral around her."

"Aye, Sir. Turning to bring us broadside. Spiral envelope."

"Even at broadside, Sir."

"She's damn handy as well as fast! Nice flying, Mr. Shin!"

"Easy as pie, Sir!"

"Weapons!"

"Weapons ready; all on line; Port broadside targeted"

"Mr. Vaughn, you may fire at will."

****

USF Excalibur
Standard Earth Date December 6 3811

"Admiral, we've been split apart with a huge volley of plasma cannon fire, 90% of our port broadside weapons are out."

"Weapons fire close by! Incoming on Starboard side!"

"Target that space and fire all you've got, Miss Finch!"

"Pulse lasers, firing! Broadside railguns, point defense railguns, all firing. Missile tubes, firing. Forward torpedo tubes, all active homing, fired!" Lt. Commander Stacy Finch listed each system as the mighty Excalibur hit the area of space that broadside came from, and hit it hard.

****

USF Fortiter
Standard Earth Date December 6 3811

"Damn, will you look at that! "

"That is one hell of a lot of firepower, Sir!"

"Yes, it is. And, it's about zero point zero, zero, zero, two five percent of our firepower. Shin, good job moving us up and out of the way of that!"

"Yes, Sir."

"Point defense, watch for fighters, and track those torpedoes, but don't engage unless they lock on us."

"Aye Sir. Tracking unless locked."

"Do you want to launch our fighters, Sir?" came the question from CAG.

"Negative; we outnumber theirs by too great a margin. Let's see what our Near Space Defense System can do against their birds."

"Damn!" whispered First Flight Leader Lieutenant Phyllis Mor when the fighter jocks sitting on the ready line heard the Captain's orders. "Even a little training, and we can't join in!" She was *aching* to take the new birds with their implant interfaces out in a battle against other pilots instead of just running simms . The Eagle II fighters were, well, light-years ahead of everything else, and she wanted to prove it!

"Did you say something, Miss Mor?" the CAG snarled.

"Just suffering from some gas, Sir!"

"Be careful how you relieve your pressure, Lieutenant!"

"Aye-aye, Sir!"

"I'll speak to Cookie about dumping that hot sauce you drown his food in, now stow it. We may be needed in a hurry." Commander Kowalski grunted back. Mor was the best pilot he had ever seen, except for his sister; but his sister had never wanted to fly fighters. Phyll had bettered Singh's scores on the Simms by almost five percent; Jen had beat Singh's score by over twelve percent when he snuck her in to settle a sibling bet, but only he and his sister would ever know it.

Keeping Mor calm had been quite a challenge since she was assigned here; she wanted, demanded action with an energy he had only seen from his dad. Missing this exercise did nothing to help him channel her energy for the good of the ship.

****

Screamin' Demons
USF Excalibur Flight Deck
Standard Earth Date December 6 3811

"OK, heads up, Screamin' Demons! We have to find this bogy, and pound the hell out of it!" CJ growled at his flight.

"Just what are we lookin' for, Boss?" Clemons asked. "Huck" Clemons had the best eyes in the fleet.

"Well, figure it out, Huckleberry! Whoever is shooting our butts off would be a good place to start!"

"Aye, Sir!"

"Hey, Boss, twelve degrees down, forty degrees starboard. Notice the stars?"

"Good work, Huck. Lets not be too obvious that we've made our target for the night, girls. Just act like bashful wallflowers hanging on the bleachers."

"You got it, Boss!"

"Attack vector Singh Gamma Seven, accelerate to zero-point-two C. On my mark."

"Mark!"

****

USF Fortiter
Standard Earth Date December 6 3811

"Fighters attacking. Looks like a varying radius spiral around a sinusoidal vector from port lower rear quarter, port upper midships, and starboard lower bow, 300,000 clicks out. Number; three groups, fifty-four fighters each. Velocity zero-point-two C. NSD has them tracked. Interceptor missiles launched and tracking."

"112 fighters hit, 120, 148. NSD railguns tracking survivors. Two hit. Six, No, twelve more. Last two out. PD reports all fighters out of action Sir!"

"Secure from Battle stations. Stand down from General Quarters. Everyone, well done! Senior Staff debriefing in my Ready Room in thirty minutes! Landing bay, prepare to receive the Admiral's skiff in forty-five minutes."

****

Screamin' Demons
Standard Earth Date December 6 3811

"Damn! What the hell just happened to us!" Thought CJ as he flew his "dead" ship back to the Excalibur.

"Comm, get me CAG. Please."

"CJ, it looks like you managed to get your flight checkmated!" The CAG growled over the link. "I thought I told you to take CARE of my pilots and my fighters!"

"There's only one way I'll ever learn just what happened here, CAG. Can you get me on that Admiral's skiff?"

"No promises, CJ. Haul your ass back here and I'll see." *Good thinking. I've already gotten your clearance. That should be an interesting meeting*, Singh thought.

USF Excalibur
Standard Earth Date December 6 3811

"Really, Jen, the whole thing was, IS too classified. Need to know only. I shouldn't even be bringing you along on this trip."

"Yes, *Sir!*"

The Admiral's comm beeped. "Singh, tell the pilot all stop."

"Aye, Admiral, all stop. CJ, all stop."

"Aye, Commander."

The shuttle hung motionless, alone in space until a huge rectangle of lights came up in front of it. A sliver of light expanded up from the bottom of the rectangle revealing the interior of a massive hanger deck.

"Admiral MacAlister, requesting permission to dock." Angus said into his comm.

"Permission granted, Admiral. Welcome aboard!" Upon hearing the reply, Jen's mouth fell open as she recognized the voice.

"My father used to say, 'you'll catch flies like that', Miss Kowalski," grinned the Admiral.

"There are no flies in space, Sir!" Jen quipped back at him as a smile spread across her face.

"CJ, get us inside please!" bellowed the CAG over the laughter in the cabin.

****

USF Fortiter
Standard Earth Date December 6 3811

"Admiral on the deck!"

"Admiral, welcome aboard, Sir!" Saluted Alex.

"Finally found a ship with enough headroom, Commander?" Angus grinned at his son towering above him as he returned his sharp salute.

"Aye, Sir." Alex smiled back. "I believe you have met my XO, Commander Peter Perry. This is my Helmsman, Lt. Commander Ito Shin, my CAG, Commander Jerome Kowalski, Jr., and my Fighter Force Commander, Lieutenant Phyllis Mor."

"Good to see you again, Alex, Peter. Damn, Jerry, you look just like your dad! Good to see you."

"Thank you sir. He's left me some big shoes to fill."

"That he did. From the reports I've been getting, you're stretching them a bit. Keep it up."

"Aye-aye, Sir!"

"Lt. Mor. I don't believe we've met." The Admiral greeted the tall, buxom pilot.

CJ's eyes widened at the name; *her*! She beat Singh's scores! He looked her over closely, then his eyes found hers, and his mind went blank. Absolutely empty of everything, except those amazing green eyes....

"Sir! The Admiral is correct, Sir!" *How did the Admiral know my name? Why did the Commander's sister smile and start shaking her head at that?*

"I appreciate your support, Lieutenant. If you see my wife, please pass that along!"

"Sir?" Mor puzzled a few seconds until the embarrassed look on her face told everyone she got the joke. That is when she saw Jones staring at her as if she had two heads. Who was this cute but rude officer who made her feel so uncomfortable?

"Alex, You know Commodore Gridley, his CAG, Commander Singh, and Lieutenant Commander Chester Jones, his Fighter Force Commander."

Jones! Chester Jones? And Singh! A thrill at meeting the two best pilots ever; aside from her and Jerry, that is. Still, here were her idols as pilots, her role models. Jones was only a year older than her, and the second youngest to make Lieutenant Commander in history, just six months older than Alex MacAlister, and ten months older than Admiral MacAlister had been! But why was Jones staring at her, looking right *inside* her? *Did I grow a third eye? Was there a zit on my forehead? Is my uniform unzipped? Did it become transparent?* She felt herself blushing brightly and sweating at that thought. Then her Tomboy took over; she made a camera gesture at Chester.

"A-HEM!" the comment from Jen was punctuated by a subtle but sharp kick to the Admiral's nearest leg.

"Oh, and my Chief Of Staff, Lieutenant Commander Jenitka Kowalski." Angus, grinning, glanced at first Jen, then Alex. *Their eyes are locked on each other so tightly you'd need a fusion torpedo to break them apart*, Angus thought. Jerry grinned at his blushing little sister.

"Ladies, gentlemen, shall we move to my ready room for the debriefing?" Alex asked as he motioned for his guests to follow the marine escort while he fell into step behind the Admiral and his COS, never taking his eyes off of Jen. CJ maneuvered himself behind Lt. Mor, where he soon discovered there was something besides her eyes that fascinated him.

Chapter Five

"Admiral, I've taken the liberty of opening some Hackberry juice from Omregon 12 for the debriefing. Non-fermented, of course."

"Good choice. Wish I knew how it always seems cold, no matter what the temp of it really is! Alex, your ship is most impressive. You and your crew have done a great job prepping her."

"But, prepping her for what, Admiral?"

"Soon enough, Captain. How did the new links work? Any problems?"

"We run at one-hundred-fifty percent of the simms command teams in combat, sir, a fifty percent efficiency increase. Their reliability has always been one-hundred percent."

"Alex, the ship is amazing. She's an order of magnitude past the Excalibur. I just hope that's enough."

"Sir?"

Angus waited until the group was seated before answering his son. He addressed that answer to the group.

"Ladies and Gentlemen," the Admiral's 'Serious-Official' tone announced as he turned to face the group, "this meeting is now compartmentalized and boxed."

"Meeting log secured, Level One. Screens applied and operational." All eyes grew wide at the computer's announcement. Everyone took a drink from the glass in front of him or her.

Even the existence of this meeting's log was above the security level of all but the Admiral and The Joint Chiefs. The room was now screened, so nothing could be transmitted out or recorded by any bug or personal recorders.

"Shall I clear the room of the lower security clearances?" Alex offered, his apprehension and confusion apparent.

"Those of you with insufficient clearance for compartmentalized and boxed information have sufficient clearance as of now."

Jones and Mor stared at each other with nervous eyes. *What was this?* Mor bit her lower lip as Jones gave her a slight shrug.

"Lieutenant Mor, you are the most recent Academy attendee here; how many civilizations have we discovered in the galaxy so far?"

"Well, two, sir."

"Really? Did we discover them?"

"Some would say they discovered us, Admiral, but when we

became aware of them, we in a sense discovered them."

"Lieutenant, you may well have a long and prosperous career in politics after you leave Star Force. Other than the Birds and the Bugs, have we found even any trace of any other civilizations?"

"No, Admiral".

"Does that strike anyone here as odd?"

"The Birds and Bugs destroyed them all, sir." CJ answered.

"Every trace? Every building, every road, every space station? The B&Bs weren't powerful or thorough enough for that. Think of this; how many habitable planets have we discovered orbiting likely stars, as compared to the predicted number? The surprising answer is two percent. Just two percent of the likely stars we've mapped have habitable planets. Most of them have only asteroid fields orbiting the liquid water zone. We think we now know why.

"There are two parts to this. Here is part one." The Admiral took out a datacard and slid it into the receptacle. "This happened seven and a half years ago."

****

Chrysler Building
55th Floor
New York City
Standard Earth Date December 4 3811

"Your *person* has failed to execute his assignment. He must be removed before he gives up any information."

"I've already arraigned for that."

"Just be sure you do not fail us again, Senator Anderson!"

****

USF Fortiter
Standard Earth Date December 6 3811

The room was silent as the probe's recording of the Sagan's destruction finished playing. Everyone in the room felt empty, hollow, and helpless. How could there be something that powerful! How could they protect their citizens from *this*? CJ had almost forgot about those eyes of Lt. Mor.

"Alex, the Victorious…"

"She's been renamed, Admiral. She is now The USF Fortiter."

"They pushed that nonsense up? That means your mother is here?"

"Aye *and* aye, Sir!"

"Well, things *are* moving quickly. The first part of this is that ship. We believe ships like it have been shattering planets with technological civilizations for eons. We believe they, and not the Bugs, are the reason the Birds never came back, and why we could never find their home world.

"The second part of this is that I am not retiring. After my official 'retirement' party, I'm quietly moving my flag to the Fortiter. Alex, you will continue to command the ship. Our mission is to get as many of the mothballed ships upgraded to her standards as quickly as possible. Those red beams will come for us. My retirement is a cover to give me time to accomplish this away from the public's gaze. Our mission is simple; defend Earth, and when we have enough ships, the other systems."

"This ship was to be a surprise at your retirement!"

"That was, and is the story. Stick to it."

"My crew is not complete yet, sir. I was to go recruiting after your retirement…"

"You will ask for volunteers, starting with certain members of the crews from the Excalibur and Enterprise; each of those ships will be going in for a ' standard' refit. Will, you will be commanding the Cygnus shipyard facilities, and overseeing those refits, as well as planning the upgrade of the entire fleet. The order of upgrade is at your discretion; the Fortiter is now the new standard. The Graveyard has been renamed; The Cygnus Shipyards are once again open for business, in a very quiet way. Two million yard workers and their families are moving in, along with half of the Academy and a large amount of sailors and reservists plus civilian support. Fifteen million in total. All under the biggest stealth umbrella we could build.

"But now, Captain, perhaps your guests would like a tour of your masterpiece? You may start by showing me the Admiral's quarters, since I assume that is where the Admiral's *wife* is?" Angus knew the room was too gloomy after seeing the Sagan recording. He tried to lighten things up a little.

"Aye-aye, Sir. And, I would be happy to give your COS a *personal* tour while you, um, *inspect* your quarters, Sir. Commander Perry, would you kindly give the rest of our guests the VIP tour?" Alex knew his father well enough to see where he was headed, and why.

"Aye, aye, Sir!"

Lt. Mor glanced at CJ, who was staring at her with that lost look again. *He **is** cute. Why did that look affect me this way?* "Permission to tag along, Sir!"

"Denied. Lieutenant, I think you should show Lieutenant Commander Jones your little gems." Alex quipped. Mor and CJ exchanged puzzled looks as Jen blushed bright red as she landed a hard punch on Alex's right shoulder. The rest of the room broke into some much needed laughter.

****

USF Fortiter
Flight Deck
Standard Earth Date December 6 3811

"Here are our birds, Lt. Commander. Vought-Boeing SF-4 Corsairs. These Corsairs are quite the improvement over your standard issue Wildcats." Mor was truly proud of these ships and what they could do. "The new power plants let us run the Gravitic Drives like the big boys do; this one could outpace Excalibur in normal drive *and* FTL. And, they have the new quatinary computers. In terms of range, speed, acceleration, maneuverability, firepower and defensive capabilities they rival a destroyer."

"FTL? No ship this size can go FTL. How can you do it?" *I would love to test her speed! What a ship!*

"Gravitic Drives work in normal space by using gravitic fields to create a sort of 'friction' against the 'fabric' of space itself; instead of pushing matter out of an exhaust for thrust, we push against space with gravitics. For FTL speeds, we stretch that 'fabric' behind us and compress it in front of us; we don't really go faster than light, we just shorten the trip."

"Or lengthen the ship."

"Or both!" *Oh, I'll bet I could lengthen your ship…STOP IT!* "Normally, you'd be correct that the power plants available for ships this size never had anything near the output required to power gravitic drives. But, these little gems do! So, what do you think? Like what you see?" *Oh, GOD! What did I just say?* Mor thought in a panic.

"A sleek, sexy design, for sure. What curves! Nice shape! How hot is it?" CJ said as he ran his hands over the *"Phyll's Killers One"* painted on the sleekly curved nose of the fighter, over a cartoonish scorpion with exaggerated lipstick-covered lips and a stinger dripping venom. He had no idea he was throwing out the type of double-entendres Mor had fought off since she was twelve. Her response surprised him as he tore his eyes off the ship to look at her. *Those damn eyes of hers again!*

"Please keep you comments, *and everything else*, confined to the fighters, Lt. Commander!" If her eyes had been plasma beams, they would have burned right through him and breeched the hull for sure.

CJ had no way of knowing she was as furious at herself as she was at him. All her life Mor had pushed any thoughts of romance or even just sex into a deep, deep pit and covered them over with a thick iron will; for that pit to be ripped open and exposed to him, totally outside of her control, was the most frustrating thing she had ever felt! CJ swallowed the huge lump that had sprouted in his throat and snapped, "At *ease*, Lieutenant! I was talking about the ship. Nothing else here interests me enough to talk about!" *Dammit, that did not come out right! She's not the kind who sleeps her way to the top! Relax, idiot!*

"Aye-*AYE*, Sir." *Did that SOB set her up?* Her reactors started overheating.... *What did he mean, 'nothing ELSE interested him'! I've had more interest than he could generate! That...*

"Look, I'm sorry, Lieutenant. I didn't, well, you didn't deserve that. I really WAS talking about the ship." *But, since you mentioned it......Slow down, CJ! Do NOT look at anything but her eyes! Oh, those eyes....two green, black holes drawing me in deeper...Mercy!*

"Let's start over; that was a built-in reaction. I've been hit up too many times by floozies looking for an "in". I don't think that's what you were doing; it was just reflex. Truce?" CJ offered his hand.

Oh, God! I'm melting! What is going on? Pull out of this nosedive, girl, before you drool on his boots! "Apology accepted, Sir. And, let me also offer one to you for the same reason." Phyll took his hand, meaning to let go after one shake. *Strong, but gentile. Big hands. This guy is special, I can feel it! Stay on target!*

"Lt., I don't doubt that for a minute. Let's agree; if one of us decides to make a pass, they'll just come right out and ask, OK?" *GAWD! Those hands, warm, soft, smooth. What a clumsy oaf! Shut up and say something safe, talk shop! Don't blow it with this one; she's the real deal!*

"Agreed, sir!" *Bite your lip before you say it, before you rip his uniform off and jump on him right here! Specs, talk specs.*

The two pilots stood with clasped hands for several long, silent seconds.

"Here, sir, let me show you my cockpi..., um, pilot's office, sir!" *I can feel my face getting redder! It's getting gawd-awful hot in here! I'll never survive this! He'll court-martial me for sure! LET GO OF HIS HAND YOU IDIOT!*

Those eyes.....I wish I could gaze into those eyes forever.....LET GO OF HER HAND, YOU MORON!

****

"I've missed you so much!" Angus managed to squeeze out between kisses.

"Emmmm. I've missed you, too, ya big hunk! Ready to 'retire'?"

"Senator, what would your constituency say?"

"'Go get 'em, girl' most likely. You are quite the wet dream fodder for us middle-aged empty-nester babes, you know."

"Senator, you *are* good for my ego. I think I'll keep you around. Would you like some Hackberry juice? It is quite refreshing. How do you unbutton this thing?"

"Hear, were you this much of a clumsy oaf in high school?" Cindy stepped back, made a mysterious movement behind her back, and dropped her sensibly stylish dark blue business suit to the floor. "Now, what formation are you thinking of deploying, Admiral?" She stepped forward, put both hands on the big man's chest, and shoved him back onto the bed.

"Are you taking the Excalibur back to Earth?" Angus grinned up at his wife. *Life is good! Oh, I am one lucky SOB.*

Cindy straddled Angus' waist, placing her hands on the bed, one on each side of his head. "No, I have to get there before you do." She leaned forward and crushed her lips to his. *I am one lucky girl! Life is good.* "Mmmm. The itinerary needs work, and I'll never get it done in your quarters. Mmmm."

"Mmmmm, Can't mmmm Barb do it? Mmmm."

"Shut up and kiss me again, Handsome!"

"Aye-aye, Gorgeous!"

****

BEEP-beep-BEEP- BEEP-BEEEEP!

Commodore Gridley's comm unit announced an urgent call from the Excalibur.

"Gridley. Go"

"Captain, I'm picking up a May-Day on civilian channel seven, Sir. A civilian colony ship called the Mayflower, destination Cygnus Zeta 114, Sir. Position about one hour from us at max velocity. They say their reactor is down, and life support is on batteries."

"Prepare to get underway. We'll be back shortly."

"Aye-aye, Sir."

****

USF Excalibur
Marine Commander's Quarters
Standard Earth Date December 6 3811

"Major! The prisoner, sir!"

Major Marx hit his comm to reply, "Evans, what is it?"

"The prisoner, Arnault, sir. He's dead!"

"On my way. Touch nothing!"

****

Fighter Hanger Bay 1
USF Fortiter
Standard Earth Date December 6 3811

"BEEP-beep-BEEP!" CJ's comm went off.

"Lieutenant, it looks like the Admiral's finished his, um, inspections and is ready to go back to the Excalibur. I'll take a rain check on that tour. Thanks for showing me this much, anyway." *Damn, I did it again! She'll have me up on charges! Those eyes, well, if I could look into them for just a few more minutes, it'd be worth it...*

He's fumbling over his words like a schoolboy! OK, Ace, you're in MY sights now. "Aye, Sir. It's been my pleasure, Sir." Mor replied confidently. "I'm hoping we'll be able to compare moves sometime. On flying, Sir!" *Bulls-eye!*

"Would you be so kind as to lead me back to our shuttle, Lieutenant?" *If my knees don't turn to jelly first. Oh, brother!*

"It's about ten minutes, Sir. Please, this way." Mor grinned as she turned and walked in front of the Lieutenant Commander. The view fascinated CJ, as she led him on a less than direct path back to his shuttle.

****

"Jen, I want to ask you something."

"Yes, Handsome?"

"Why don't we have the wedding here. During Dad's retirement party?"

"Alex MacAlister! *That* party is for your *father*. It's *his* day."

"But, it's not a *real* retirement. Besides, it was Mom's idea."

"It was not! She told me you asked her about it, and that you had asked your father, too. Alex MacAlister, you promise me you'll never lie to me again!"

"Yes, Baby-Doll".

"So, then, will Jerry be your best man?"

"BEEP-beep-BEEP!" Jen's comm went off.

"Jen, we have a civilian SOS call to answer. We have to get back to the Excalibur."

"Aye-aye, Admiral. On my way."

"It looks like it'll take CJ about ten minutes to meet us in the hangar bay."

"Understood, Sir!" Jen replied as she reached her arms up, draping them over Alex's broad, muscular shoulders, and around Alex's neck, drawing his head down for a very passionate kiss.

"Turn your comm off please, Lieutenant Commander!" Angus laughed.

Alex's laugh echoed his father's.

Jen turned her comm off, because she *always* complied with the Admiral's orders, even when she didn't hear them.

****

"OK, boys and girl, you have your nav coordinates loaded. Your teddy bears and blankies are on a freighter headed there now. Any questions?"

"No, Sir!"

"Then fire 'em up and let's get 'em outta the corral."

Twelve silver SF-12 Mustangs tore through the Upstate New York sky on their way to their new home, Cygnus 78. But first they joined up with another 1,960 Mustangs from other units, as well as 1,880 Thunderbolts, 930 of the gorgeous new Lightnings, just in his formation alone.

"Well, will you look at that! Are *any* of the new fighters staying on Earth, sir?"

"None of your beeswax, Yeager. I'd say over 15,000 altogether are coming with us. That would leave about 12,000 each of the older Hawks and Cobras in Sol system."

"Sir, as far as I can see on Infonet, this is the first interstellar trip for one man ships, sir."

"Stow it, Adamy. But yeah, it is."

****

USF Excalibur
Standard Earth Date December 6 3811

The Marine Corporal looked both ways down the empty maintenance corridor of the Excalibur before slipping into the sensor data junction room. A directional comm signal could be sent out of the ship from here, up the data conduit to the external sensor receivers. The signal would be difficult to detect, and nearly impossible to trace. His non-regulation comm unit had nearly finished booting up when a huge shadow passed over him, and an over-sized hand clamped over the unit.

Before the Corporal could react, a second huge hand grabbed the back of his head, slamming his face into the electronics rack.

"Jesus, Ellis, did you kill him?"

"Not yet, sir. Am I cleared to?"

"I'll have to see if he will confirm our intel first. After that, I may just space the SOB myself, Dave."

"Aye-aye, Sir."

"Bring him to Interview room four. I'll notify Major Marx."

Charlie Sims, Space Force Intelligence, turned and followed behind the huge agent in a sailor's uniform carrying the prisoner over his shoulder. Charlie was pissed off. *Very* pissed off.

****

USF Excalibur

"The last shuttle is in the bay, Captain. We have all of the children aboard, and accommodations are being set up in the Delta Mess, Sir."

"How many children, all together, Steve?" Will Gridley asked.

"It looks like the final count is 384, Sir. The youngest is six, the oldest is fourteen. Why evacuate the kids, Sir, and not the parents?"

"That ship uses an old reactor design. They never should have brought the kids on board; that radiation can screw up adolescent and younger kids pretty bad, fry their glands. That would have been a one-generation colony! Most of the parents left on an earlier flight, to have the colony started before the kids arrived. The parents onboard all had to stay with the ship, to repair it and get it to Cigna Z-114; leasing it represents the group's entire life savings. We'll bring the kids to the Cigna Z-114 after the Admiral's retirement. I want to have a little 'chat' with the leasing firm first. We are heading in that general direction, anyway."

"Aye-aye, Sir."

****

USF Excalibur
Admiral's Quarters
Standard Earth Date December 6 3811

"Come!" Angus replied to his cabin's door chime.

"Admiral, I just want to report on the children from that colony ship we picked up. The children are comfortable in Delta Mess for now. We've set it up like a camp-out, complete with a holo of the CZ-114 night sky. Steve Walton did a great job coming up with that, Sir."

"Good. You are overseeing the care of the kids, then."

"Well, not officially, Sir. I'm just trying to help out..."

"That was not a question, Jen. You like it, you have the time, so take it."

"Aye-aye, Sir!" Jen beamed. "By the way, what are your plans for dinner tonight?" she asked.

"I hadn't thought of it, Jen, to be honest," Angus lied. *Just don't tell me it's another social event with the reporters.*

"The bridge crew has asked me to convey a request to you, sir; they want you to attend a little farewell party on the bridge. They've gone to a lot of effort, Sir; I suggest you go. It starts in thirty minutes. Hotaling *claims* to have real haggis." With that Jen turned and walked out of his quarters before he could assemble any response.

"I'd love to!" Angus said to a closed door. "I just hope I can tie these Ghillie Brogues in time!" the Admiral mumbled through his smile as he thought of the looks on their faces when he stepped onto the bridge, wearing his dress kilt!

****

USF Excalibur
Airlock 37
Standard Earth Date December 6 3811

United Space Marine Corps Major General Bill Marx wore a major's uniform, as he stood expressionless at the airlock view port as he watched the body drift away. Of the million or so thoughts streaming through his mind, empathy for that person was not included.

William Marx was in fact the Major General in command of the USMC Intel division, undercover as a major for eight years while investigating a deep conspiracy to assassinate The Admiral. This was possible only because all USMC Intel officers were promoted off the record; only The Commandant USMC knew of them. Marx's last official promotion came nine years ago. For all anyone knew, he was a major in command of a combat unit.

"Bill." Charlie Sims said quietly from behind Marx.

"Sims. I'm not happy about this. Not at all. How did this plant end up in *my* command?"

"There are people high up involved, Bill. VERY high up. That's all I can tell you. We know about them, who they are, their general objectives, but not their specific plans. We're collecting evidence, but it takes time."

"How long will it take?"

"It could be soon, if they make another mistake. They don't make many, so it may be a while."

"I just pray I can protect him until you're ready."

"So do I, Major. So do I."

****

Admiral's Quarters
USF Excalibur
Standard Earth Date December 7 3811

Admiral Angus MacAlister stood in front of his full-length mirror, turning back and forth as he inspected his Argyle Kilt outfit. He smiled at the look, just as he had imagined it!

"OK, Angus! Show-time!" he whispered as he walked to the door with a small smirk of self-satisfaction on his face.

As Angus stepped out of his quarters, the Marine Guards snapped smartly to attention as they had done countless times before. Angus took two steps towards the bridge before it hit him; he stopped, thinking of the vision of the two expressionless soldiers, smartly dressed in sleeveless combat shirts over impeccable MacAlister Clan Kilts! *Was that a tattoo on their right shoulders? Nah!"* He thought as he walked on to the bridge in confusion, never daring to turn and look at the guards. As the automatic doors opened to admit him to the bridge, he suddenly stopped mid-stride.

****

USF Farragut
Near Altair System
Standard Earth Date December 7 3811

Senator Cindy Grabelle reclined on her bed, scanning the itinerary for her husband's retirement reception, wearing her favorite, rather unstylish, but decidedly comfortable nightgown and robe. She used her maiden name for purely political reasons; to avoid immediate identification with her famous military spouse, and also as proof of her independence from him.

Her room aboard the USF Farragut, transporting her back to Earth for the reception, was small, but comfortable and quiet. Until the alarms went off.

Her aide Barb Hopkins entered the room, her face carrying the expression of breathless panic that seemed perpetually frozen to it; "What's going on?"

"Do I look like the ship's captain, Barb? Relax. I'm sure everything is under control. Let me find out.

"Captain Stathus, should we be concerned about the alarms?"

"Captain?"

"This is odd. Computer, ship's status report."

"The ship is on auto pilot. The current alarms indicate probable collision with Altair 66 Gamma within three hours if course is not corrected."

"Why haven't you corrected the course?"

"Course has been locked."

"Over ride the lock."

"The lock was set with command level authority. It can not be overridden."

"Fleet Level Emergency over ride."

"Commodore or higher rank is required for Fleet Level Emergency over ride."

"Crew status?"

"All crew members departed in shuttles forty minutes ago."

"I'm getting too damn old for this shit, Barb. Looks like I *am* the pilot now. Come with me."

The two women ran to the bridge, but the doors would not open.

"Computer, open Bridge doors!"

"Bridge door access requires Commodore Level rank or higher."

"Being an Admiral's wife has advantages, sometimes. Computer, Command Level over ride code......"

"STOP!" Barb screamed.

Cindy shot her friend a puzzled look. Then it dawned on her.

"Computer, environmental status of Command Bridge?"

"Command Bridge is currently in a vacuum. The Command Bridge Esc-Mod bays are empty and open to space."

"CCCC environmental status?"

"Combat Command and Control Center is currently in a vacuum. The Combat Command and Control Center Esc-Mod bays are empty and open to space."

"Computer, Flag Level over ride code 1243965."

"Over ride code accepted. Pass code please."

"Pass code; eat my haggis you son of a bitch."

"Access granted Admiral MacAlister. Orders?"

"General distress signal broadcast."

"All comm equipment is unresponsive."

"Esc-Mod activation."

"All Esc-Mods have ejected."

"Damn it!"

"I have insufficient authority or equipment to damn the ship."

"Do not hit Altair 66 Gamma."

"Insufficient time to achieve planetary escape velocity with available thrust."

"Can you land us on it?"

"Landing is possible."

"Environmental conditions on Altair 66 Gamma?"

"Atmosphere: Pressure 9,000 feet Earth equivalent altitude; eighty percent nitrogen, sixteen percent oxygen, four percent carbon dioxide. Temperature range at equator; high 44C, low 12C. Gravity zero-point-six Earth. Average length of day twenty Earth hours. Radiation exposure one-point-four equatorial Earth. Indigenous life forms; none recorded. Imported life forms; none recorded. Liquid water; none recorded."

"Display the three most suitable landing sites. Barb, start packing."

****

CAG Quarters
USF Fortiter
Standard Earth Date December 7 3811

"Lieutenant Mor, reporting as ordered, Sir!"

"At ease, Lieutenant. Sit", Lieutenant Commander Jerry Kowalski was very short in his order. "Computer, all recording off!"

"Confirmed."

"Lieutenant, you have been in a fog thicker than oatmeal. What has you so distracted?"

"Um, Sir, I, ah.."

"This is off the record, Phyll. It started after the Admiral's visit. Is it the grey ships? Damn, Phyll, they have us all edgy, but you've always been so focused on your flying, on your pilots. Phyll, you almost ended up a deck stain today! What is it?"

"Sir, I, um, I have some confused feelings, Sir. About, um, ah…about a, um…. a man, Sir!"

"There is someone you need to talk to. Hell of a pilot, yes, better than you! But she went through the same thing. And, you need a woman to talk this over with." Jerry handed Phyll a piece of paper with a comm number on it. "Call her. You can tell her anything. It's personal, off the record, girl-to-girl. That's an order."

"Aye-aye, Sir!" Phyll saluted, turned and left the room. *He is a great CO. I am lucky to work for him.* Outside, she looked at the paper and grinned. The next to the comm number was written, "Jen".

Jerry Kowalski sat back in his chair as Phyllis walked out of his quarters. *That is one lucky guy. Looks like nice guys do finish last. At least she'll be happy.*

****

Command Bridge

Two marine guards stood expressionless outside the bridge, dressed in sleeveless combat shirts that displayed a circular shaped tattoo on their right shoulders and spotless Argyle Kilts in the MacAlister Tartan, each complete with Claymore, dirk, and sgian dubh.

Angus entered the bridge between two Marine guards identically dressed to the pair outside. As he scanned the bridge, each station with it's combination chair and life support/escape module, he found Jen, Will, and the entire bridge crew, along with what must have been half of the rest of the crew, all standing at attention. Each wore a sleeveless dress shirt (*was there even such a thing? Angus wondered*) and a perfect MacAlister Clan Kilt, complete with Claymores, dirks, and sgian dubhs!

And the smell! Angus scanned the bridge, and found the table holding the haggis, that ancient mixture of onions and oats with sheep liver, heart and lungs seasoned with good Scotch whiskey. *I don't believe this!*

"Admiral on the bridge!" Jen's voice boomed out with an authority betraying her short height. In response, everyone there stood and turned to the bridge entrance.

"Atten-SHUN!" Gridley bellowed. At that, every crewmember snapped to attention with a perfect salute.

A speechless Angus stared at the sight before him, trying to stay composed as he returned the salute with perfect precision. As the crew's right arms came down, Angus noted the tattoos on the right shoulder of everyone present; a circle with a dagger thrust up through its center, and the word "FORTITER" within the top half of the circle.

"At ease, as you were!" Angus managed to croak out. He fixed his eyes on Jen moving once to her tattoo and then looking back to her face. The Admiral shook his head slightly as he grinned at her. *I believe my son is in for a very interesting life!*

It took a few minutes for the "Hip-hip Hoo-rahs" to die down. Angus had a very hard time keeping his face dry.

The party had been the most enjoyable affair Angus had ever been to; no one demanded speeches, dances, or acknowledgments. Everyone there simply came up to the Admiral and gave him their best wishes. The entire crew seemed to have shown up over the past 40 minutes, but to Angus it seemed to pass in a heartbeat. He couldn't believe they had gone to this much effort for him. He only did what he thought should be done; he wasn't a hero, he was just a man who did his job as best he could. He didn't deserve this. He just did his job.

During a rare break he had asked Will about the shirts and kilts. Jen had answered that it was the "dress of the day" throughout the *fleet*! Angus was very happy to hear that the tattoos were voluntary, but he almost lost all composure when Will told him that *every* crewmember in this fleet requested one; the demand was so high, the certified tattoo artists on board have a backlog of 6 weeks!

Angus wondered at Jen's ability to handle the logistics of this without him having a clue; he was very impressed with his future daughter-in-law. Pulling *this* off took some doing.

"Passing Neptune's orbit, Sir. Inner Sol system in four minutes, Admiral", announced Ensign Alan Hotaling. *Why can't I pick up any chatter, any well-wishes for The Admiral?* Alan thought. *Well, I'm not going to spoil his moment with that question-Earth must have some kind of surprise planned.*

"On main view screen, Helm", Will directed.

The large view screen at the focal point of the bridge lit up with, at first, a full-scale view of the Sol system. Other than a slightly brighter star centered in the display, there was not much to take note of. Until the view zoomed in on Mars.

That is when they saw what all 'hell breaking loose' looked like.

"Sir! Reading *nothing* in Mars orbit! No sign of the Mars Dry-Docks, Transit Station, or Orbital Defense Stations, Sir!" Ensign Hotaling exclaimed.

"Deep scans, entire system!" Commodore Gridley's voice carried an added touch of urgency that had the hair on every crewmember's neck standing up. He opened the protective cover over the "battle-station" switch.

"Aye-aye, Sir!" the kilted crew moved smoothly into the confident, professional mode of well-trained soldiers in combat without missing a beat.

"Reading no ships or stations from ADS 1437 to low Earth orbit, Sir!

"Anything active, Hotaling?" Gridley enquired.

"Nothing, Sir. No energy readings at all above ambient!" Hotaling's voice was heard as an awed whisper, reflecting the anxiety of everyone on the bridge.

Then, as multiple alarms rang out, his excited voice burst out, "Reading large energy spike near Mars. SIR! Mars! It just BLEW UP!"

Chapter Six

"Attention! THIS IS NOT A DRILL! Battle stations! Battle stations! Battle stations!" The automated voice of The Admiral went out to the fleet at hand.

Angus had uncovered and hit the large red button on his Fleet Command Station chair, initiating the automated call to battle stations. At the same time, curved walls shot up and down encasing the bridge stations with armored walls holding command and sensor instrumentation. There were gaps directly behind Angus, to his front left corner where Captain Gridley's station was configured similarly, and directly to his right.

Elsewhere in the ship, men and women moved with well-practiced efficiency to their posts. GravTorp tubes were loaded, with the bus-sized second-shot rounds moved into place. Grav and Photon screens flickered to life. HPABs and HPL Grids came online. Bulkheads sealed, stand-by reactors powered up, and Marines took their positions either at likely boarding sites or within LCPAs. The same was repeated on every ship in the fleet.

"Will, is anything *visually* moving?" Angus dreaded the only possible answer. As he asked, a Mark 7 Fleet Command Helmut dropped in front of Angus. He moved efficiently to put it on.

The Mark 7 provided Angus with many sensory inputs as well as a 3D view of surrounding space.

Gridley knew what the Admiral was thinking; the huge grey spheres. A chill ran down his spine as he imagined one orbiting Earth. "Hotaling, any visual anomalies?" Will managed in a voice on the verge of cracking.

"Here, Sir! Near Earth! On screen now!" An edge of-something; terror?-colored Hotaling's voice. "Large energy spikes near...Earth" Alan's voice broke slightly as he reported his sensor data to his Captain.

"SIR! The moon, it's GONE, Sir!"

The view screen showed *two* huge grey spherical shapes near Earth, a third leaving the debris field where Mars *used* to be, and another huge debris field around that planet, around their home!

There was no sign of the hundreds of defense satellites, the defense and commerce stations, as well as the fleet vessels and fighters that were *always* stationed there.

"Sir, no response from Earth, Lunar Control, Fleet, Mars-there's nothing responding, Sir!" Comm Officer Lieutenant Orson Appleby reported.

"Keep an ear open, Apps". Will replied.

"Fleet priority ALPHA ONE! This is the Admiral speaking. This is NOT a drill!" The Admiral's voice boomed across the gravitic wave comm system to every vessel and every station in the fleet, no matter the star system. Angus himself ground out the words in a voice he had not used since his last football game; "Earth is under attack by unknown forces. Most likely these are alien forces of unknown capabilities. We will move to intercept and defend shortly. You've all trained very *hard* for just this event. The time to use that training is now. You know what to do. Earth has never had a better, a more capable force to defend her. Fortiter!"

"Channel Force Alpha;" Angus now spoke directly to the fleet units he had designated. "Excalibur and Edinburgh break to engage targets Alpha and Beta in low Earth orbit; Brooklyn, Prince Eugen, Constellation, Tiger, Sheffield, Bonhomme Richard, in support. Support vessels Mars, Venus, Jupiter, and Saturn, form Force Delta, hit full stealth mode, make for Jovian orbit."

Angus took a big breath before continuing.

"Enterprise and the remainder of the fleet will form as Force Beta and engage target Delta. Good hunting, Andria!"

"Good hunting, Admiral! We'll make you proud!" Angus saw through his helmet the fire that shone through Commodore Andrea Nelson's tear stained face as she replied.

"I know you will! Good hunting, my friend!" Angus replied. "Force Delta, execute! Force Beta, Execute! Force Alpha, Execute!"

Three 200-kilometer wide shimmering grey spheres hung near Earth. Two were in low Earth orbit, the third half way between Earth and Mars. All shimmered as if they were behind a huge mass of hot air rising off of sun-baked summer pavement.

"Will, fight your Force!" Angus directed Gridley to coordinate the attack with Edinburgh.

****

The Screamin' Demons
The Battle of Earth
Standard Earth Date December 7 3811

"Singh, launch *all* fighters, CAP HOT-RED". Captain Gridley ordered.

"Aye-aye, Captain" replied the CAG."

"CJ, you heard the man. This is your show today. Keep anything that shows up off our backs here. And CJ....."

"Yes, Cap?"

"If anything get close, give those bastards some hell for me."

"Aye-aye, Sir." CJ took a quick gulp, then said in his best 'cool and collected' commander's voice, "OK, heads up, Screamin' Demons! We are to keep anything smaller than a Destroyer out of Excalibur's way. The Mad Hatters have CAP on Edinburgh. Keep your eyes open people. No friendlies. Good hunting."

"Aye-aye, CJ"

"You gottit, Boss"

"Let me at 'em!"

"We'll burn those bastards a new exhaust port, LC!"

Fifty 'Gung-Ho' answers, one from each six ship element, CJ thought. For a split second, he pondered the meaning of 'Gung-Ho'; it was very old, he knew. He promised himself for the umpteenth time that he'd look it up later; he had a job to do, so back to work.

CJ did a mental checklist of his command. Fifty sharp fighter jocks, each in charge of six Wildcat fighters. They were ready, he was sure of that. "Demons, you've got the talent. You've got the hardware. You have the training. Now, you have the opportunity. And, it *is* for real. Let's show them how it's done!"

Three hundred sleek dark shapes moved into position just off the port bow of Excalibur. And there they waited, like hornets patrolling to protect their nest.

****

USF Excalibur Bridge
The Battle of Earth
Standard Earth Date December 7 3811

"Force Alpha, make for midway point between targets Alpha and Beta at War Emergency Accel. Execute! Edinburgh, we'll use attack maneuvers Angus Seven! Cross it sharp, Paully!" Gridley said in a sharp, professional voice. Angus thought, *he's doing a fine job.*

The face of Captain John "Paully" Jones, commanding the Edinburgh, appeared in the helmets of Angus and Will, replying, "Let's hit 'em hard, Will!" Angus thought he had never seen this normally quiet man look so angry.

While the smaller vessels spread out to a position to intercept any attack by fighter and torpedo craft, the six Gravity Pulsar Drive Units on each vessel glowed brighter than the Sun under war emergency power, pushing the two great cruisers at a tremendous rate of acceleration, even as the Edinburgh rotated ninety degrees in relation to the Excalibur. This formation, controlled by secure nav-computer link, allowed the two ships to bring maximum firepower to bear on each alien sphere as they passed between the two targets; by rotating each ship at the same rate, this untold devastation would be unleashed upon the two alien vessels on one pass. Soon, the GPDUs turned 180 degrees to begin the deceleration that would plant the two five km long, crossed heavy cruisers right between the two 180 km wide alien ships.

"GravTorps locked and loaded across Force Alpha, Sir."

"Force Alpha, fire GravTorps."

"Torpedoes away, Sir!" Weapons Station Chief Nimitz declared. Each cruiser unleashed fifty stealth-GravTorps, and the smaller screening vessels added theirs to the total; these independent weapons would spread around the programmed position of the targets, and accelerate quickly to strike when they had a good target lock. If a lock did not happen within a pre-determined time, the torpedoes would converge upon the programmed location of the target. 80 of these were now spreading around the locations of each of the two grey spheres, each ready to place a small black hole on the enemy's hull.

"You may fire when ready, Gridley!" Angus ordered, completely aware of the historical connotations of using Admiral Dewey's words; *I just hope the results are the same*, Angus thought.

Angus had never felt fear during his life; now, his fear was that he would be too little, and too late. Deciding he did not like fear at all, The Admiral buried it deep within his mind.

"Gentlemen, weapons free, you may fire at will; *FIRE, FIRE, FIRE.*" Gridley calmly ordered.

As the crossed pair of USF cruisers moved between the alien ships, they let loose a torrent of destruction. The broadside of one cruiser was therefore added to the central firepower of the other to send wave upon wave of devastation out to…

Nothing.

All the railgun projectiles, missiles, and laser fire seemed to pass straight through the alien spheres. It looked as if they were not really there.

"Will, they could be using dimensional shielding. Hiding in another dimension, so we can't reach them."

74

"And they have to move back into normal space to fire! Weapons; GravTorp status?"

"GravTorps are still holding, Sir, looking for a target to lock onto."

"Will, if we can get them to fire, the GravTorps should pull them into normal space!"

Then the sensors lit up, and alarms sounded.

"Sir! There is a part of the sphere showing up on sensors now, Sir!"

"Target exposed area! NOW!" Angus's voice boomed across the Sol System.

The areas that looked like a surfacing sub on an ocean started glowing a bright red. Then the beams reached out.

Excalibur and Edinburgh fired everything in their considerable arsenals at the exposed sections of the alien ships, but it was too late.

One red beam from each alien reached out and touched the Earth, converging near The Bahamas. The Atlantic Ocean disappeared, boiled away in less than a second. The structure of the planet vaporized down to the Earth's core. What had been dry land was now a sea of fire.

After forty seconds, the beams stopped, leaving a trench over 22,500-kilometers long by 7,000-kilometers wide. The Earth's spinning, molten nickel-iron core, super heated by the beams, was squeezed out of the opening like toothpaste.

The Earth was doomed.

Pressure from the Earth's crust pushed down, and the mantle and core of the planet responded by spewing liquid rock up and out of the gaping wound. Pressure down, movement up and out, the rotational mass changing, and the internal structure weakened; within minutes the earth cracked, then imploded, and finally crumbled out into a vast, glowing debris field.

After ten minutes, the Earth, along with it's population of twenty-three billion men, women, and children, was reduced to a cloud of rapidly cooling molten rock fragments drifting in orbit around the Sun.

But the alien ships were not to leave scot-free; the USF Fleet demanded a price be paid.

As the USF cruisers Excalibur and Edinburgh unleashed their futile firepower, the GravTorps lurking about found and targeted the sections of the alien ships exposed while firing on the Earth.

They homed in with a vengeance bordering on malignant cognizance.

The two alien ships stopped shimmering as they were dragged by the immense gravitational pull of the GravTorps warheads completely into the Sol system space.

Then the firepower of the Excalibur and Edinburgh began to extract a modest revenge.

****

"There's your target! POUR IT ON! Weapons Free: *FIRE, FIRE, FIRE!*" Commodore Will Gridley directed his crew.

"AYE-AYE, SIR!" Excalibur's well-trained crew knew what had just happened, and they moved with deadly efficiency to extract as many pounds of flesh as they could from this alien scourge.

The Excalibur's HPL Grids began unleashed hell in thousands of half-second bursts as the heavy railgun rounds from the Edinburgh pounded into one of the exposed alien ships, the kinetic energy exploding in flashes of solar brilliance as heavy railgun rounds from the other end of the great ship impacted the other one. Broadsides of HPAB lasers, missiles, and railgun rounds from the Excalibur hit both huge ships as well.

Unbearably bright flashes of tremendous energy marked the missile strikes and impacts of the railgun rounds. Where the flashes died down, huge chunks of the grey spheres were gone. On the alien sphere near the moon's orbit, impact after impact had began an incandescent glow near the center of a huge crater on the sphere as the two cruiser's weapons centered on their target.

The inevitable result; the hundreds of nuclear missile hits, railgun impacts and laser strikes that gouged deeper and deeper into the vast sphere were followed by dozens of gravity warheads. As they started detonating, the sphere began imploding.

"Captain! Something's coming out Sir! Can't tell if they're escape pods, missiles, or fighters, Sir." Hotaling called out.

Thousands of small black cylinders had sped out from the collapsing sphere.

"Sizes, about two-point-five meters long by a meter wide, cylindrical in shape. No detected protrusions, indentations, or openings, Sir."

"Thank you, Alan. Singh, did you get that?"

"Roger. CAP is already on 'em, Skipper".

****

"Bogeys inbound on vector zero-zero-one-three, velocity zero-point-zero-zero-zero-two C. Warm 'em up, gentlemen. We're gonna dance *real* soon!" CJ alerted his group to the information coming in. "We will use formation Singh Gamma Four Mod Delta. Flight leaders ack-nowledge!"

"Roger that, Boss!"

"Copy, CJ. Singh Gamma Four Mod Delta"

"Gothchya, CJ. SGFMD"

Fifty emotionally cracked voices checked in with the professionalism born of effective and extensive training. These pilots were not only the best in the fleet; they were Chester Jones' pilots, Singh's pilots; the group defined multi-level fighter unit teamwork.

"OK you son's o' bitches, let's take some fuckin' alien names!" CJ surprised himself with that outburst, but the "Ooh-RAH!" he heard echoed three hundred times over the comm from his group made the hairs on his neck stand up so hard he worried he'd lose his helmet.

He hit the throttle and accelerated into the path of the alien swarm.

"Damn, there are a *lot* of them, CJ."

"Short bursts, save your ammo. Make it count. Just like training!"

Ok, CJ thought. *Combat with an alien race.* He let out a big breath he didn't remember taking in. *Let's go!*

"Weapons free, Demons. Make it count. Good hunting." *Those eyes! If I buy it here, it was worth it for seeing those eyes.*

Alien cylinders began exploding by the dozens. There were an awful lot of alien cylinders, though.

****

Angus thought he could hear the cheering from the entire fleet through the walls of the ship as the huge grey sphere kept shrinking, falling in upon itself at an ever-increasing rate. Within a few seconds, only a glowing red ball a few hundred meters across remained.

"Weapons free, target Alpha! *FIRE, FIRE, FIRE!*" Will commanded in a calm, yet loud and authoritative voice. The earlier rage in his voice from the destruction of the Earth was almost totally replaced by workmanlike precision. "Let's squeeze the fucking bastards, HARD!" *Almost* replaced.

Angus moved his attention to the Enterprise; the sensor helmet gave him a computer-compressed view of the battle to make the entire engagement comprehensible. "Andrea, sit-rep!"

Angus felt the lump move up his throat as he saw the red beam reach out from the alien ship as he spoke.

"Admir............Noth.......fired.......hit................."

The static that followed told Angus the same story the sensor data did; the Enterprise, with her entire escort, was gone. The Photon Screen, the twenty meter-thick gravity-compressed hull couldn't stop a beam that could bore through a planet in fractions of a second. The Admiral watched the shimmering grey sphere fire at the light cruisers, destroyers and frigates that had been escorting Enterprise. Three more times the red beam lashed out, and all the ships of Force Beta were gone. Then the grey sphere simply 'winked' out of sight.

"Will, we *have* to get this one. Enterprise, Force Beta, they're gone." Angus swallowed hard.

"Understood, Admiral!" Will replied.

As Will finished that statement, that red beam reached out and hit the Edinburgh. When it stopped, nothing was left of the great ship or it's fighter screen.

Over 20,000 sailors. *His sailors. Earth. His responsibility.* Will's words flashed back to Angus; '*Admiral, they all have a very personal connection with you.' And I have failed them!*

Throughout his life, except for his proposal to Gina, Angus had never lost. He struggled now to keep the losing feeling from overwhelming and paralyzing him. *By losing Gina, I found Cindy. Lord, give me something here.*

"Captain-those small objects from target Alpha are heading for us, Sir!" Hotaling stated as if he were reciting a dinner menu.

"All hands! Prepare to repel boarders!" Will announced ship wide.

Angus looked around the bridge, and realized he had lost track of Jen. A quick check on his sensor showed her at the Delta Mess. She was where he had assigned her, with the kids.

"Will, we need to keep him *here*."

"GravTorps! Fire!"

"GravTorps, all fifty away, Sir! Tubes reloading."

The red beam came out again, and the Brooklyn, Constellation, and Sheffield all disappeared. Again the red beam came. This time, Prince Eugen, Tiger, Bonhomme Richard. All gone with one blast! Still it came.

Now it came for the Excalibur.

But this was The Admiral's crew. No orders had needed to be given; this crew knew when to take action before it was too late, they knew how to fight their ship. Helm had taken evasive action when the first red beam hit their escorts, accelerating instinctively. But the mighty flagship did not escape injury.

Alarms blared as the aft third of the Excalibur was vaporized. The great ship rocked, but remained in action, the nav computers compensating for the altered mass and lost thrust of the damaged flagship.

The nearest surface of the alien began flashing with brilliant releases of energy as the rounds from Excalibur's railguns found the range. The 50 GravTorps activated around the huge grey globe, holding it in one spot while the Excalibur fired everything she had. But the alien vessel was so huge, it would take a lot of time for Excalibur to destroy it by herself. It was time that Excalibur simply would not have.

The red beam fired again, and the three hundred strong fighter screen around Excalibur vanished. Another red beam, and a large section near the center of Excalibur vanished, as if a giant shark had bitten a chunk out of the ship. More alarms sounded on the bridge as the Helm and Navigation stations blew up. Another explosion hit the Admiral's armored command station. The Admiral's Esc-Mod closed and ejected amidst a second explosion that opened the bridge to space, leaving it in a vacuum.

****

USF Excalibur Delta Mess
The Battle of Earth
Standard Earth Date December 7 3811

Lieutenant Commander Jenitka Kowalski had made the trip from the bridge in record time, even if the heavy sword hanging from her kilt belt had left her thigh bruised and sore. She had wasted no time in getting the older children to help her organize the younger ones. *They've been through so much already. Now the grey ships. Please, Lord, if it comes to that, make it quick for the children!* Jen prayed.

****

The Screamin' Demons 1
The Battle of Earth

Lieutenant Commander Chester Jones sat helpless as what was left of his Wildcat drifted powerless away from the battered Excalibur. He kept trying system after system, but only his flight suit had power. Still, following the re-boot procedures kept his eyes from staring at his ship, his *home*, from thinking of all his friends dead and dying there. And that kept him from thinking of the Screamin' Demons, thinking of how he felt watching that red beam sweep across and vaporize them all. And it kept him from thinking that if he had been quicker, maybe they'd still be alive, maybe he'd still have the 70 percent of his ship it burned away. And Mor. He *needed* to see her again, to at least hope for the chance. The re-boot procedures kept him from thinking of all those things. Almost.

My pilots had pledged to follow me into hell, if that's where I had to lead them. Well, I sure had done that, but I'm still here, and they weren't.

CJ decided that the shaking those thoughts caused was what he hated the most. But the sobbing was almost as bad.

****

USF Excalibur Bridge
The Battle of Earth
Standard Earth Date December 7 3811

The crew stations instantly closed over the bridge crew occupants, the escape modules providing emergency air, but remaining attached to their bridge station so the well-trained crew could keep fighting their ship. The crew never missed a beat, as The Admiral had drilled them on this situation countless times.

But the Excalibur had been hurt badly. Another hit would kill her, as the Excalibur could not dodge away anymore.

"Damage report, Alan!" Will called over the emergency comm. He was bleeding from a shard of plastic stuck in his left arm. *Why had the Admiral's pod jettisoned? I have no indicator he triggered it. Must have been damage from those explosions. And what the hell caused those?*

"Not much coming through, Sir. I've got some…Beta and Delta Mess are intact, Marines quarters Alpha and Propulsion Unit Alpha have atmosphere. No data from power plants at all, everything is on local battery power. I have zero weapons online. Negative maneuvering, not even gas jets responding. No data coming in from the fighter decks or the hangers. Two decks below us still have atmosphere through to Delta Mess."

Gridley looked at his Esc-Mod's tactical display as he almost made a call to the fleet. Protocol required him to inform the fleet that the Admiral was out of action, and that he had taken command of the fleet. What stopped Will also sank his heart; there was no fleet left to call.

He noticed then that he was rubbing the tattoo on his right shoulder. He looked at the remnants of his bridge crew, and saw many of them doing the same. *Damn if I'll give up now! That's not what he taught me!*

"Hotaling, do you have any sensors? Can you find the Admiral's capsule?"

"I have nothing but visual, Sir, and I can't re-direct it." Alan's frustrated voice was almost a sob.

The huge grey sphere of the alien moved closer on the view screen. And then a large section of the alien vessel began glowing, the Excalibur bridge crew seeing it quickly spread, transforming the entire alien ship into a brilliant sphere of rolling hell, a glowing plasma under unprecedented firepower as the Excalibur's view screen showed the huge shape of the USF Fortiter streaking past, decelerating hard to concentrate on pouring immense amounts of energy into the alien ship. The view got better as three groups of twenty-four fighters swarmed out of her hangers. The Corsairs were accelerating hard for the Excalibur.

That was when the alien cylinders began hitting the Excalibur.

****

Phyll's Killer's
The Battle of Earth
Standard Earth Date December 7 3811

"Attack formation Jones Alpha, max acceleration. Target those cylinders!" Lieutenant Phyllis Mor barked out over her flight's comm channel. *It figures that **his** formation would fit this mission best. Where are you, Demons?*

"Aye-aye, Skip!" her wingman, Alan Adamy affirmed.

"Right with ya, Boss!"

"Let's fry the bastards!"

Twelve pilots, the six-ship element leaders, chimed in, their thirst for revenge dripping from their replies, barely checked by their professionalism.

"OK, Killers, you know what to do; you have the training, the tools and the talent to do it. Fire free!" A million thoughts flashed just under Phyll's concentration on her job. One thought pushed up; *Where was he? Was he in the hanger when it was hit?*

Seventy-two Corsairs curved in on the cylinders, destroying hundreds of them every few seconds. But hundreds more were crashing into what was left of the Excalibur.

Mor locked on to a group of six cylinders, firing precise plasma cannon bursts. The six flares of their destruction cleared her assigned area, so she turned her sensors to the Excalibur. *Of course he was out here, leading his group during the battle. Stop this! Concentrate! You have a damned job to do.*

"Fortiter CAG to PK 1."

"PK 1. Go, CAG" Mor replied.

"We show all cylinders either destroyed or impacted on the Excalibur. Good shooting, Killers. Mission shift; scan for survivors, specifically escape modules."

"Roger that, CAG. PK 1 to Killers. Sensor sweep. Look for escape modules." Sigh! "Begin Operation Heartbreak." *Did I say that? Oh, Shit!* Tears welled up on her eyes.

"Aye-aye on that Boss. We *all* hear ya," the quiet reply.

The flood of her tears made it very hard to read her sensors. But Lieutenant Phyllis Mor *never* gave up on her objectives.

****

USF Fortiter
The Battle of Earth
Standard Earth Date December 7 3811

"Never before in the history of warfare had the destruction been so indiscriminate and universal."

The line from the ancient novel, "War of The Worlds" sat in Alex MacAlister's mind as he looked at what used to be "home". The six-foot, eight-inch Commander had to consciously unclench his jaws before his teeth popped. *Earth. The Moon. Mars. Nothing was left. Dozens of stations and ships. Jen. Dad. Mom. All gone. Home Fleet; gone.*

WE SHOULD HAVE PREVENTED THIS. THAT WAS OUR JOB his mind screamed, while his massive intellect said that he couldn't have, they couldn't have, that they had done the best they could with the cards dealt them.

I think I'd better stick with that last thought.

"Mr. Perry, ready a boarding party for Excalibur."

"Aye, aye, Sir."

Think, plan on worst case scenario, his father's words came to him. *Then, whatever happens will not be as devastating.*

He needed more resources.

"Comm, get me Cygnus 78 United Aero Space Command."

"On comm two, Skipper."

****

USF Excalibur Delta Mess

The Battle of Delta Mess

Standard Earth Date December 7 3811

"Lieutenant Commander! Something's coming down the hallway, and fast! A bunch of things!" Johnny Alexander was a tall boy for fourteen. He was athletic and, Jen had decided, very bright. Plus, he moved well in the half G they now found themselves in. She made him her Second, and had a serious talk about what may happen; a lot of 'what may happen's. She thought he took it pretty well. "Manned-up", she said.

"John, you, Jim and Carl take the rest of the Troops into The Keep." Jen's computer-like combat voice ordered. She thought calling them Troops instead of kids would help keep them calm; and by calling the boys by the 'grown-up' version of their names, she hoped they would keep acting the part. *"This doesn't look like it's going to be quick at all"*, she thought. She was starting to get angry thinking about the children being harmed.

"Yes, Command, eh, Lt. Commander!" Johnny began leading the few older children still outside the kitchen, or 'The Keep' as Jen had renamed it, into that last room. The older boys and girls had moved the younger children into the walk-in freezer, which had been turned off and emptied when they came aboard. Each Trooper over ten was armed with a kitchen implement; knives, cleavers, long forks, and rolling pins. Janice Wilson, a pretty thirteen-year old, bright-eyed, raven-haired girl, had taken the younger children as her responsibility, keeping them distracted and showing a cheerful face in The Keep. Johnny decided he was impressed with that. He stood a little taller when thinking of her, as he carried the half-meter long dirk Jen gave him with a determined pride; *They will **not** get past me* he promised himself as he watched Janice. *I won't let the Lieutenant Commander or Janice down! I must protect them!* he thought with that unflappable teenage confidence.

The older Troops took their place, waiting for Lt. Commander Kowalski to join them. After a few minutes, Johnny got worried. "Stay here. I'm gonna check outside" he told Carl.

He opened the door, and saw the Lt. Commander standing ready in the center of the mess hall, both hands holding the broadsword at the ready. John watched as she brought the weapon up very quickly; a movement at the outer door caught his eye.

The grey-brown thing entering the mess hall was about a meter and a half long, about a half meter wide. *It looks like a lumpy grey leather bag full of grapefruit*, John thought. There were three short arms, or legs on each side, the middle set slightly towards the 'top' of the thing. It had a head, sort of; it looked a lot like one of the legs, but poked out of the thing's front, shorter and fatter than the legs. And, where the legs ended in six sharp looking two cm coal black claws, the 'head' had an opening ringed with a dozen of them. Just behind this 'mouth', equally set around the 'head', were three shiny, dark-brown, round lumps. *Must be the eyes*, John thought.

There wasn't just one of these things. They were plowing into the mess, one over another, seeming to swim through the air. As their arms/legs moved, the black, shiny claws extended out and retracted back in with the movements.

A loud, angry scream chilled John to his core and pulled his attention back to the Lieutenant Commander in time to see Jen swing her sword up in an arc that came down and cut the first thing neatly in half, spraying blood everywhere as dozens of the things burst through the door.

John turned and opened the door as his mind processed the blur of motion that was Jen's sword. He looked straight at Carl;

"Carl, lock this door. Don't open it. No matter what." *How can she move the sword so fast?*

John pulled back into the mess hall as Carl locked the door behind him. *There is no one else here to do this. It's up to the LC and me.* John thought with a new maturity born of necessity. *OK, then! Here I go.*

Jen stood near the door to Delta Mess, positioned so she could strike without being seen; at least she *hoped* that was the case.

This is different from those fighters attacking The Admiral. No, actually, it's not; kill or be killed. OK, you alien sacks-of-whatever kind of excrement you are, you want a piece of me? HERE I FUCKIN' AM!

A creature moved silently through the door, and Jen screamed as she swung the broadsword at it with all her might. The 'thing' fell in two neat halves at her feet; but three more came through in the time it took her to swing the sword. *This thing's heavy, even in ½ G. I need to pace myself* Jen thought.

She took two steps back and swung again. It seemed to work, as another beast fell to the floor. *How are they floating?*

Jen repeated her moves of 'slash, step back, and slash again' until she felt her back hit the door to The Keep. *That's as far as I'm retreating.*

The sword made a distinct sound as it flew through the air at the end of Jenitka Kowalski's arms. The sound it made as it sliced through alien flesh was much more welcome to Jen's ears, however. Her arms began burning with the effort. *How many? Twenty? Forty? Keep slashing!*

The bodies piled up around Jen as more and more of the creatures filled the mess hall. She swung again, a little slower this time, and a monster bit her from behind. The pain made her scream, but also brought new energy as she spun and stabbed the big broadsword through the offending creature. Another clawed at her from the left, and another from behind again, along with one from the right. *There are too many, too many different directions!*

An alien monster bit down on her arm, and Jen screamed in pain and anguish; *I can't let them get the children!*

She saw a blur next to her, coming out from behind; Johnny thrust the dirk up into a creature right behind Jen, then pulled it out and struck again. Jen felt…*something*. A new energy revitalized her body, her exhausted, aching arms. She swung the sword at incredible speed, the silver blade a barely visible blur as she hacked one creature after another even as more and more clawed and bit into her flesh. She was aware only that Johnny was behind her, at least twice killing alien monsters trying to eat her alive. By then, her mind had blanked out, and moved into an autopilot-like state; *KILL! KILL! KILL!*

Inside The Keep, the noise of the struggle poured through the doors; Jen's War Whoops and screams of pain, mingled with the alien creatures' attack growls and death howls, and other savage yells from Johnny. One of the younger girls began sobbing, but a soothing voice soon calmed her. Carl tightened his grip on the butcher's cleaver he held. He thought it sounded like Janice's voice calming the child; but he kept his eyes on the doors.

On the bridge of the USF Fortiter, Commander Alex MacAlister covered his ears. It didn't help; the screaming came from within his head, not his ears. And it wouldn't stop. He knew that agonized, screaming voice as if it were his own…and that made the screaming unbearable.

****

Angus gasped for breath. *No air. Dark. Cold. Quick, hold your breath. Suit needs to be on. It is. Where am I? Esc-Mod. Why? No air. No power. Can't see. Suit helmet gone. Get helmet on. Hole in module…..piece of helmet in it……head hurts bad……head bleeding….dizzy…….where's helmet….pieces of it….like it exploded….taste blood…..that's not good…….Have to get nanny………didn't even get any damn haggis…….I blew this…..badly………Earth…..Alex…..Jen………Cindy…………..…..Cindy……*
…Must see her one more time at least……..My Cindy….
I'm here, my love! Hold on! Please, I need you!

****

CJ saw the last hit on the Excalibur out of the corner of his eye. He turned to look, and saw the huge grey sphere. *It's going to finish her off.*
"SHOOT ME! FIRE HERE, YOU MOTHERLESS BASTARDS! YOU ALL SHOULD BURN IN FUCKING HELL…" CJ was screaming at the alien nightmare ship when he saw large bright flashes appear and begin to merge across its surface. Huge chunks of the grey ship where cut and gouged out of the giant globe. When he saw the long shape of the Fortiter become visible as it unleashed its wrath he cheered, and when the alien vanished behind the largest plasma ball he had ever seen, CJ screamed so loud he thought he'd bust the canopy.
Now, if only I could signal somehow…
She's here. She would see it!
CJ just knew that somehow.

****

"Sparks, can you get me any info?" Major Bill Marx asked his ELO, Lieutenant Hiram Greenberg. Greenberg was trying to get readings from his Battlefield Sensor Array, or BSA.

"I've set it up for boarding party use, Sir. I've got nothing showing aft of bulkhead 1286. Forward is good to bulkhead 507. Down is good two decks only. Up is zero decks. Damn!"

"Spit it out, Greenie."

"Those kids are in Delta Mess, Major. I'm picking them up, around 350, 400 of them, and about 200 other readings. Warm, life of some kind. Moving. A lot of movement by them *in* Delta Mess. Not.....not human, Sir. Another hundred or so heading towards the bridge."

"Groups Alpha and Bravo, split up. Objective Delta Mess. Mission; repel boarders!"

Damn! Not the kids!

****

USF Excalibur Bridge
The Battle of Excalibur
Standard Earth Date December 7 3811

Commodore Gridley surveyed his bridge, or what was left of it. At least six dead, several injured, and the Admiral ejected. Battle damage and unexplained explosions; there had been no volatile substances in that area, nothing that should have exploded. And the aliens had only used that red beam weapon; that just vaporized everything. Will had read the briefings; he knew some one was after Angus. They just may have succeeded. *Little good it would do them now. You want to rule the Earth? Bastards!*

"Sir, I have some comm within the ship. From Major Marx, Sir. He's moving to repel boarders near Delta Mess."

"Those kids? Alan, let's get out of these Esc-Mods and form into a unit. We can't do anything productive here. Maybe we can lend a hand there."

The bridge crew was out of their escape modules before Will finished his sentence. Hotaling opened the bridge armory and began dispensing the automatic mag pistols. Everyone had forgotten they were all dressed in kilts with swords hanging from their waists.

Will moved up to the bridge exit. "Let's go!" he yelled as he led what was left of the bridge crew through the opening.

Hotaling followed closely behind Gridley. As they rounded a corner a dark shape seemed to grab Will's head and pull him away.

Hotaling fired round after round as three more of the things closed over what was left of the Commodore, watching the rounds hit the things and have no effect at all. When his magazine was empty, Hotaling tossed the gun away and pulled his sword out. He started walking forward, hacking as he went.

The rest of the bridge crew followed him, wading into a wall of alien death.

****

The Screamin' Demons 1
Operation Heartbreak
Standard Earth Date December 7 3811

"Damn piece of fucking C R A P!" CJ pounded his fist on the instrument panel in front of him. "OK, half a piece of crap!" Absolutely nothing worked outside of his suit. *Think, moron, think! Training. Remember all that training Singh had piled on you! Survival training. Well, I'm not in a desert or a jungle, not adrift at sea on my little yellow raft.*

You have things to do, DAMN IT! You have to make them pay! THINK!

OK, take stock of what you do have! Your suit. The raft is beneath your seat. SURVIVAL KIT!

"What a moron!" CJ said out loud. It may be hard to reach, but he should be able to......*stretch just a little more...GOTIT!*

Pulling up the small package was a little difficult in the close fitting cockpit, but CJ managed. Opening the zipper, he tossed out the candy bars and cash. The gun and knife he set in his lap. Two MREs........here it is! A flashlight and a mirror.

CJ held the light up to his canopy, pointed it at the Excalibur, and began the series of on-off flashes that held his only hope.

She will see it. Those green eyes won't miss it. Those eyes...

****

Marine Combat Logistics Company 23
Roughnecks
The Battle of Excalibur
Standard Earth Date December 7 3811

"Button up, Roughnecks! Combat support mission; relief of USF Excalibur. By the numbers! ETA twenty minutes!" Captain Vito "Connie" Constantino barked.

"Ooh-RAH!" the response came in chorus.

The Landing Craft Personnel Armored, or LCPA 47 Rhino shot out of the hanger bay, leaving the USF Fortiter a rapidly dwindling speck behind them.

The LCPA 47 was used to insert and extract 120 combat Marines under fire. The hull is formed by gravity-compressed titanium alloy a foot thick, equivalent to twenty-foot thick armor plate. Armament includes a twin 4.5 plasma cannon turret on the roof, and a single 6.75 plasma cannon turret under the floor, along with various countermeasures.

All this comes at a price; while the Rhinos can boast of a high top speed, it takes a long time to get there. The LCPA 47 is, however, very maneuverable.

"What are we going into, Connie? Scuttlebutt say we got aliens on board" PFC Simon Jefferson asked.

"Yeah, Connie. We gonna get a chance for our 'pound o' flesh'?" Sally Ross chimed in.

"Cool it, kids. Excalibur has been boarded. That's all we know. I doubt we will find any humans that are not part of her crew. That's all I'm sayin'. Now, button up, run your checklists one more time, and stay alert."

****

Phyll's Killer's 1
Operation Heartbreak
Standard Earth Date December 7 3811

"SARA! Contact at 322.7 vector 43 degrees north velocity 2KPM. Command Esc-Mod with severe damage, venting atmosphere. Slight tumble. Life signs….." Phyll had to swallow before finishing in a whisper, "negative…." Phyll took a look at the sensor reading. *Don't give up. Ever! Find a way!* "at this range."

"Understood, PK 1. We're on our way, ETA four minutes." The Search And Rescue Air And Space, simplified to SARA in fighter jock lingo, replied.

"Hurry up, SARA! There could be more out there." *There has to be! At least one more! Please!*

"Roger that, Lieutenant. Damn, looks like the Admiral bought it! He can't be…. Aw, Geeze, Bill, how long we gonna stay out here? We haven't found even a bolt yet…"

"SARA 7, your comm is open." Alex MacAlister's emotionless voice stated flatly.

"Shit. Sorry, Skipper, PK 1. Just, um, blowin' off steam."

"It's.....OK, SARA. We're all stressed and tired. Forget it. I have."
Phyll chipped in, covering them so the Skipper didn't have to respond.

"Roger that. Thanks."

"Just keep....looking, OK?" *The Skipper's dad is dead in front of me, and I'm crying over a guy I've spent two hours with. And I do NOT want to think of what is NOT behind me. DAMN IT ALL!*

"We ain't gonna stop, Lieutenant. I promise." Jody's voice snapped Phyll back to reality.

"Thanks, Jody." Phyll's reply was barely audible.

****

USF Excalibur
Outside Delta Mess
The Battle of Excalibur
Standard Earth Date December 7 3811

"Any movement, Sparks?" Marks whispered.

"Two inside, very little movement Sir. The targets are adult-small, Sir. Hell of a lot of *warm* stuff in there, too."

"Charlie, take Beta group and set up a perimeter. We don't need any more surprises today."

"Yes, Sir. Copy that."

"Sparks, set up here, near the door. Boyd, Jenkins, follow me. I'm going in."

Major Bill Marx pushed on the door. It moved an inch only. He pushed a little harder, and the door slid enough for him to see some of what was inside. He pulled back, taking big, deep breaths.

"There are a lot of, *things* in there." *Deep breath.* "All cut up. Hacked to pieces, like they flew into a sawmill. Damn bloody, red blood everywhere!" *Deep breath. OK, now. Better.* "And, it smells *really* bad!"

"Jenkins, give me a hand. Let's open this door. Be warned, it's real gruesome in there."

As the two men shoved the door open wider, they found the reason the door was so hard to open; bodies, like big sacks of grey-brown leather. Aliens, hacked and slashed, piled up against the door. The Marines followed their Major into the open doorway, uneasy with what they had seen so far. What they saw inside made half of them retch.

****

90

Phyll's Killer's 1
Operation Heartbreak
Standard Earth Date December 7 3811

"We have the Admiral's Esc-Mod, PK 1. You're free to resume your...Hey........Bill, what was that?"

"Jody, What have you got?"

"I thought I saw.....there! It's there again! A flashing light, a SOS, bearing 12 by...42 by.... 87!"

"I don't...GOT IT! I'm on my way, SARA."

"PK 1, Skipper, we have the Admiral's Esc-Mod open. He's alive, Skip! Pretty bad off, but he's still here!"

"Copy....SARA 7. Thank you." Alex's normally booming baritone voice was a quivering whisper over the comm, but Jody could hear the cheers in the background. *Thank you, God. Thankyouthankyouthankyou.*

"PK 1, time estimate to signal?" *How many more can we find? Please Lord, let us find them all!*

"About twenty minutes out, Skipper."

"PK 1, that signal's a lot farther out than that. Don't bust a reactor, Phyll! We don't need to be giving you a ride home, too!"

"Just follow me out, SARA." *I know how to fly my damn ship! She'll make it!* "I'll let you know what's there in case you need to turn back." *If the Admiral can make it, maybe there's a chance for CJ. This has to be him! I know it is. I can....feel him.*

"Negative, PK 1. The Admiral needs to get to the Fortiter *now*. He's lost a lot of blood, he has a big head wound and facial burns. I'm stabilizing him, but he needs to be in Sick Bay ASAP."

"SARA 7, are there any other SARAs in the area?" Alex had to ask, even though he already knew there weren't.

"Negative, Skipper. Nearest is two hours out."

"Estimate of time delay in returning to Fortiter if you pick up that signal?"

"About an hour, Skipper. I think The Old Man might make it, but I'm not sure. It's about fifty-fifty, Sir." *Am I damn glad I'm not you, Skip,* Bill thought.

"SARA 7, follow direction from PK 1. Phyll, no unnecessary risks, understood? I need you leading these fighters when we fry these......." Alex's voice was quieter than anyone ever remembered hearing it.

"Understood, Skip. Thanks, Boss!" *I owe that big lug a kiss.*

****

USF Excalibur
Outside Delta Mess
The Battle of Excalibur
Standard Earth Date December 7 3811

"Lieutenant Commander! Jen! Can you hear me!"

Jen moved under the load of several alien bodies, trying to get free. "Arrgh!"

"Jenkins, Boyd, Finch, help me get these *things* off of the LC." The big Marines moved quickly to begin digging Jen out of the bloody, smelly pile of alien body parts.

"Angus? Alex?"

"Major Marx, Sir."

"The Marines are here. It's 'bout damn time!" Jen, now free from the weight of a dozen or so mangled alien bodies, gasped as she stood up, spent muscles shaking her body from exhaustion.

"Easy, LC. MEDIC!" Bill steadied her by her arm as Jenkins grabbed her waist. "Miss Kowalski, you look like hell, Sir!" *She looks like she's been in a cement mixer with a hundred angry machetes.* She was covered with cuts and scratches, some pretty deep. One gash on her right arm showed bone. *What Hell did she go through here?*

"Yeah, well, you hack your way through these crap grinders and see how good *you* look!" Jen whispered. "Find John."

"Ma'am? John?"

"The oldest young teen with the kids. Saved my life at least twice. JOHN! JOHN!" Jen wobbled, then fell down, collapsed from exhaustion.

"Major! Over here!" Finch shouted as he pointed to a bloody foot sticking out from under a pile of alien body parts.

****

SARA 7
Operation Heartbreak
Standard Earth Date December 7 3811

"Admiral, can you hear me, Sir! Admiral!" Jody Sims-Campbell called to Angus. She focused on him completely; it kept her mind off of her kids, off her month old grandchild, off the fact that they lived in Florida. This was the man her father had spoken of as if he were a God. This was the man her father stayed in service well past retirement age to protect. She couldn't lose him, not and face her dad. *If* her dad was still alive. Excalibur was pretty banged up, half gone. *Don't think like that! Do your job!*

"Hrunghlph!" crept out of the Admiral's lips. "Helmet. Exploded. Get nanny."

"You got the nanny paste, Admiral. You slowed the leak." Nanny paste, or nanite pressure repair paste, was a simple paste of nano-shaped molecules that could stop, or drastically reduce, the leaking air from a small hole in a space suit or a ship.

"Easy, Admiral. You've lost a lot of blood. We've got one more pilot to pick up, then we'll get you to Sick Bay on the Fortiter."

"Excalibur?"

"Badly damaged, Sir. Rescue parties dispatched. SARAs are out picking up Esc-Mods and damaged fighters." *No sense telling him we haven't found any yet, or about the boarding.*

"Need to secure the area. Fortiter and fighters may not be enough. Bring Force Delta, Jupiter."

"Easy, Admiral. Skipper has that under control. Get some rest now, Sir." *A little NeoMorph in your IV will help with that.*

"Bill, The Old Man's OK, sleeping. Just keep the bumps to a minimum."

"Roger that, Jody. ETA ten minutes to PK 1."

"Bill, don't push it. I want to eat dinner tonight."

"It's under control, Jody. And, just so you know, *I* ain't cookin' *tonight!*" Bill gave the throttle another nudge past redline.

****

The Hounds of Heaven
Operation Heartbreak
Standard Earth Date December 7 3811

"OK, Doggies, form up. Formation Gamma 3, Mission is CAP and Search for survivors. Lead-wingman, two ship elements. Any ship bigger than you are that you don't recognize, get your ass back to Fortiter. Assigned sector is Alpha Seven. Execute!"

Why couldn't we have been delayed on departure? We may have made a difference! Major Warren Bong thought as he watched the sensor show his twenty-three fighters spread out to their assigned search patterns. His tactical display showed another 230 fighter groups, Mustangs and Thunderbolts, spreading out in different directions, covering a globe shaped perimeter of the battle-space. Then came the 100 groups of

Lightnings, forming a tighter sphere around the Fortiter and Excalibur. He would have liked a better, heavier weapons mix after the briefing, but there wasn't time.

"Fortiter CAG, 524th reporting on-station." Bong announced.

"Roger, Hounds. Glad to see you." Jerry answered.

****

SARA 7
Operation Heartbreak
Standard Earth Date December 7 3811

"PK 1, CAG,"

"PK 1. Go, CAG."

"We have a pair of Mustangs inbound to your sector, CAP/Search relief. Come on in, Phyll. Get some chow and a shower."

"Roger that, Jerry. I'll cover SARA 7's return." *I'm not leaving here until I know he's on SARA 7. This **is** him, I feel it.*

"Affirmative, PK 1. 524th comm is channel 3. Relief call sign is Freddy. Wingman is Letta."

"Copy, CAG." Phyll switched her comm to channel 3. "Freddy, PK 1."

"Freddy. Go, PK 1."

"I've got a flashing light here, SARA 7 following if there's a pilot. I'm back with SARA after."

"Copy, PK 1. Anything we can do for you, Ma'am?"

"Just find 'em all, Freddy. That's all. Just find 'em all."

"Copy that, PK 1. We'll look sharp."

Phyll checked her scanners, and switched her external lights on as she began her decel.

Just a few more minutes, CJ.

****

USF Excalibur
Delta Mess
The Battle of Excalibur
Standard Earth Date December 7 3811

"Three hundred and thirty four, Major, best we can tell. Most of 'em are hacked up pretty bad, chopped to pieces, like some one really wanted to hurt 'em, make 'em feel pain."

94

JESUS! Marx thought, *She did all this, with only the kid watchin' her back?*

"She'll be OK, Bill. I've sealed up the biggest wounds, given her an AB shot, some potassium, and some fluids. She does need some rest, though." Lieutenant Mike "Mickey" Reynolds informed Major Marx.

"Understood. Mickey, what about the kid? How's he doing?"

"He'll be fine, Major. He's about as cut up as the LC is. Most of the blood on both is from the aliens. One brave kid, Sir."

"Copy that, Mickey." *The kid did himself proud by any measure. How do I tell him the Mayflower was vaporized, his parents are gone? Damn bein' in command!*

"Jenkins, can you open up that kitchen door?"

"I don't wanna hurt any of the kids in there, Major. I'm just tryin' to cut the bolts." The big marine knelt by the door, using his multi-tool to add a burnt paint and metal smell to the mess hall ambiance as he burned the door hinge bolts off.

"Get it open. Those kids must be terrified." *They had to hear what happened out here. I wonder if these things made any noise when they died.* Somehow, it seemed more satisfying if they had screamed. More so if they had screamed a lot.

"Major! Contacts approaching. Looks like seven, no, nine Sir. People, no doubt." Sparks' excited voice came over the comm.

"OK. Boyd, get out there and make sure they know we're friendly. Bring them in, see if they need any help."

"Aye-aye, Sir."

****

The Screamin' Demons 1
Operation Heartbreak
Standard Earth Date December 7 3811

I can't see anything. This could be hopeless. Air is almost gone. As CJ watched the oxygen warning light in his helmet go from yellow to red, he felt his hope dropping with his oxygen levels.

Doug Coon. He was going to marry that girl tomorrow, after the Admiral's party. She practically melted when he gave her that ring. Now, Doug's gone, and Alice most likely as well. They should have had the real thing there. DAMN IT ALL!

Just a few more minutes, CJ.

What? CJ fought through his hypoxic fog.

Almost there.

Hurry.

The light was hardly noticeable at first. Then he saw what it was; it kept growing larger and brighter. *There! A GravDrive firing!* Tears started rolling down CJ's face. He didn't try to hold them back. Not now.

"What ship are you?" CJ said out loud, opening his suit comm. *I know it's her. Of course it's a Corsair! Now, calm down and conserve your air!*

"SD 1, PK 1. Can you respond? Over."

My suit comm works! "SD 1. Go, PK 1" *I can see the ship's name, I hear her voice! 'A voice so thrilling ne'er was heard, In spring-time from the Cuckoo-bird'* ...

I can see his ship, see the Screamin' Demons 1. His voice! He's OK. Phyll's heart leapt up high into her throat. "Nice to see you again, LC", her cracking voice managed to get out.

"Lieutenant, you look just great in a fighter. In fact, you've never looked better. Are you up for dinner tonight?"

"I *was* planning on eating sometime. The company would be nice. SARA 7 will be here in a few. You're riding back with The Admiral, CJ."

"Then it'll be a smooth trip. I'm buying tonight, OK Phyll? Just for the record, I *am* definitely making a pass at you."

I won't drop it, CJ! "Copy that, SD 1." Phyll whispered back, then took a big breath.

"PK 1, SARA 7."

"PK 1. Go, SARA"

"Keep you pants buttoned, Phyll. We're two minutes out." Phyll could hear the wide smile in Bill's voice; it let the tension out, and Phyllis finally exhaled.

"Pushin' it a little, Bill?"

"Just for you, Sugar!" *She's back, OK. Good.*

"That's sweet! Jody's not in the cockpit, is she."

"Ha-ha. You got me, PK 1."

"I owe you two. Join us for dinner?"

"Thanks, but neg on that tonight. We've got some healing of our own to do, Phyll. The kind we can only do for each other."

DAMN! I forgot their kids lived in Florida. A new grandson! "Understood, Bill. If there's anything…"

"Roger that, Phyll. Thanks. We'll let you know. Right now, we've got a job to do, and that helps a little. Tears can… tears can wait."

"Roger that, SARA."

****

"Ahoy! Who goes there!"

"Boyd? It's Hotaling. I've got the Bridge Crew with me." *What's left of us*, Alan thought.

"This way, Lieutenant. We've got a base of sorts in Delta Mess."

"We have wounded with us."

"We've got a medic, but not a lot of supplies."

"Well, that's something."

****

"Captain, I can only let you stay a few minutes. He's a little groggy from the meds, and we need to get him into surgery ASAP" Commander Leo Rottello, M.D., firmly told his CO.

"Understood, Leo. Thanks" the big man said quietly.

Alex walked into the prep room of Surgery Suite One. It took him several seconds to get used to the sight before him. He'd always seen his dad as an indestructible force of nature, invincible, strong, always right, always winning. He always had looked up to him, even after he had grown to be the taller one. To see him this way just seemed wrong....

Angus lay naked on the table with his left eye closed. Technicians worked to clean the dried blood that covered his head and torso. The right side of his head was an ugly, swollen and burned mess of featureless red, yellow, and black. There was a piece of his helmet sticking out of his chest just below his right shoulder, with pink foamy bubbles pushing out around it on every breath. Another piece stuck out of the right side of his head, where his ear should be. The skin on the right side of his neck hung as if it had been peeled back. Numerous small puncture wounds peppered his neck and shoulders, and the three outer fingers on his left hand were white from frost bite/space exposure. Both of his legs also had that bloodless white, dead color.

"Dad…….."

"Alex. Thanks for coming." Angus' voice gurgled out of his throat.

"Dad? How are you?"

"Doc tells me I'll be OK in a while. Mom?"

"No data on her shuttle."

"I feel her. She's scared"

"Me too." *Is he hallucinating?*

"Force Delta?"

"Under heavy UASF fighter escort to Cygnus Shipyards."

"Excalibur?"

"Rescue shuttles are there now. Badly damaged. Dad, she was boarded."

"And?"

"We don't know yet."

"Jen?"

"I….I don't know", the big man's voice cracked out his reply. *I can't tell him about the screams, I can't tell him she's probably…*

"She's tough. Damned resourceful. Pity the bastards that pissed her off." Angus took a deep breath. "Alex, Will's not able, you're Admiral of the Fleet."

"We don't know yet, Sir."

"We need more firepower. Build the fleet up. Analyze their weapons. Find out where they live. Then we go kill those bastards. Alex."

"Dad?"

Angus reached up with his left hand, grabbed Alex by the collar with his good finger and thumb. His left eye opened and focused on the face of his son as he pulled him close with more strength than Alex expected.

"I do NOT like to loose."

****

USF Excalibur
Delta Mess
The Battle of Excalibur
Standard Earth Date December 7 3811

"Major, it's the Bridge Crew!"

"The Admiral? Is he with them?"

"Negative, Sir."

Boyd's reply hit Marx like a brick in the head. *What the hell. The Old*

Man. DAMN! We need him now!

"Lieutenant Hotaling, Major. This is what we have left. We fought our way from the bridge. Ran into a couple hundred of those *things*." Alan looked around, noticing the carnage in the mess, now piled up to one side. "We lost seven, including Commodore Gridley. Mag guns don't stop 'em, Sir. You have to cut them up. Thank God we had the swords."

The Admiral and Gridley. DAMN IT! This keeps getting worse and worse.

"Alan, are any of those things left alive?"

"No, Sir. We hacked them all. It was hard to stop, Sir. They....they eat you, Sir."

"Copy that, son." *So that explains why they went after the kids. Where the hell did these things come from?*

Marx moved off to the side, an area of the mess hall away from everyone else. He removed a black comm unit from a pocket on the inside of his shirt.

"Charlie, Bill."

C'mon. DAMN IT ALL!

"Charlie, Bill. Respond. Code Zeta."

"Bill." It was a whispered response.

"Location."

"Beta Mess. Kitchen. Hiding. Things, Bill. Strange things moving around outside. No weapons."

"Copy. On my way. Boyd! Jenkins! Finch! You're with me! On the double! Adamy, you're in charge."

****

Roughnecks
The Battle of Excalibur
Standard Earth Date December 7 3811

"Docking ring, secured, Captain."

"OK, Roughnecks! MOVE! MOVE! MOVE!" Connie yelled.

The 120 Marines sped through the boarding hatch at the rate of four per second. Each was armed and angry as hell; they all saw where Earth *should* have been when they were launched. They all had family there.

"Perimeter secured, Cap'in."

"Move out! Follow your maps. Objective, Delta Mess."

****

"CJ? How do you feel?" Phyll whispered. *'Anoxic brain injury', the Doc said. 'He may wake up. He may not. He may wake up for a little bit, then slip away'........ He may wake up later. He may never wake up. I wasn't fast enough. He is the one, I'm sure. I don't know why, but something tells me he is. We need him to fight those things. I need him. He's so handsome! If only I had pushed it a little more....*

"Hmm. Like a squadron used my head for 'touch-n-go' landing practice." CJ's voice sounded like he had a mouthful of pebbles. *Wake up. She's here. Think of her eyes. Those eyes, the eyes of an angel. Nothing else matters. Everything will be OK if she's here.* CJ's eyes opened briefly, and when he focused on Phyll's face, he smiled and moved his hand.

Phyllis picked up his hand and held it as CJ's eyes closed. She held off her tears; she knew that all across the fleet, countless hearts were broken, crushed by this battle. She felt guilty about her petty, selfish feelings compared to the vastness of that heartbreak, and she piled that guilt up high, using it as a dam to hold her tears back.

And then, she felt him squeeze her hand. Then the dam broke, and the tears poured out.

No one noticed. Alex had ordered that no one bother her for 24 hours.

Phyllis sat next to Chester and just watched him sleep for the next six hours.

After that, she slept in the chair next to his bed for the next twelve hours, until Jerry Kowalski came and ordered her to get some food.

Then Jerry sat down and stayed with Chester. Because it would make *her* feel better to know he was not alone.

****

"AaaarK!"

The scream grabbed every marine and sailor's attention.

John Alexander sat up with a start. He was sore, and felt a lot of cuts hurting all over. But the visions of those…*things*…they just kept coming, more and more of them, it would never end. *I must kill them! Kill 'em all…I must protect them.*

"John, It's OK. You did very well, lad!" Corporal Otis Finch sat down next to the young teen, placing his well-muscled hands around the young man's shoulders. "You are relieved, Soldier!" Otis said in his best 'Big Brother' voice. *He's a pretty strong kid for his age,* Finch thought.

John looked at the Marine uniform, then up at the face under the helmet. He recognized Finch from the Mayflower evacuation.

"I'm OK." *Deep breath. It's OK, if the Marines are here.* "Where is the Lieutenant Commander?"

"She's fine, son. She said you saved her life twice. Good job. We're proud of you."

"The Keep! Carl won't open it except for me!" John tried to get up, but Otis laid a big hand on his shoulder and calmly kept the teen seated.

"We've opened it up, son. The kids are fine." He pointed over to where a young girl was standing amidst the group of sitting children. "They were asking for you, one was pretty insistent. She is very concerned."

"Janice?" Johnny's eyes brightened as she came nearer.

"Johnny!" the girl squealed as she rushed to him, brushing aside the large marine and nearly smothering Johnny with her hug. *Her hair sure does smell nice! What a funny thing to notice now.* Johnny thought. *Her arms around me, hugging me, soft and warm, taking all the pain and the hurt away. Her smell. And, those….her chest, pushing into me; I feel a million feet tall! A guy could get used to this, real fast.*

Right behind Janice, Carl and the rest of the kids had stood up and were coming over. The marines hadn't time to hide the bodies of the aliens from the children. The kids dealt with the sight and smells better than anyone could figure; they looked at Jen and Johnny as superheroes.

Then again, so did the marines.

****

Roughnecks
Delta Mess
Excalibur
Standard Earth Date December 8 3811

"Excalibur is clear, Sir! We've found a total of 383 alien bodies, give or take a few. Two alive and in quarantine. Total of crew, marines, and passengers recovered is 506. All logs and files have been downloaded and transferred. Ship's data has been erased."

"Understood, Connie. Good work. Lets bring those people home."

"Aye, aye Captain. One more thing, Sir."

"Yes, Connie."

"Alex, It's Jen."

"Connie" Alex whispered.

"She used a sword to kill over three hundred of those things! She's a little roughed up, but she'll be OK, Skip."

Jen!

"Skipper?'

Jen's alive!

"Sir?"

I can breathe again!

"Captain?"

I....Oh, Jen!

Alex!

"Alex?"

"Thank you, Connie." Alex finally managed a quiet reply.

"Yes, Sir. That woman was amazing, Sir. You wouldn't believe what she did."

"Yeah, Connie, yes I would." *Thank you, Lord!* "Any word of Commodore Gridley?"

"KIA, Sir. They had some pretty gruesome hand-to-hand combat, Sir. The bridge crew tells me he fought very well."

"Marty Wells?"

"No sign of him, Sir. His station was in the section that the beam hit first. We have Charlie Sims, though."

Marty! Damn it! "Thanks, Connie. Get back here safely."

"Aye, aye Sir."

****

The Hounds of Heaven
Operation Heartbreak
Standard Earth Date December 8 3811

"Freddy, I've got something here. 42 by 55 by 89."

"I see it, Letta. Can we grapple it?"

"Do you think that's safe, Sir?"

"Right. I guess I'd better call it in instead. CAG, Freddy."

"CAG. Go, Freddy."

"We have one of those cylinders here. Looks undamaged. Just drifting. Shall we retrieve?"

"Hold on, Freddy."

"Freddy, negative on retrieve. Keep an eye on it, SARA 9 will retrieve. Escort SARA 9 back to Fortiter."

"Understood, CAG."

****

LCPA 47
Sol System
Standard Earth Date December 8 3811

Where is Alex? Is he OK? I thought I heard him call to me. Where is Angus? Is he all right? Cindy, where is she? Alex, I need you! Oh, Alex!!!

Jen, I'm here! I heard your screams. I thought….Oh, Jen!

Jenitka Kowalski awoke with a start. The sparsely lit room was moving, jostling her about, and all the while clanging like a bag of pots and pans in a windstorm. It smelled of oil and burnt metal, of blood and sweat, and of other foul things Jen could only imagine the sources of. She sat up, looking around, uncertain of her whereabouts for a moment.

Her eyes widened as it all came back to her.

"Johnny!" She yelled.

Everyone on the LCPA 47 turned to look at her.

"Lieutenant Commander, I'm here, Ma'am" John Alexander replied, raising his hand. He was sitting next to Janice, his hand on her shoulder, as she comforted a younger child who kept asking for her mommy.

Jen tried to get up, but Corporal Jim Jenkins, sitting next to her, placed a massive blood stained hand on her shoulder, holding her down.

"Not a good idea to move around now, LC. Landing sequence and all" Jenkins's deep bass voice advised.

"Right. Thanks, Jimmy. Johnny, um, John, are you all right?"

"I'm fine, LC. How do you feel, Ma'am?"

"I don't know yet, John. Ha-hah, I think I need more information." *He sounds so grown up now!*

"I'm sure everyone will be OK, LC." John said. *She's worried about the people she cares about. Dear God, let them all be OK, please!* He noticed that Janice was squeezing his hand now. He felt like he could take on the universe when she touched him. He smiled without realizing it.

Jen closed her eyes tightly. *Alex, I need you to hold me now, so much! As soon as possible, my love!*

Jen's eyes opened wide. Had she really heard that in her mind? *Angus?*

He's OK. Badly hurt, but he's here in sickbay, in surgery. You can see him soon.

Will? Marty?

KIA, both.

Oh, God!

Easy, my love. I need you. I thought....

I need you, too.

Soon.

"Please!"

"Jen?" Bill Marx gently shook her shoulder.

I had to have been hallucinating.

"Major. Sorry. It's been a, a long day. Any news of Charlie?"

"Copy that, LC. Three aliens had him trapped. Roughnecks helped us get him out. We captured two of those, *things*. He's injured, but he'll be fine. You OK?"

"Yes, Bill. I'm better, now. You?"

"All my family was," the tired marine paused a moment, "on Earth. Not a rare statement today, I'd bet. But still…"

"Bill, I'm so sorry. So many. They had no chance. Why?"

"We may never know."

"Copy that, Major." Quietly, Jen continued, "God, I need Alex."

I'm here, my love. I always will be.

"Understood, LC. With The Admiral and Gridley gone, we all need him. We *will* settle this score."

Alex, what will we do?

We'll find and kill the Bastards, Jen. I've started the prep for that already.

"I want a piece of that!" Jen growled out loud.

"Ooh-*RAH!*" chorused loud and clear throughout the LCPA.

Jen closed her eyes and leaned back to rest her head on the bulkhead behind her.

"Bill, Angus is on the Fortiter. He's in sickbay."

Marx snapped his head around and looked at Jenitka as if she had just grown a second head. Jen didn't notice; she still had her eyes closed. She felt much better now.

****

USF Fortiter
Between Cygnus and Sol
Standard Earth Date December 9 3811

"Are you sure leaving Excalibur there like that was the best move, Skipper?" Commander Peter Perry asked his Captain.

"If they come back, I want them to find those bodies. I want them to feel some fear, Pete. I want them to *know* we're coming after them. And, when they return to check their work, I want to know where they go home to." Alex's determination was obvious.

Peter Perry knew his CO well enough; even the laws of physics couldn't stand up to that man's determination. *Just like his old man.* "Roger that, Skip. 24 Mk 17 SCRDs are in place. And, Skip, I have the final recovery numbers, Sir; 2 Esc-Mods recovered, The Admiral and a Warrant Officer Stiles; seven fighter pilots, and 507 souls from the Excalibur."

"Not much left from a system of 30 billion and a fleet of over 50,000. That's a big bill some one owes us, Pete."

"Roger That, Sir. I can't wait to collect. More news, Alex. Contact has been lost with every single inhabited planet. We've dispatched SCRDs, but, well… On the positive side, the Heavy Cruisers Edmonton, Detroit, Denver, and Fairbanks, the Light Cruisers De Ruyter, Rochester and Syracuse, and the destroyers Gearing and Frankfort have arrived in system undamaged, as have the commercial ships Marcus Daly, Mary Ball, General Vallejo, Samuel Huntington, and John Burke. Also, the new carriers Wasp and Hornet have just returned from trials with their six escorting destroyers."

"How many people do we have at the Shipyards?"

"Last estimate I'd heard was 12.5 million plus. And the R & D, training centers, and al support services are operational. We have a decent fleet, Sir, and the means to expand it, and support it. They're just awaiting your orders."

"Understood, Pete. Comm, raise The Graveyard."

"Aye, aye, Sir!"

"Sir, there is another urgent matter." Pete reached out and grabbed his friend's arm.

"What else, Pete?"

"Sir, Doc sent me the Sick Bay HR recordings; the Admiral was absolutely specific, Sir. You have to tell them you *are* the Admiral now."

"That can wait, Pete." *Dad must have activated the HR recordings before I came in. Damn it! The bridge crew is hearing this, even if they pretend not to.*

"No, Sir, it can not. The Fleet needs to know they aren't headless."

"The Admiral is still with us, Mr. Perry."

"But he's not capable of command right now, Sir. Alex, we need *you!" And, this bridge crew needs to see your honest reluctance to 'take the crown'.*

"Pete, what would you have me do, create a monarchy here, where rule passes from father to son? I can't do that." *If I accept this, I can't look for mom.* Every eye on the bridge was now unabashedly focused upon their Captain and his XO.

"With all due respect, Sir, that is a load of Capitol B-bull and Capitol S-shit, and you know it. Alex, you taking command now *is* the proper chain of command. More importantly, you *are* the right person for the job. If The Admiral can come back and take command, you can step down. If he doesn't, we have not wasted several months waiting and several more sorting through the politics of the four other Commanders. Alex, you *must* do this."

Alex glanced around the bridge. He was not at all comfortable with this conversation taking place in front of the bridge crew, and Pete had to have known that. Looking at them, each and every one hanging on every word of this conversation. He met each of their eyes, and saw each determined face, each clenched jaw, nod once when he did. *DAMN IT! But, Pete is right.* Alex still sensed their tension.

"I have The Graveyard, Sir." Comm stated.

"Patch me into the entire Fleet, Comm."

"Channel open, Sir."

Did she do it that fast, or had she started the connection some time ago? Miss Hastings always seemed a step ahead.

"Fleet, this is Commander Alex MacAlister. As of this moment, I am assuming command of all United Space Forces and United Humanity Forces until Admiral Angus MacAlister returns to duty. That is all."

"Was that OK, Pete?"

"Ask them, *Admiral!*" Pete yelled over the cheers of the crew as he took the pair of silver stars from his pocket and pinned them on Alex.

We'll find you, mom.

****

Chapel Alpha
USF Fortiter

"Did you tell Lieutenant Mor?" Bill asked Jody as they walked down the passage towards Chapel Alpha.

"Yes, and I sent a note to the Captain and the CAG as well. Did you tell Tracy? Rick?"

"Yes. They each said they may tell a few......oh, my!" Bill gasped as Jody grabbed his arm.

The pair stopped and stared at the hundreds of people in the passageway. A powerfully confident yet calm, peaceful voice swept over the quiet gathering;

"People, there are too many here for the chapel to hold. Please, follow me to the Alpha Mess, where we've set up an altar for this service." With that, Mother Mary Halloran led the gathered crew to the mess hall.

Bill looked at Jody, and took her hand as they followed. When they arrived at Alpha Mess, it was packed.

They had all come to mourn Earth.

Chapter Seven

"Caruso Base"
Altair 66 Gamma
Standard Earth Date December 9 3811

"Forget the comm gear, Barb" *Angus will find us. It will just take some time.*

"If we can get....it working.............it may speed....them up some." Working was hard enough in the low oxygen levels. Talking just made it harder. At least the lower gravity helped.

"I don't want.........whoever took that....shot.........at me.........to know they've.....missed." *And I don't want any big grey ships shimmering around here either.* "Help me...set this......tripod up......in front of the cave."

"So.....tell me again..." Barb paused for breath, "why we.....don't just......live in the ship?"

"It needs to look......like it's crashed." Cindy set the point railgun onto the tripod, and sank panting to the ground.

"There's more...." Barb sat down panting next to her friend, "you're not telling.....me."

Should I tell her everything?

Yes.

I don't like what that answer means. Either way.

I will send Jen and the best pilots to find you. It will take some time. It would take me too long. Alex is needed here.

How bad?

Everything is....gone. Except Cygnus.

Angus! Oh, Angus!

"It's Ok. Whenever you're ready." Barb put her arm around her sobbing friend as Cindy buried her head into her friend's shoulder.

The nights here were very cold.

****

Reed Hospital
The Cygnus Shipyards
Standard Earth Date December 11 3811

"He talks to me without words, sometimes. I don't know how, but it's like we have conversations without talking. Am I crazy, Doc?"

"Lieutenant, your neural and psych scans are all normal, aside from showing a moderate case of sleep deprivation. All you need is a good night's sleep in a real bed every few days. It won't help your friend if you're in sickbay when he wakes up."

"Will he wake up?" Phyllis asked in a whisper while studying the hem of her sweatshirt.

"Nothing's changed, Phyll. We just can't tell."

"He'll wake up. But, I'm *not* nutzoid?"

"You're stressed, and you're tired. You look like hell. That's all."

"Thanks, Doc!" Phyll jumped up and kissed the physician on his cheek before running out of the exam room.

...

*I need to wake up! DAMNIT! I'm supposed to **do** something!*

...

It hurts!

...

I can almost hear them talking. I can almost feel....me.

...

WAKE UP! MY HEAD HURTS!

...

Why can't I wake up? Why does it hurt so?

...

So alone!

...

Crawl up, get out, wake up!

...

So hard.

...

So alone....

...

"Hi, Phyll. Don't stay too long tonight, that's an order. You need a shower and some *quality* sleep, or you'll put a dent into one of my Corsairs."

"Aye, aye, Cap, um, Sorry Sir, Admiral."

"In this room, call me Alex, Phyll."

"Yes, Alex. Thanks for watching him, Sir."

"Good night, Lieutenant."

"Sir?" Phyll called as Alex walked past her. As he stopped and turned his head, Phyll jumped up and kissed his cheek. "Thanks" Phyll whispered as she turned and sat in her chair next to CJ's bed. Alex watched from the doorway for a few seconds before heading off to his own nightly vigil.

"I'm here, CJ. Can you hear me?" She said as she picked up his hand.

Trying. So hard. So alone!

You're not alone. I'm here.

PHYLLIS!

CJ. I was worried when I couldn't hear you.

It's like I'm at the bottom of a well. I need to crawl out to wake up. I have to find some one. You have to help me.

"Shhh! Quiet, CJ. Rest, get better."

A passing nurse heard Phyll, and asked her hopefully, "Did he say something, Lieutenant?"

"Not really." Phyll looked at the nurse's nametag. "Alice, we sort of, well, we talk, um, without talking." *She seems sort of sad. A big engagement ring, but no wedding ring. Today, that's not good.*

"I said I have to find some one, and that you have to help me!" CJ's weak voice was raspy from disuse.

"Aaarrk!" Phyllis screamed as she jumped up in shock.

CJ lay there, as motionless as ever. The nurse walked to Chester's bedside and checked his vitals.

"Alice, did you hear him?"

"Yes, Lieutenant" the nurse grinned at Phyll. "But he doesn't seem to be completely awake yet. Still, it's a good sign." The nurse wrote on her datatab, and turned to leave the room. "Are you all right, Lieutenant?" Phyll nodded without taking her eyes off of Chester. "You have two hours, then I'm kicking you out. Your hair is a mess, and you need a shower and some sleep, and you won't get any of that here. If he wakes up and sees you like this, you may just scare him back into a coma! I'll have Doc write for something if you need it."

"Thanks, Alice."

Phyll?

I'm here.

Did I talk?

Yes, CJ.

I could hear you and….someone else. I don't know who.

That was Alice, your nurse. They're kicking me out in two hours, CJ. I need sleep.

"Then you should get into bed now."

"Are you making a pass at me, Lieutenant Commander?"

"Not tonight dear, I've such a terrible headache."

"Can you open your eyes?"

"I'm afraid to."

"Why?"

I'm afraid I wont be able to talk with you like this anymore.

110

I would miss that, too. It feels very special. Like a secret. Our secret.
Phyllis felt her heart beating wildly.

What are you wearing?

Oh, shit! I, uhh, um, "I have to hit the head. I'll be right back!"

"I'll be here!" CJ said as a grin pushed through the pain to spread over his face.

Phyllis didn't notice; she was flying to her quarters at near light speed.

****

ICU
Reed Hospital
The Cygnus Shipyards
Standard Earth Date December 11 3811

Alex walked into the Intensive Care Unit and came over to his father's bed. "Any change, Ensign Sorbello?"

"He's made some progress, Admiral. Not a lot, but some. We hope to back some of his meds down tonight. If all goes well, we hope to extubate tomorrow evening. After that tube is out, the rest is just a matter of time."

"What's so special about that tube?"

"With all the technological advances we've made, that tube is still the only way to support ventilation in many trauma patients. We've been able to heal the punctured lung and subsequent pneumo- and hemo-thoraces, but that tube limits what we can do, what level of consciousness we can allow, therefore what progress he can make. Once that tube is out, recovery will be much better."

"Thanks, Joe."

"Want some private time, Sir?"

"Please. Thanks again, Joe."

So, now you're a Respiratory Therapist!

I don't think so, but I need to know some things.

You pretty much know everything, or so you used to tell me!

Not even close. There's a lot I wish I knew.

Like if I'll ever get out of this bed?

Well, yeah.

I will. I worry about your mom.

Me too. I know she's out there, but I can't find her.

Mom and Barb are on a rock, low oxygen, low gravity, no water. She's blown up the ship to hide from any grey snoopers. The star is green. A something 66 something.

Does she have supplies?

She's scavenged the ship, so they're OK for about two months, baring any visitors. Send Jen; use CJ and Mor as escorts; that's important.

You're expecting trouble?

She's my life. I'd send the entire fleet, but that would draw attention we can't afford for a while. Those four could handle a lot with a small footprint.

Jerry will go too. CJ's still in a coma. No sign of waking up.

He'll be asking to fly by breakfast. I've given him the assignment already. He has a newfound strength.

I've got some ground-based fighter jocks I can keep as backup. Their new ships are pretty fast.

Good idea. Now, go to bed.

"Aye-aye, Sir!" Alex said as he saluted, spun crisply on his heel, and walked to his quarters.

I may actually sleep tonight he was thinking as a copper-topped, high-heeled flash in a short mint-green skirt and a smart black sleeveless top under a white sweater. *Was that Mor? Wearing perfume? CJ must be awake.*

****

Reed Hospital
The Cygnus Shipyards
Standard Earth Date December 11 3811

"CJ?"

"Phyll? How'd everything come out?"

What?

In the head?

Ha, ha, and ha!

"One of my dad's old lines. I couldn't resist, sorry."

"Have you opened your eyes yet?"

"I was waiting for you."

"I'm right here" *darling.* Phyllis whispered as she squeezed CJ's hand. *Please like it, please don't think I'm an ugly toad! Please, please, please!*

Chester slowly opened his eyes. It wasn't hard adjusting to the dimmed lighting that was the shipboard version of "night".

What made it hard to breath was the vision in front of him.

Oh, my!

"CJ?"

"Phyll, is that you? I've never seen you with….and your hair down....and.... WOW! It's red!" *You are so beautiful! Those eyes are like green flames warming my soul! If only I could gaze into them forever!*

"I can hear that, CJ!" *But, please, don't stop saying that! Ever!*

Aye-aye, Ma'am! "I need to see Doc. I have to get checked out in a Corsair ASAP." CJ tried to sit up, but found gravity a much more formidable opponent than he had remembered. *OW!*

"What's the rush? It'll take some time."

"I have to help find some one. You and CAG have to help, too."

"Help what? Who are we going to find? Who are we looking for? Everyone not here is..." *dead.*

I know. I had a ringside seat. "LC Kowalski. We have to help her find the Senator."

"The Admiral's wife?"

"Owww! Maybe tomorrow." CJ laid back.

Tomorrow will be fine, Lieutenant Commander.

Thank you, Admiral.

OH! MY! GOD! I'm talking to The Admiral IN MY HEAD!

Enjoy your company tonight, Mr. Jones, Miss Mor. That is an order.

Aye-aye, Sir! CJ fell asleep with Phyll holding his hand.

Half an hour later, two nurses came in and gently moved the sleeping Lieutenant Mor onto the hospital bed in the next room. It was good that she had the next day off. She slept very late that morning.

When CJ woke up, a nurse named Alice was waiting to talk to him.

****

Reed Hospital
The Cygnus Shipyards
Standard Earth Date December 11 3811

"We talk, sometimes. I know he's sedated and not conscious, but we talk. It's him, no doubt, as if he could see things...." Alex paused, unsure how to explain it.

"That no one else could see?" Doctor Rottello finished the sentence for Alex.

"Am I crazy, Leo?"

"All your tests are quite good for the strain you've been under. I wouldn't worry about it."

"I am worried, Leo. Worried what he will do when he finds out; I don't think I can hide it from him any longer," Alex hung his head and stared down as one tear drop hit the top of his left shoe.

"If he does communicate somehow, as you say, you won't be able to hide it from him. So tell him. Flat out. I know that's what you'd want; it's what he would want."

"Leo, thanks again. You're sure I'm not crazy?"

"Go ask Lieutenant Mor. And Jen. I don't know what's going on, but I do know none of you are crazy!"

Alex looked up and stared into Leo's eyes for several seconds.

"All right then. Thank you." Alex walked out, on his way to speak with his father.

****

Iso–Pod 43
The Cygnus Shipyards
Standard Earth Date December 11 3811

"So, what do you think? Can we get any of this thing to make sense?"

"Beats me. I can't think of any angle on this that we haven't tried."

"Is the 'thing' alive in there?"

"Every once in a while it moves, so I think so."

"If we let it out, will it just die like the other two?"

"Most likely, yes. It seems to be a programmed response."

"Haahhh. Get the dissection suite ready."

****

ICU
Reed Hospital
The Cygnus Shipyards
Standard Earth Date December 14 3811

Dad?

Alex. You're worried. Don't be; it's OK.

Dad, I have to tell you something.

I know, Jen's OK. You should be with her instead of here.

I'll see her after we talk.

It's that bad?

Dad, when you wake up….

Yes. I'm looking forward to it.

Dad, you won't be able to….

Move? Hell I knew that! I think I'll have some use of my left arm and hand. Shame I lost both legs and those three fingers. Not bad though,

114

considering."

Dad!

Alex, Hmm! Er, Admiral! Nice! Perry must have badgered you unmercifully!

Dad. I love you!

I know, Son. I love you too. Things are what they are. Now, go make that little fireplug you're engaged to smile! That's an order. I still outrank you!

Aye.....aye-aye, Sir!

Jen, he's on his way. He needs you.

Angus, I'll cheer him up. When can I see you? Soon?

After you get back, stop by. Not before. I'm not presentable yet. I do have a reputation to uphold, you know.

Admiral, I, I've finished revising your...speech....heh...huhh...Oh, Angus!

Nothing to cry about, little one. Dry your eyes. Put on that sunbeam smile! Your most important assignment is almost there, and he needs your full and complete attention.

****

Rehab Gym
Reed Hospital
The Cygnus Shipyards
Standard Earth Date December 14 3811

"See, I'm fine, really!" Lieutenant Commander Chester Jones quipped as he jumped from one foot to the other in a crude imitation of bad Irish dancing.

"CJ! Be careful! You're not 100% yet!" Al Morrison cautioned. The Physical Therapist had never seen a faster recovery than this pilot had; just two days ago he could barely stand, and now he had a 0.9 meter vertical leap!

"OK, Al. I'll be good. Can I go get cleared for flight now, please?"

" I can't do anything with you. Go see Doc Leo."

"Whoo-hoo!"

****

Visiting Officer Quarters
USF Fortiter
The Cygnus Shipyards

"There isn't a thing you can do about it, Alex. So, stop moping about and come comfort your fiancé!"

"Jen, I can't imagine him like that. I don't know how he'll take it, being paralyzed. He thinks he'll have the use of one arm. He...I...."

"No, Alex, you don't know how he'll take it. So, stop worrying about it. You know him well enough; he won't let this beat him."

"What?"

"I said, he will *not* allow this to beat him, to make him quit."

"'I do not like to lose', he told me. He knew then, even though he could move some then. Jen, I love you!"

If you're in love, show me! Show me now!
Now, wouldn't that be loverly!

****

Admiral's Mess
USF Fortiter
The Cygnus Shipyards
Standard Earth Date December 14 3811

"Thank you, Lord, for all the wonders that you have placed before me. Amen."

CJ and Phyllis sat in their Dress White uniforms at the elegantly set table for two.

"CJ, you make me blush by saying Grace!"

"Who, Me?" *You look so great tonight! Like an angel!*

"I can't believe the Admiral let us use his mess tonight!" *When have you seen an angel?*

"Well, I had a little talk with the big guy. And, you saving his father likely helped the cause." *I saw an angel while I was waiting to be rescued. It was the single most beautiful thing I can imagine! You are my angel, Phyll. YOU are the single most beautiful thing I can imagine!*

"It took you a week to get me that dinner you promised!" *Lazy bones, sleeping your life away. If I had known you were this romantic...*

"Oh, that promise doesn't count; hypoxia, you know." *It wouldn't hold up in any court.*

WHAT?

"So, now that I have a perfectly fine bill of health, I'll make you a new promise." CJ leaned forward and took Phyll's left hand in both of his as he stared deeply into *those beautiful eyes.* "Exactly like the other one. For as long as I live," CJ reached back with his left hand and took something out of his left jacket pocket, "I will tell you this every single day for as long as I live; I'm buying tonight, OK Phyll? Just for the record, I *am* definitely making a pass at you."

"CJ, what…every day? You're not making sense!" *My face must be red as a landing wave-off. Is he? Oh, God, I'm going to faint! I can't breathe! Is he? PLEASE! Why am I crying? Make that pass; I won't drop it, CJ! He can't be! No, Don't expect THAT! Oh, this is the most romantic night I can imagine!*

"Lieutenant Phyllis Mor, I want nothing but to spend every day of the rest of my life making pass after pass at you." CJ slipped the ring on Phyll's finger " Lieutenant Phyllis Mor, will…" …*you marry me?*

"AARRK!!!YES!" Phyll screamed as she leapt over the dinner table, making a perfect landing in CJ's lap with both arms wrapped around him and her lips plastered to his. *Oh, yes, yes, YES, YES!!!*

It took quite a while for either of them to notice that CJ's chair had fallen backwards from the impact.

****

Corsair Simm Station
K.L. Reusser Flight Training Center
The Cygnus Shipyards
Standard Earth Date December 16 3811

"These two are amazing!" Lieutenant Commander Jenitka Kowalski exclaimed as she watched the monitor of the simm mission they were using to acclimate Lieutenant Commander Chester Jones to the SF-4 Corsair star fighter. "I've never seen a pair of pilots work together like this."

"Well, they are the two top scoring pilots of all time still living, you know!" Lieutenant Commander Jerry Kowalski couldn't help but rib his kid sister a bit.

"Ahem!"

"Officially, that is!"

"Look at them, Jerry, it's like they fly as one pilot!" *As if they could….read each other's mind!*

"What?"

Jen's eyes widened as she turned to face her brother. *Don't say it, think it!*

You have got to be kidding me!

Jerry, you and I need simm time together, Now!

****

"Computer, record; debriefing of Captain Demos Stathus, commanding officer, USF Farragut. Lieutenant Commander Jenitka Kowalski presiding. Captain, what happened to your ship?"

"We had some radiation issues, then the nav stopped responding. We had to, um, abandon ship. All crew members were able to evacuate, but our passengers could not be, uh, found."

"Captain, You were recovered with only six of your crew. What happened to the other 317?"

"We hit a, uh, a debris field of some kind, and the other shuttles were destroyed."

"I see. What happened to your ship, The USF Farragut?"

"She crashed into Altair 66 Gamma."

"Tell me about your efforts to locate your VIP passengers, Senator Grabelle and her aide."

"We, um, we searched high and low, but the radiation…"

"Captain, need I remind you that your shuttle carries a copy of the Farragut's log recordings?" Jen's voice stayed very level in tone and volume.

"We erased….um, what recordings, Ma'am?"

"Captain Stathus, who gave you the orders to kill the Senator?" Jen asked in the same tone as every other question.

"I, uh, Ma'am, I…"

"Mr. Stathus", Jen was practically whispering now, "you do know that the maximum penalty for military personnel attempting political assassination is death, do you not? And, in the event several officers are involved, that the highest ranking officer will face that maximum penalty without option?"

"Uh, hem, ah, Ma'am, you are SURE Earth is gone? No one had time to leave?"

"You've seen the recordings, *Mr. Stathus.*"

"It was, Senator A…a…"

"Captain!" Jen barked at the man.

"Ach! Vansh! Egh!"

"Medic!"

118

Behind the one-way mirror, Charlie Simms removed his hand from his right coat pocket as he limped out of the room.

****

USF Pickering
Near Altair 66
Standard Earth Date December 22 3811

The cutter USF Pickering hovered just outside the Altair 66 system, escorted by two Corsair fighters. Jen and Jerry served as pilot and copilot, Bill and Jody Campbell served as sensor officers and medics, while the remainder of those on board consisted of Major Marx and a squad of marines.

"Long range grav-sensor sweep Altair 66 system complete. No hostiles detected, Jen. Preparing to enter system upon Gravoptic scan completion." This was the fourth system they had identified as possible locations for the USF Farragut.

"All stop! Emergency stealth complete shut down!" *Jerry, CJ, Phyll! Optical scanners show a grey ship is in system, orbiting Altair 66 Gamma!*

Everything is shut down. CJ and I are dark and quiet.

Jerry, did they see us?

"I don't think so. Jen. We went dark pretty quick." Jerry whispered to his kid sister.

The USF Pickering was small as cutters go, just a little larger than a SARA, but it was very maneuverable and had excellent FTL performance. Its minimal armament was adequate against lightly armed shuttles, but nothing capable of confronting a grey globe. But the main reason it was a perfect long-range 'Search and Rescue' craft was it's excellent sensor suite.

"They're over Gamma. Did you get any readings on it?"

"Charts say it's cold, low O2, low grav, lifeless."

"Lifeless? Where'd the oxygen come from?"

"Dunno. Just readin' the charts, sis."

It's moving!

It's gone!

Jen, stay put for eight hours.

Alex, where did you come up with eight hours?

It just popped into my head. Like asking you out that first time; totally arbitrary.

You....

Relax sis. He's your CO now.

Just wait until I get him off duty, Jerry, I'll show him who's CO. Arbitrary my ass!

Nah, your ass is far from arbitrary! It's actually very...

ALEX! DON'T YOU DARE!

Children, enough!

Mom!

MOM!

I'll see you in eight hours, Jen. Alex, mind your manners!

Yes, Ma'am.

Angus, this could get to be kind of fun!

I know.

****

Iso–Pod 43
The Cygnus Shipyards
Standard Earth Date December 22 3811

"The cylinder seems constructed of a type of nano material, but it has been deactivated. Like it ran out of power."

"Do you want to try feeding it a little juice?"

"NO! The information we have of the Excalibur boarding shows these things eat into the hull, boring through and sealing it. We don't need it doing that in here!"

"OK, then cut it open."

"Here goes; using the gravitic peeler to pull one layer of nano off at a time from the "front" end, to our left."

"Are all security protocols active and in place?"

"Yes; there are a dozen angry looking marines holding swords covering every compartment surrounding this lab."

"It's open! Will you *look* at that!"

"Are you thinking what I'm thinking? That thing looks like a giant..."

"Six-legged waterbear?"

"Exactly. How is it moving in the air like that?"

"I'm picking up a kind of magnetic field, possibly holding it up and providing motive force. It seems sort of sluggish, like it wasn't designed to function in gravity."

"I'm going to try talking to it." The exobiologist opened the comm into the cell. "What are you?"

The alien stopped, turned to 'face' the scientists, and hung motionless for several seconds.

"It seemed to hear that, if not understand it."

"You food. I eat food."

"Jesus!"

"It's trying to eat through the window!"

"It has no intake of gasses, Sheila. Nothing coming out, either."

"I wonder what happens after it eats? Does it grow?"

****

Meeting Room Beta
Central Administration Complex
The Cygnus Shipyards
Standard Earth Date December 22 3811

"We've interviewed all the crew. At the point they look ready to break, they die. Any ideas, Charlie?" Alex seemed frustrated with the lack of progress.

"Admiral, this looks like a dead end, pardon the pun. There is no one left to get information from. We may never know who was behind this."

"Charlie, I thought you said you knew, but were gathering evidence..."

"Uh, right, Bill. But, without something concrete, it's all just guesswork, isn't it?"

Bill Marx stood up, followed by Alex and Jen. "Well, I guess there's nothing left for it, then."

"Right." Alex said as he moved closer to Sims.

"Absolutely" Jen confirmed, while sliding around the other side of the table. Within a second, Charlie Sims was surrounded.

"What..."

"Mr. Sims, come with me." Bill Marx said with more than a touch of disgust in his voice.

"Alex, Bill, I, Jen!"

"Sims!" Alex snapped as Marx reached into Charlie's pocket and retrieved the remote poison release control. "Who was behind this, Charlie!" Alex's voice sounded larger than his considerable size.

"I should have had that MVP! It should have....Ugh!...been....AWeK!......MINE! Aark! AlBlt!"

"MEDIC!"

****

BEEP!-beep-BEEP-BEEP! Alex's comm demanded attention with the 'urgent' ring.

"Alex here. Go."

"Admiral, Leo. Your father has woken up. We've been able to remove the breathing tube."

"Thanks, Leo. I'll be right there."

****

ICU
Reed Hospital
The Cygnus Shipyards
Standard Earth Date December 22 3811

"Dad! How do you feel?"

"Like mud on the practice field at the end of the season."

"That good?"

"Eh! I had to be awake when your mother gets home. She has certain, um, expectations, you know!"

"They'll be here in about twenty hours."

"And the day after, you and Jen have your wedding."

"We can't spare time for that now, dad! I can't have my personal life take precedence over...."

"Bull shit. Alex, you are the leader of everyone now. They need something joyful to celebrate. They need to know it's OK to find a little happiness after all of this."

"Dad..."

"I insist. If I have to, I'll order you to do it!" *Not like that has worked with you since you turned ten!*

"OK, I'll tell Jen. But, what do we tell everyone about you?" *I hope I'm over trying to become the Alpha Male of the house!*

"Don't worry about that. Worry about the prosthetics being able to get my new legs and arm working properly so I can enjoy a dance with my new daughter-in-law! And, Alex, one more thing." *You are now the ultimate Alpha Male, Alex!*

"Yes, Sir?"

"Mor and Jones."

"A double wedding?"

"Your mother was right, you are bright! Mor and Jen are close. CJ looks at the world differently since The Battle of Earth. He is immensely important, Alex."

"Dad, All that is not a problem. But something is worrying me." *Why can we talk like this? How do you seem to know what's going to happen, what will be important?*

Something happened to us. It was the Hackberry juice; we have symbiots inside us. They make this possible.

Is that, well, is it safe?

"Alex, I think our survival as a species depends upon it!"

****

Fleet Admiral's Quarters
The Cygnus Shipyards
Standard Earth Date December 22 3811

"I am so glad you are home, and even more glad that we are away from all those others."

"Angus, we need to talk."

"Was it that bad, Hon?"

"You know what I mean. I know you better than anyone else, no matter what Jen tells you I said. I know what you think, and I know *how* you think, deep down inside. I always have, even in high school. Now, let it out."

"Cindy, I want to love you so much, but...."

"I know. If you haven't noticed, you don't have to think at me for me to know what you're thinking. Everyone else you do, but not me. Angus, I know you're paralyzed. I know how much that hurts you. But you know that was only a part of us, a very nice part, but just a part. You and I are so much more, my love, you give me, you fulfill me so much beyond that. Angus, I love *you*, not just physically, but totally, deeply, entirely, madly; I need you. I always will. And you know it!"

"Somehow, having you tell me, makes it more real. You are my life; I *need* you to be happy and fulfilled."

"Oh, Angus, I *am* happy and fulfilled because I have *you*!"

"I don't deserve you, you know!"

"Then tell me the rest."

"Vance. Why, Cindy? He'd been my best friend since I was eight years old! And Charlie. Good Lord, Charlie!"

"Some mistake, some wrong turn Vance made, Angus, allowed some one to put more pressure on him than he could take. You know he had been running in, well, 'faster' circles the past few years, and, as you yourself said, he was letting his ambition overcome his sense of service; I couldn't tell you that we were investigating him on bribery and kickback charges. And Charlie hid his jealousy from everyone, including himself, since that football game. He let it out for some reason, by attacking you. But, Angus, think of this; if Charlie Sims had wanted you dead, would you be here, talking now?"

"No. I certainly would not. Vance and Charlie may have been playing a delaying game with whoever was behind....." Angus looked down at the unresponsive stumps, which used to be his legs. *Behind this.*

"So, now will you tell me about what is *really* bothering you!"

"Those prosthetic legs cut an inch off my height, I think. I....."

"ANGUS! STOP IT! I know you! Losing your legs, losing our sex life, finding out that two of your best friends had been involved with trying to kill you are all hard to take. But not for YOU! Your view of life won't permit it! NOW, TELL ME!"

"I, I..........I've failed. I've failed at the one basic purpose of my job, my life's work; Earth is.....it's....it's gone! Gone because I wasn't good enough! So many dead, gone forever! My f-fault." Angus broke down, sobbing heavily, as Cindy pulled him to her breast, and held him, rocking gently, in her arms.

"Let it out, my love. When you are ready, I'll tell you how wrong you are about *that*, and how much better our world is because of *you*, how we are all alive *only* because of *you*...."

The two of them just held each other close the entire night, as they had many times before; this night, out of all the others, was the most special of them all.

****

CAG's Quarters
USF Fortiter
The Cygnus Shipyards
Standard Earth Date December 22 3811

"I'm sorry, Jody. It was a pulmonary embolism we missed. He was gone before we could do anything."

Sniff! "Th-thanks, LC. I, um...I, awe...oh!" Jody Sims-Campbell was overwhelmed by the sobs flooding out of her, releasing her grief al at once.

"Bill, take care of her. You two have as much time as you need."

"Thanks, Jerry. It's been a tough couple of weeks."

"No problem. Let me know if you need anything else."

Jerry watched Bill Campbell lead his wife back to their quarters.

That was the best way to handle it, Alex. Jody had nothing to do with the mess her father got caught up in. Jerry thought.

We've been through his quarters already. It was Senator Vance Anderson. Marx's suspicions are that some one else pulled his strings as well. Jen confirmed.

That wouldn't matter much now, would it?

I would still keep an eye on things, Jerry. You just never know.

****

Newton Research Station
The Cygnus Shipyards
Standard Earth Date December 23 3811

"Alex, it works! We have the red beam, just like you said! Not only that, but we have screens that will stop it!" Troy Praetor exclaimed.

"Good work, Troy! Great news! How long do you think it will take us to deploy them?"

"Well, about twenty minutes per vessel, I figure."

"What?"

"Alex, it's just a software rewrite! We have about twenty times the power in a Fortiter Class than they have in one of their big grey globes. We could kill them with a fleet of Light Cruisers if we wanted. And the dimensional shift; not only can we duplicate it, but we can nullify it over a cubic AU."

"Troy, you've just moved up a pay-grade!"

"Admiral, it was all your ideas, your theories, your direction!"

"But you did the hard work, Troy, you and your team. Don't be afraid to take the credit for it. Remember Earth!"

"Remember Earth! Alex. And, Merry Christmas!"

"Merry Christmas, Troy."

****

Theresa Chapel
The Cygnus Shipyards
Standard Earth Date December 23 3811

"Jerry, I can't stop shaking!"

"Alex, relax. This is the easy part! She's still cute; wait about sixty years!"

"CJ, will you smack this guy for me, please?"

"Admiral, that's my bride's boss you're talking about. I must show restraint!"

The three men laughed as only three truly happy people can.

"OK, you two. It's time to go. Are you two ready?"

"No!" The two grooms chimed in perfect chorus.

"Imagine how I feel, best man for two weddings, I have to give two speeches, dance with two Maids Of Honor, and I'm only able to get drunk once!"

"C'mon, let's go."

The two grooms, in spotless white dress uniforms, walked out onto the altar as Jerry went through the back halls to find the parents in the chapel atrium.

"CJ, are you...."

"Yes, Admiral, I certainly am."

Jerry Kowalski Jr. stopped behind the door for a moment before opening it to find the Admiral and Senator MacAlister in the vestibule, talking with a middle-aged officer in a Merchant Marine white dress uniform.

"Admiral! Mrs. MacAlister! Hello!" Jerry offered.

"Jerry! You look so very nice in your dress whites!" Cindy complimented the Lieutenant Commander.

"Jerry! I'd like you to meet Captain Philippe Mor, of the freighter SS Marcus Daly. Mr. Mor, this is Lieutenant Commander Jerry Kowalski, CAG of the Fortiter, and Jen's older brother."

"Thank you, Madam Senator! Pleased to meet you, Captain Mor."

"Pleased to meet you, Sir! It is an honor." The man said as he enthusiastically shook Jerry's hand.

"Jerry, This is Phyll's father. She does not know he's here. She believes that I will walk Jen down the aisle, and then come back for her. Instead, Mr. Mor will step out and walk her down to give her away."

"Admiral, that is fantastic! Phyll has not said much of her family, except that her mother died while she was in the academy, and her father was working in space." *I'm so happy for her.*

"She may be reluctant to do so, gentlemen. I have not seen her since she was sixteen years old; these older freight companies pay well, but have twelve-year contracts. If she bears any resentment..."

"Mr. Mor, I know your daughter very well. Trust me on this, she will be very happy to see you." Jerry smiled at the nervous father. "But Sir, please tell me; has she always screamed when she gets excited?"

"She still does that? Ha-ha ha! I would have hoped she had outgrown it! I do miss it, though."

"It is one of her unique mannerisms we all love, Sir. Your daughter is an incredible pilot, and an excellent officer." Angus offered.

"This means a lot to me, Sirs. I can't thank you enough."

"Don't mention it, Captain Mor."

Just then the music began playing, and the ushers came to pair with the bridesmaids. The girls came out dressed in the same flowing gowns, the first two in a seafoam colored gown, followed by two in lemon yellow, then two in sky blue, and finally two in coral pink. Phyll's maid of honor, Jody Sims-Campbell, wearing a bright royal blue gown, followed them. She walked over to Jen's Maid of Honor, Cindy MacAlister, looking stunning in her lilac purple gown. The eight pairs of ushers and bridesmaids formed duel lines, walking down the aisle as paired pairs, and as the music changed, began their promenade down the aisle. Jerry grinned as he prepared to walk down the aisle with two lovely ladies, Jody on his left, and Cindy MacAlister, on his right. *Not a bad assignment,* he decided.

Then the music changed once again, and the two brides appeared.

Jen looked at Angus, her eyes widened in surprise; she had expected him to be in a grav-chair, as he was during the rehearsal. "Angus, you're.... you're walking!"

"Well, I do have a reputation to uphold, you know!"

You big softy; you didn't want to take attention from me. They tell me it is very hard to learn how to use prosthetic leg. I love you, you sweet old lug!

Angus could not keep from beaming a huge grin as he gazed at Jen; all her career she had purposely covered her beauty. Not so today! Stunningly golden hair cascaded over her lightly freckled face. Her white lace gown highlighted her voluptuous curves, accentuated perfectly by a neckline that revealed the perfect amount of cleavage. Angus found himself forgetting to breathe at the sight.

"Jen! You are, amazing! What a vision you make!" Angus beamed as he hugged his former Chief of Staff. *Alex is one lucky man!*

"Thank you, Angus! For so much" *I had to rehearse that to not say 'Admiral'! Thank you so much for giving me away! And teaching me, everything! For being the father I lost!*

"Come, my dear. Your life is waiting." Angus smiled as he offered his arm to Jenitka Kowalski, and, as she took it, began the slow march down the aisle on his prosthetic legs. As he walked, he reached up to wipe a tear; he was thinking of his old quarterback, his friend, Jerry Kowalski Senior.

As Jen approached, Alex looked at his father first, holding his breath. He watched closely for a few steps, until he was convinced the old man would be OK. Then Alex looked at her. *My God! I don't deserve this angel! Such beauty!* The vision she presented would be the *only* thing he remembered about the entire ceremony.

Jen walked the first quarter of the aisle concentrating on Angus, her hand on his arm ready to catch him if he fell.

Not so tightly, little one! You'll cut off the circulation to my two good fingers!

Sorry, Dad. He's fine. I can't believe he learned those so fast! Jen glanced at the guests, all a blur, as her gaze moved up to the altar and found Alex.

Oh! So handsome! So tall, so strong! I can't breathe! He loves ME! Oh, Dad, don't let me fall!

Never, little one.

Just as Jen reached the Altar, Phyllis came out into the vestibule. As she stopped and looked at Angus and Jen take their last few steps, she felt a presence next to her. As she looked to her left, she noticed a uniformed arm was offered to her. She started to accept by moving her hand to it as she looked up at the face of her escort.

"Dad? AARRK!" Phyllis squeaked out as she jumped in the air, wrapping her arms around her father as she landed, sobbing with joy.

"Daddy! Daddy! Daddy! Daddy! Daddy! Daddy!"

"P-Pod! You are so gorgeous, my little one! Look at you, all grown up! What a fine young lady you have become! This man, he is a very lucky man, indeed. Does he realize this?"

"Oh, Daddy! You're here! All my prayers over you! Daddy! Yes, daddy, he is the most wonderful man I can imagine!"

"Come, little P-Pod. Your knight in shining armor waits! You have caught quite the big fish, they tell me, Phyllis! I could not be any happier for you."

"Oh, daddy! I love him so much!"

"As I loved your mommy. You will make each other very happy, I can tell, but only if we get moving, my little girl! So proud am I!"

And so the father and daughter walked down the aisle, to join the Admiral and his bride to be on the altar. Not only were those present actively wiping their tears, but nearly every person on ships and anywhere on the Shipyards Complex was watching. All had heard Phyllis' squeal of surprise when she saw her father; the few who knew the cause wore broad smiles.

They all needed something to celebrate; the wedding of the new Admiral and the two pilots gave the perfect chance for all to smile and share a little joy.

Chester Jones looked down the aisle and his heart stopped. Always made breathless by Phyllis' beauty, seeing her lacey white gown with thin, bright green trim set against her bright copper hair nearly toppled him. *How do I rate this? I am the luckiest man alive!* CJ thought as she came closer. Then he gazed into those eyes, bright green, the trim on her dress perfectly matched to their glow…those eyes that had captured him from the moment he looked into them…. *were they really for him only?* And nearly fell over. Only the fast reactions, and large size of Alex kept him upright.

We are two amazingly lucky men, aren't we?

Yes, Admiral, that we are.

The almost eleven million people that now comprised the human race all smiled for the next several hours.

Especially the ring bearer, John Alexander. After all, the reception would include dancing. Dancing with Janice. A lot of close dancing with Janice, if he was lucky!

****

Fleet Admiral's Quarters
The Cygnus Shipyards
Standard Earth Date December 23 3811

"Angus, how long do you think they'll stay at the reception?"

"They're younger than we are, dear. I can't play that late anymore. It could be five minutes, or five hours! Cindy, would you help me with these legs, please? They are killing me."

"ANGUS!" Cindy stopped and stared at her husband's face with wide eyes.

"What?"

"WHAT DID YOU SAY?"

"Huh?"

"You said those legs are killing you. Angus, are your stumps sore?"

"Well, yeah! I've been on these things all day, dancing, and…..Oh. OH, MY!"

"Angus, you can feel your stumps!"

"Well. Umm. Ah. Well. YES!"

"Here. Let me help you with that. First, let's disconnect the neural inputs at the neck….now, the legs. Lay back. There. One. The other. Better?" Cindy asked as she looked at the red, irritated skin where the prosthetics had rubbed harshly. Moving so Angus could not see, she pinched the red, irritated area on his left stump.

"OW! What are...you didn't believe me? Ha-ha. Watch this!" Angus wiggled both stumps.

"Oh, Angus! That's marvelous!"

"Now, can you help me get ready for bed? I am dog tired!"

"I'll just bet you are. Did you see....Ahh! Oh, my! Aaahh! Aaaaaaaaaah! Aaah! Ah! Oh. Oh. Oh, Lord! What was THAT?"

"Um, Cindy, that was Alex and Jen. I'd say they've left the reception."

"You mean? Ah! Oh, Not again! Aaaaah! AAAAAAAAAAAAAARK! Oh dear! Oh. Was that..."

"Yeah, Chester and Phyll. I guess it's a little overwhelming when you can feel each other's thoughts while..."

"Um, Angus?"

"Yes, my love?"

"Cuddle-buns, it looks like 'something's come uh-up'!"

"Something that requires your immediate and concentrated attention, I presume!"

"Absolutely! Admiral, permission to come aboard, Sir!"

"Permission granted, gorgeous!"

****

Rear Admiral's Quarters
The Cygnus Shipyards
Standard Earth Date December 23 3811

"Oh, Alex! That was..."

"Absolutely breathtaking!"

"I think CJ and Phyll enjoyed themselves as well!"

"Alex, did they 'feel' us, too?"

"I would think so, Jen. We'll have to try and control that. It could take a lot of practice!"

"Oh, you big hunk! Have you, um, reloaded yet? Ah, Oh, OH! OH! Aaah! OH! Ahh! OH! OH! Oh. Well. Um, What was THAT?

"Oh, GOD! That was my parents. Jen, does Jerry have a girlfriend?"

"Alex, your father!"

"They said it wasn't possible for him to walk, either." *He just does NOT...*

"...like to lose. I know. OK, so a half dozen people, including your parents, know when we, um, eh-hem. We need to figure a 'privacy screen'. Are you up for research?"

"Count me in, Ma'am!"

****

Guest Officer's Quarters
The Cygnus Shipyards
Standard Earth Date December 23 3811

"Thank you, Chester." Phyllis Jones gazed into her husband's eyes.

"For what, love?" Chester panted, as he gazed into those endless green eyes.

"For saving me."

"Hey, Angel, you saved me, remember?"

"If you hadn't rescued me, I would have suffocated inside that armored shell I used to keep everyone out. I never would have known...." *..this.* Phyll ran her fingers lightly over husband's chest. *Not just talking this way, CJ. I feel you inside me.*

Not for a few minutes, you've worn me out!

Not that way, though that's incredible too! But I feel your soul in here with me. All the time.

I know. It is so much more than I had imagined.

"CJ, I never knew I could be so happy! Oh! Ah, um, ah, OH! OH! OH! Aaah! OH! Ahh! OH! Oh. Ah. Um, Ah, CJ, what was that?"

"I think that was The Old Man and The Senator."

"But, I thought..." *.....I thought he was paralyzed. How could he...? OH! MY GOD, CJ, did they, were we, that way, too?*

I would think so, Angel.

"AAARRRK!"

****

RSP-15 Lightning
"Super Snooper"
Near Norma 7
Standard Earth Date January 10 3812

"OK, ACE, do your stuff!" Captain Johnny Mustafa whispered. It was silly, he knew, but every recce pilot worth a pretzel whispered when this close to an objective. Even though the sound couldn't possibly travel past the confines of the cockpit, it made them feel better to whisper.

ACE was the Artificial intelligence Crew Enhancement. A new computer system based on the quatinary system developed by Alex

MacAlister, coupled with software developed by R & D, and placed into a stealth drone, ACE had the capability, in theory, to penetrate any system, record data, and even infiltrate alien networks, then get out and report that data by gravitic burst before it self-destructed.

The self-destruct feature was due to the discovery of a small probe attached to the Mk 12 SCRD deployed by the Sagan. Humanity could not afford to let the Grey Globes find them. Not just yet.

Captain Mustafa released his ACE probe and waited. His mission was to wait there for thirty-six hours while ACE did its thing.

The probe locked on to the star Norma 7, and began a two-G acceleration using a direct gravity beam on the star's mass.

Communication frequencies....very low frequency range......there. Large amount of traffic. Indeterminate purpose......language analysis......likely binary data...........language reconstruction ninety-four percent reliability. Proceeding to phase two.

Strategic dispersal information.........340 large grey spheres.........320 deployed in war throughout large area near Circinus X-1......three deployed to Sol system....danger greater there than anticipated, two lost, yet objective achieved, threat civilization eliminated, food recovered.......losses unacceptable......can not survive a second front......terror at Circinus X-1.........pull ten to war at Circinus X-1.....leave eight searching......home at Norma 7 dangerously vulnerable........

Objective achieved... gravity burst transmit...destruct in Three, Two, One......

Twenty-two hours into the mission Super Snooper picked up the gravity burst from ACE 1. Johnny checked his passive sensors once more, and then lit his engines at maximum power. He would be home with the information in fourteen hours. If he didn't make it, the gravitic burst would be received in twelve days.

****

CAG's Office
USF Wasp
The Cygnus Shipyards
Standard Earth Date February 10 3812

"John, if you take the differential of that...."

"Oh, I see! Then I get to find the answer on the curve! I've got it now, Sir. Thank you so much."

"No problem. Same time tomorrow?"

"If it's not too much trouble, Sir. I need to keep my average up if

I'm going to The Academy!"

"I have a feeling that won't be a problem, Mr. Alexander."

"Sir, one more thing, if I may?"

"What's got your goat, son?"

"Goat, Commander? I've never had a goat. I did have a hamster once."

"It's just an expression, John. What is on your mind?"

"Well, Sir, it's about, eh, it's about, um, about girls, Sir."

"That's a broad subject, young man. It's a joke, John. Humf! Computer, recording off. Now, tell me what your problem is."

"Well, I want to ask Janice to go to the dance, but every time I try, well, I just sort of..."

"Oh, well. John, this is how you manage that issue... no, wait, not that. Let's see... AH! Here's what I did...ahh...um, no, no, don't do that...Well, the best thing, son, is to be yourself. Be honest and respectful, but be your self..."

****

Fleet Admiral's Conference Room
The Cygnus Shipyards
Standard Earth Date February 12 3812

"Gentlemen, Ladies." Angus began the Command Briefing with the age old, boring greeting. "You have just seen the raw information from ACE 1, the interior monitors aboard the Excalibur, and our combat probes at The Battle For Earth. This is the information we have in a coherent package;

"The Grey Globes are huge vessels because they have a large number of very large fusion reactors.

"The red beams are a focused form of super-excited photons.

"The shimmering effect is not a shield, but a dimensional shift in partial stasis. It is the method of defense as well as the method of transport the Grey Globes use.

"The black cylinders are nano-constructed boarding pods. The nano-construct is not unlike our nanny-paste.

"The 'water-bears' are NOT the intelligence behind the Grey Globes. They are essentially biological robot warriors designed to function in a variety of zero-G environments. They are sluggish in as little as one-half G."

"They didn't seem sluggish to me! Commander Jenitka MacAlister mumbled under her breath.

"It would seem that, while they are designed to survive beam and projectile strikes, they are not designed to win a sword fight. *I still can't believe you did that, Jen.*

Admiral, a girl must uphold her reputation. They tried to look under my kilt!

Angus managed to suppress his laugh, but just barely. "From intercepted intelligence, the aliens behind the Globes are thin mammal-like and have six limbs. Two are used exclusively for locomotion, two are used for locomotion or tool manipulation, and two are exclusively used as arms. The faces are somewhat feline in form, except that they contain three eyes and three ears. Fully erect, they stand about 1.5 meters tall."

"How tall are they flaccid?" Lieutenant Commander Chester Jones asked in a serious tone. The entire room erupted in laughter.

"Clever, Chester." *Funny how he's become 'Chester' instead of 'CJ' since he got married.* "The crew of a Grey Globe is four."

A gasp escaped the audience as one, and a low murmur began.

"Focus on topic, people!" Angus' old attention-getter had a conditioned response, and every lip zipped shut, while all eyes focused on Angus. "The aliens use a trinary computer system. In short, there is not so much an 'advancement in technology' gap as a difference in the direction of our technologies.

"Their total Grey Globe strength is 337 units. 330 of those are engaged in a war near the center of the galaxy, in the vicinity of Circinus X-1, approximately 30,000 light years from eh, Sol, and approximately 48,000 from here.. From what we can tell, that war is not going well for them.

"Under no circumstances is any ship to go within 30,000 light years of Circinus X-1. Is that clear?"

"Aye-aye, SIR!" Chorused the officers present.

"Politically, they run on a caste system, with military leaders at the top. Total population runs about seven million."

The crowd gasped. It was an incredibly small number.

"The cultural age estimate is about 12 billion years. Average lifespan of an individual is estimated at three thousand years. Reproduction..." the Admiral fixed his gaze on a grinning Chester, *don't even think of it, CJ!* "...is sexual, with two sexes. Rate is one child per twelve hundred years, beginning after age five hundred. Their birth rate has been declining."

"We are retooling our fleet with new defensive and offensive weapons, in addition to our familiar and proven plasma cannon, railguns and GravTorps. We have a goal of the following fleet to be completed by June 30, 3813;

"Twenty eight interconnected turrets surrounding Cygnus 78 capable of defeating Grey Globes when they attempt to fire;

"Three defense stations equipped with Red Beams around each Cygnus Shipyard installation, civilian and military;

"Defensive screens proof against the Red Beams on every Cygnus Shipyard installation, civilian and military;

"Three thousand armored vehicles per Marine design;

"All forty Fortiter Class BB Battleships;

"All thirty-six Lexington Class CB Battle Cruisers;

"Four Sol Class CA Heavy Cruisers, plus 68 additional as new builds;

"Ten Gridley Class DD Destroyers;

"Two Wasp Class CV Carriers;

"Twelve thousand six hundred ground-based interstellar fighters: Mustangs, Thunderbolts, and Lightnings;

"Six thousand fleet interstellar Corsair fighters;

"Eight thousand attack craft: Havocs, Dauntlesses, and Invaders;

"Two thousand Landing Craft, Personnel, Armored;

"Six hundred Landing Craft, Vehicle;

"Two hundred thirty SARAs;

"Twenty-four Cutters;

"Two hundred and seven Patrol Craft;

"Eight commercial freighters;

"Four Fleet Support ships.

"What we do not have are the trained crews to man them. That is your job now.

"Fleet COC will be as follows;

"Civilian Authority; Chancellor Cindy MacAlister.

"Commander In Chief: Admiral Of The Fleet Angus MacAlister.

"Commander, Fleet, R & D and Cygnus Shipyards Operations: Rear Admiral Alex MacAlister.

"Commandant, Marine Corps: General William Marx.

"Commander, First Fleet: Commodore Jenitka MacAlister.

"Commander, Task Force One: Captain Wilson Alimonte.

"Commander, Task Force Two: Captain Sheila Driscol.

"Commander, Combined Aerospace Operations: Commodore Jerry Kowalski.

"Commander, Aerospace Group, Task Force One: Commander Chester Jones.

"Commander, Aerospace Group, Task Force Two: Lieutenant Commander Phyllis Jones." *Chester, Phyll, I'm sorry about splitting you up, but I had to. I have something in mind.*

We understand, Admiral

"The Office of Chancellor will be up for election. The election will take place June 1, 3814. When the results are affirmed, the serving Chancellor and Commander In Chief will retire upon the swearing into office of their replacements.

"People, You have your assignments; they were made based upon talent, ability and Fleet requirements only. Get your ships ready for combat, and train your crews. Keep an eye out for talented teachers, we will need them.

"I expect detailed plans and time estimates on my desk at 0800 tomorrow morning. Dismissed." Angus gave a big sigh; it was over. A million problems could have bitten his ass off; the heavy cruiser captains or any number of other officers could have objected to his Chain Of Command, anyone could have objected to an appointed civilian, and they even could have objected to his retirement.

In the end, their eagerness to attack the Grey Globes held any objections in check; the items Angus laid out, even the seemingly impossible tasks of preparing two fleets, were seen by all as just the steppingstone to their common objective; strike at the Grey Globes, and hit them hard. Very, very hard.

And that was exactly what Angus needed to win this war.

****

Rehab And Prosthetics Clinic
Reed Hospital
The Cygnus Shipyards
Standard Earth Date February 14 3812

"I can't explain it, Angus. It could be those symbiots causing your nerves to grow back. There is something else; Angus, you legs and arm are growing. I don't know what the end result will be, but your leg stumps are four inches longer and your arm is three inches longer. And your fingers look about halfway regenerated."

"Leo, I think I'll just go with it. I'm not complaining."

"I wouldn't either! Come back every other day. We'll keep adjusting your prosthetics as much as we can. At some point, you may need a week or two off to get your space legs back, so to speak!"

****

SS Marcus Daly
Altair 66 Gamma
Standard Earth Date February 15 3812

"Payload away, Sir!"

"Thank you, Mr. Johnson. Estimated time to impact?"

"47 minutes, Mr. Mor."

"Let's hope that ice asteroid hitting Gamma works. Lord knows we need another planet, especially one that the Grey Globes have looked at and left."

"Yes, Sir!"

****

USF Wasp
Office of CAG Task Force One
The Cygnus Shipyards
Standard Earth Date March 22 3812

"BING-bing, BING"

"Come" Chester Jones responded to his door chime without looking up from the training readiness reports on his datatab.

"Commander, I, um, I need your help, Sir."

The stress in the young woman's voice made Chester drop his datatab and look up.

"My God, Cheri! What happened! Comm, Medic to CAG's office ASAP. Injured Sailor." Chester rushed around his desk and helped warrant officer Cheri Stiles sit down. She was shaking, her uniform torn, her lower lip split, swollen and bruised.

"Medic on the way Sir."

"Cheri, what happened?"

"He, he, he hit me Sir, when I wouldn't...do...things!"

"Who hit you, Sailor?"

"Ensign Wally Martin, Sir."

"The Medics are here now, Cheri, relax, you're safe now. Comm, HR recording from WO Stile's arrival."

"HR recording is automatic when subordinate enters threshold outside CAG's office."

"Good. Request a Marine detail to accompany me, and a one to cover Miss Stiles. Locate Ensign Martin."

"Marine details report as on the way. There are four Ensign Martins aboard the Wasp. Which would you like the location of?"

"Wallace Martin." *Damn, I need to get used to this computer, and this rank, and fast.*

"Ensign Wallace Martin is on L deck near bulkhead 12-487. His current position and movements indicate he was heading for Sick Bay 12."

"Was?"

"Ensign Wallace Martin's life signs have stopped."

Oh, Lord, NO!

****

Fleet Admiral's Conference Room
The Cygnus Shipyards
Standard Earth Date May 10 3812

Ding! Ding! Ding! "Computer is recording as judicial proceedings."

"This inquiry is now opened. Presiding are Admiral Angus MacAlister, Captain Wilson Alimonte, and Captain Sheila Driscol.

"This is to review the evidence for and refuting the charges brought against Warrant Officer Cheri Stiles. Miss Stiles, we have read your statements; do you have anything further to say at this time?"

"No, Admiral" Cheri offered in a small voice.

"Captain Driscol, will you review the charges, please?"

"Admiral, Captain Alimonte. Warrant Officer Stiles alleges that Ensign Wallace Martin attacked and sexually assaulted her on the twenty-second day of March, 3812. Warrant Officer Stiles alleges that Ensign Wallace Martin assaulted her on L deck near bulkhead 12-487 aboard the USF Wasp.

"Warrant Officer Stiles states that Ensign Martin approached her and demanded sexual favors from her. When she refused his advances, Warrant Officer Stiles alleges that Ensign Martin hit her repeatedly. Miss Stiles alleges that she picked up a maintenance tool and struck and killed Ensign Martin in self-defense.

"Captain Alimonte, Please read the statements of Commander Jones before we offer him time to revise or extend his testimony."

"Admiral, Captain Driscol. Commander Jones states that he was working in his office when Warrant Officer Stiles entered and reported an attack by..."

"Stop! Please! Stop! I lied! Commander Jones just tried to help me. The Medics will tell you that. Wally beat me because I wouldn't pay him. I had some gambling problems, and the bookies said the way out of them was for me to plant explosives on the Excalibur bridge! I figured once Earth was gone it didn't matter, but Wally found out, and threatened to tell unless I paid him to keep quiet. Wally kept pushing it, and pushing it. He wanted me to have sex. He said he owned me now. So I picked up a piece of energy conduit, and I hit him with it, and he staggered back. He was bleeding, a lot. I hit him again. I made Wally pay for the deaths of my family on Earth, for the bad things I did. Over and over again I hit him, but it didn't help! I just kept hitting him, and it didn't help! I'm sorry. So sorry!" Cheri Stiles collapsed sobbing in her chair.

****

USF Edmonton
Altair 66 System
Standard Earth Date June 15 3812

"Systems report!" Captain David Johnson demanded.

"Edmonton ready, Sir! CAG reports fighters deployed in defensive perimeter. 524th fighters and attack bombers in position for follow-up strike."

"Very well, Miss Gilson. You may begin our attack run."

"Remember Earth!" chorused from each voice on the bridge.

The USF Edmonton, the last surviving Excalibur class Heavy Cruiser, accelerated with her newly installed upgraded Gravitic Drives. Acceleration at a hundred times her original specs carried the powerful ship in a 0.97C close pass by Altair 66 Gamma.

Training systems engaged, the Heavy Cruiser dropped a minefield of dimensional-shift inhibitors as she began firing training versions of red beams and plasma cannon across the planet's surface. One hundred forty-four Corsair fighters formed a protective screen around the ship, which had rotated to fire its primary railgun as it released its GravTorps at the doomed planet. Had Altair 66 G been inhabited by more than the microbes that Senator Grabelle and her aide left behind, those life forms would have been devastated by an actual attack.

Immediately following the Edmonton were 60 GravTorps, looking for anything bold enough to attempt a pursuit. And, just in case, a formation of 240 Mustangs with 120 Thunderbolts escorting 160 Lightnings and 320 Invader attack bombers followed at 0.97C. For a system reeling from a lightning strike, this would have been a devastating follow-up attack to the lightning swift primary strike, easily capable of destroying lighter combat ships, tugs, communication arrays, and various supply and repair facilities.

"Nice job, Dave. All unit commanders, debriefing in my ready room on the Fortiter in 30 minutes!" Commodore Jenitka Kowalski ordered.

Alex, it looks as good as it can in a dry run against computer generated opposition.

Jen, just tell me if you think it's good enough.

I don't think we can get any better, Admiral. If the technology works as planned, we should do all right.

I'll let The Old Man know.

Chapter Eight

Task Force Vengeance
Outside Norma 7 System
Standard Earth Date January 4 3813

"Status, Captain Alimonte." Jenitka MacAlister requested.

"All task force elements report in position and ready, Commodore. Stealth drones have seeded Dimen-Shift Dampers." Captain Alimonte's response reflected the determination felt throughout the fleet.

"Task Force Vengeance, this is Commodore MacAlister. Operation Remember Earth is authorized; all units, execute Operation Remember Earth. Execute. Execute. Execute."

Four Fortiter Class battleships began accelerating towards Norma 7. Each was covered by 240 Corsair fighters, accelerating to match the big ships.

"Dimen-Shift Dampers ready! Weapons hot! Gunners, stand by!" Captain Alimonte advised.

"Time to extract our pound of flesh, Will."

"Roger that, Commodore."

****

UASC 524th Space Fighter Group
"The Hounds of Heaven"
Operation Vengeance
Standard Earth Date January 4 3813

"Ok, you puppies, look sharp! Form up and stay alert!" Colonel Bong snapped over the comm.

"Yes, Sir! On the ball, you Rummies!" Captain Fred Yeager echoed.

"We are to escort and protect the Invader Bombers in the second wave. Stay on mission, *no* freelancing!" Yeager reminded his pilots.

180 Invader attack bombers began moving out after the battleships. Each carried a Mark 7 GravTorp and four twenty-kiloton fusion missiles. 240 Mustang and 160 Thunderbolt fighters moved into escort position around the Invaders.

The plan was for the Invaders to attack fifteen minutes after the battleships' lightning strike with a pass at 'targets of opportunity'. Twenty minutes after that, the Edmonton and her fighter screen would sweep through and clean up. Nice and neat; within forty minutes, Earth would be avenged.

Such were the plans they made.

****

The Carrier USF Wasp followed the four Fortiter Class battleships into the Norma System. The Wasp was the same size as the thirty-kilometer long battleships. The primary difference was that the Wasp replaced the centerline railguns with increased hangar capacity. Fleet carriers brought twice the fighter and three times the attack bomber capacity to a battle compared to the battleships. With the fitting of Red Beam technology, the relative firepower was much debated within the fleet.

Today the Wasp served as flagship for Task Force Vengeance. This formation was designed around the lightning fast strike idea first proposed by Captain Alimonte, and approved by The Admiral's Council.

Task Force Vengeance comprised the carrier Wasp; the battleships Nelson, Warspite, Missouri, and Washington; the heavy cruiser Edmonton, the fleet replenishment vessel Mars, 180 attack bombers and 400 escorting fighters.

The plan was simple enough. The Wasp and the battleships would accelerate to nearly light speed for an attack run on Norma 7 Charlie, the Wasp's fighters providing minesweeping and escort coverage. Following the battleships. The bombers, escorted by the fighters, would hit targets of opportunity exposed by the first wave of the attack. Finally, the Edmonton would repeat the battleships' attack run, hitting again on Norma 7. All units would move at best speed to Sol immediately after the attack, then regroup and move to Cygnus 78.

****

VF-33
"The Wildcats"
Operation Vengeance
Standard Earth Date January 4 3813

"Form up, 'cats. Look sharp!" Commander Chester Jones reminded his pilots. *Lord, let this have a different outcome for my pilots from the last*

142

combat I was in.

"On station, Boss!"

"In position, Skipper."

"Right on, Commander."

The answers came in from each member of his squadron. These men and women were well trained when Chester took command of them, and he was happy that they had improved significantly since. He kept his 'family' arrangement for dealing with personal issues. After a lot of soul-searching, he had decided the only negatives stemmed from his emotions after losing every one of his pilots at Earth; he decided that the benefits were worth that pain.

"Our mission is to screen the big guys. Keep close, no glory-hunting."

"You got it, Skip!"

"Affirmative, Commander."

These are a really good group of pilots. I am privileged to lead them. How do I tell them that?

"CAG to Group; you have the training, you have the talent, you have the motivation, you have the tools. We sit upon the brink of the opportunity. I could not be prouder than to have this chance to lead this Group into battle. Remember Earth!"

"Oooh-RAH!" The ancient Marine cheer chorused back over the comm to Chester's ears. The hairs on his neck raised on the sound.

Here we go, my love!

Be careful, CJ! Come back to me!

That is always my plan, Angel.

****

Task Force Vengeance
The Battle of Norma 7 Charlie
Standard Earth Date January 4 3813

"Presets entered and engaged, Captain"

"FTL will hold until we are one AU from Norma 7 Charlie, then we make our firing pass at zero-point-nine-seven C. We re-engage FTL at zero point three AU past Norma 7 Charlie."

"Helm and Nav agree."

"Time to zero-point-nine-seven C is thirty seconds, Sir."

"Battle stations! Battle stations! This is not a drill! Combat in fifteen seconds!" Captain Alimonte announced.

The five thirty kilometer long ships slowed to zero-point-nine-seven times the speed of light. The planet Norma 7 Charlie, their target, was about three minutes away at that speed. A lot could happen in three minutes.

"Sensors, report!" Captain Alimonte barked. He needed information. The faster he got it, the more time he had to make a decision; the more time he had, the better decision he would make.

"A large number of small objects in our path, Skipper. Could be mines or boarding pods." Lieutenant Halsey sounded nervous, yet under control as he reported to his Captain.

"CAG, can the fighters clear them?"

"On it, Skipper!" Chester Jones replied.

"Full grav shields, Miss Williams. What else, sensors?"

"Reading zero ship traffic, Sir. No Grey Globes on optical or any other sensor. Dimen-Shift Dampers active." Halsey replied, a bit calmer as he sank into the routine of his tasks.

Alimonte has trained them well. They're doing a good job. I have to stay out of their way. Jen thought.

Good thinking, Jen. You were paying attention. Angus MacAlister confirmed Jen's instincts.

"Weapons, targets acquired?" Captain Alimonte asked.

"Aye, Captain, targets are locked. Firing position in…" Lieutenant Andrews never finished his statement as alarms sounded across the bridge of the Wasp.

"Four Grey Globes at twenty-thousand kilometers and closing at zero-point-two C. Red Beams fired." The excitement level in Halsey's voice had risen once again.

"Shields holding. Weapons; return fire. Weapons free!" Captain Alimonte commanded.

"Aye, Sir. Returning fire with plasma beams." Andrews replied.

"Warspite and Nelson firing Red Beams. Grey Globes targeting our fighter screen, Sir!" Halsey's nervousness was gone as his training took over.

"CAG, get behind our screens! The aliens are targeting you!" The Captain's voice rose to convey the urgency of his message. Those fighters were vulnerable!

"Copy, Captain. Group….."

"CAG! Come in! Wildcats, respond!"

CJ! Jen reached out for his thoughts and found nothing.

CJ! Chester! Phyllis called without reply.

"I have no readings on any fighters, Sir." Halsey stated in a very quiet voice.

"Damn! Sensors, status of objects ahead?"

144

"Fighters have destroyed most, Sir. The rest we can push off with our shields." Lieutenant Carry Williams reported.

"Grey Globes status?" The Captain inquired.

Jen, the fighters were a mistake! Call off the follow-up waves.

Not yet.

"They look dead in space, Sir. I'm picking up huge gouges in their hulls." Halsey reported on the damage to the alien ships.

"Weapons, on objective?" Alimonte asked.

"Aye, Sir!" Andrews' determined voice responded.

"Fire at will!" The Captain ordered.

"Aye! Firing!" Andrews announced.

"Missiles incoming!" Halsey interrupted.

"Defensive systems engage!" Alimonte directed his crew.

"Tracking, Sir!" Williams frantically replied.

"Approaching departure point." Helmsman Jennifer Stewart announced.

"Sensors, rescan for fighters!"

"Still nothing there, Sir." Halsey replied to the Captain.

"All missiles destroyed, Sir!" Williams voice was a mixture of relief, surprise, and triumph.

"CAPTAIN!"

Large objects suddenly appeared in front of the five large ships. The objects were close enough that the task force could not avoid them. The amount of energy released upon impact.....

"Nelson is hit! Warspite hit! Missouri hit!"

The Wasp shook as if a mighty fist had slammed into it. Alarms sounded throughout the ship.

"Damage report!"

"Large object impact amidships. Halsey replied. "Hanger decks destroyed. Decks G through RRR depressurized between bulkheads 12-200 and 18. Maneuvering reduced, but operational. Screens down. Red Beams and Plasma cannon on line, railguns offline."

They will attack now, Jen. Washington can turn this.

Understood, Angus. I'll keep Pete behind the damaged ships until he's in position to finish this.

"Washington, This is The Commodore. Look sharp, Pete; expect an attack. Suggest you stay behind the damaged BBs, move to optimum firing position."

"Roger that, Commodore. You guys OK over there?" Captain Peter Perry asked.

"We'll survive, Pete. Be sharp!"

"Aye, Sir!"

145

Jen was now immersed into commanding the task force. "Damage reports from Missouri, Nelson, and Warspite?"

"Severe but not fatal damage to all three ships. Warspite has screens; Missouri has power to all systems. Nelson is the worst off, power at 45%, structure damage limits FTL to estimated one Parsec/Day."

"Do any ships have any fighter screen left?"

"Negative, Commodore."

A thousand pilots, dead. And a thousand more heading in. How did they see us, and react to us in that short a time?

Dimen-Shift Dampers. We sent them in too soon, Jen.

The follow-up strike should be OK; they won't expect it or detect it, Admiral.

"Captain, Grey Globe ahead, ten degrees off the starboard bow!" Halsey was concentrating on his data now, keeping the information flowing to both the Captain and the Commodore as he had been trained to.

"Wasp, we have the bogie. We're moving up behind Nelson and Missouri. I don't think they'll see us."

"Give 'em hell, Pete."

"Roger that, Wasp."

"Captain, departure point reached."

Captain Alimonte looked at Jen over his right shoulder. Jen just shook her head slightly. *I can't leave them. Not yet.*

"Helm, hold here. Repeat to Washington, Warspite, Nelson and Missouri"

"Aye-aye, Skipper. All ships affirm, hold here."

"Washington is engaging bogie, Sir!"

The view screen at the focus of the bridge zoomed into show the Washington spiraling into the Grey Globe, firing her Red Beams and plasma cannon. The crimson energy sliced completely through the huge grey ship. After ten seconds, the Grey Globe was cut into several glowing hot pieces.

"Bogie eliminated, Commodore!" Captain Perry sounded more relieved than boastful in his report.

"All major units make to rendezvous point Alpha."

The five USF capital ships limped home.

****

USF Hornet
The Cygnus Shipyards

"Lieutenant Commander Jones, may I enter?"

"Phyllis, may I enter?!"

Phyll, please.

OK.

You have to tell the comm system to let me in.

"Come in."

"Phyll, I don't know what to say."

"Me too."

"How can I help?"

"Just hold me, please."

Of course.

He didn't know. I just found out, half an hour before the mission. I never had the chance to tell him.

Tell him?

I'm pregnant. I'm going to have our baby, and CJ'll never know!

Oh, Phyllis!

Phyllis Jones cried and sobbed, as Cindy MacAlister held her for a very long time.

****

The Hounds of Heaven
The Battle of Norma 7 Charlie
Standard Earth Date January 4 3818

"Let loose the Hounds!" Colonel Bong announced as the attack bombers accelerated into the Norma 7 System.

Give 'em hell, Hounds! Every pilot was surprised to hear The Admiral's voice. So many units, he couldn't call them all! Each pilot sat a little taller in their cockpit as their fighters streaked towards the enemy.

The SFA-6 Invader attack bomber was an amazing piece of technology. Twice the size of a Mustang, it was nearly as maneuverable, and accelerated almost as well. The true marvel was in it's armament; four dual Four-point-five Plasma Cannon turrets, eight Eight-point-five Plasma Cannon fixed firing forward, and hard points for a full sized Mk 7 GravTorp plus four twenty kiloton fusion missiles. As if that was not enough, the Invader carried a Heavy Railgun on its centerline. This fired a half-ton projectile at zero-point-nine C, giving the Invader the ability to devastate almost any target.

The advanced computer system of the Mustangs and Thunderbolts gave them the ability to shadow the Invaders, keeping the optimal escort position as the bombers flew their attack runs.

"Hounds locked into escort mode. Here we go, people. Sensors sharp; that info is as valuable as any targets we take out." Bong reminded his pilots.

"On mark, Boss." Arleta confirmed.

"Double H 1, this is Flying Knights 1."

"Flying Knights 1, Double H 1. Go."

"Twenty seconds to objectives. Sensor sweep shows zero ship traffic other than four Grey Globe hulks and the wreckage of a fifth."

"Copy, FK1. Any info on Charlie?"

"Coming up on it now. Looks pretty bad down there, fires, looks like a lot of molten rock all over. Those Fortiters really worked it over."

"What are your targets, FK 1?"

"There is nothing in system besides debris and Charlie. We're targeting that."

"Copy."

"FK 1, Commodore. Assessment; is Edmonton follow-up required?"

"I don't see any worth while targets other than Charlie, Sir. That looks pretty well wiped out."

"Copy, FK 1. Give 'em a hard kick in the ass and come home."

"Roger that, Sir."

Chapter Nine

Fleet Admiral's Quarters
The Cygnus Shipyards
Standard Earth Date January 4 3813

"Welcome to the strike assessment for Operation Vengeance." Angus MacAlister began somberly. He was very uncomfortable over the casualties suffered on the raid. It was supposed to be so quick and, well, easy.

"First, the results; post strike assessment indicates that Norma 7 Charlie is not able to sustain life, and will not be for centuries. Second, we did not observe any shipyards or other significant facilities within the Norma 7 System. Third, we engaged and destroyed five Grey Globes, as well as hundreds of boarding pods.

"We were hurt, however. The Nelson and Warspite are badly damaged. Repair time is estimated at six months plus. The Missouri and Wasp suffered moderate damage. Their repair time is estimated at fifty days. Washington is nearly unscathed. We lost 964 fighters and two attack bombers; four fighters and two bombers were lost in collisions in combat, the rest were lost due to enemy action.

"The two pressing issues are these; first, how did the Grey Globes show up with our Dimen-Shift Dampers in place? And second, what was the weapon that damaged the carrier and battleships? Alex, do we have any ideas from analyzing the battle data?"

"Thank you, Admiral. Battlespace recordings show approximately twenty large, dense objects simply appeared in the path of our capital ships. How they got there is a complete mystery.

"As for the alien Globes, they also just appeared. However, their maneuverability was just as sluggish as we predicted. Therefore, we know the Dimen-Shift Dampers were working. So, there is another process involved other than dimensional shifting."

"You all have the data. We will break now for some important business. We will reconvene in three days. Dismissed."

****

Theresa Chapel
The Cygnus Shipyards
Standard Earth Date January 5 3813

"Phyllis, the service will start soon. The Admirals are here. So are

Jen and Jerry. And young John Alexander is here, as well."

"OK, Cindy. Thanks for your support. I don't know what I would have done without it." *I think I know, but I don't want to think about that.*

Cindy led Phyll over to where John, Alex, Angus, Jerry and Jen were standing in front of a stone pedestal. The top of the pedestal was engraved with an armored fist thrusting a dirk up through the center of a circle; the circle was inscribed with "FORTITER". Below the fist was inscribed "STARCLAN".

John, Alex, Angus, Jerry and Jen all moved to comfort her, but when Angus gave her a hug, Phyllis froze.

All of you, come, touch Phyllis! Angus ordered.

Silently the group each touched the grieving mother-to-be.

There! Can you feel it?

Something!

It's like a conversation that I can hear, but can't quite make out the words. Angus thought.

What is it? Jen asked.

You know what it is! Alex replied.

The Symbiots? Jerry wondered.

Will some one tell me what is going on? I'm getting nervous! John thought.

He's hearing us without Symbiots?

John tentatively laid his hand upon Jen's shoulder, and everything that was just out of their perception became crystal clear.

"Aaaaarrk!" Phyllis screamed and fainted. Angus caught her before she hit the ground.

OH, MY! Cindy gasped.

Phyll's eyes opened and she stood up on wobbly legs. *I have to get Jody and Bill.* Phyllis' eyes illustrated her panic.

"Alex, Jerry, you're with me. Jen, Cindy, stay with Phyll; don't let her do anything rash. John, you're with me too." *I do NOT like to lose! And now I've got the goal line in sight!*

****

Norma 12 System
Standard Earth Date January 5 3813

So cold.

...

Why do they hurt me this way?

...

150

So dark!

...

Where am I?

...

What do they want?

...

It hurts so much. STOP IT!

...

 So alone....

...

Phyllis...........where are you?

...

ARRGH! STOP HURTING ME!

  ...

****

LCS-1
USF W.S. Bush
Circinus X-1 System
Standard Earth Date January 6 3813

Commodore Jenitka MacAlister gingerly maneuvered the invisible shuttle closer to the immense battle.

Easy, not TOO close!

I've got it, Admiral! Will you look at that!

Alex and Jen looked, as the Grey Globes were busy trying to overwhelm one very large, oval shaped white ship, which moved slowly among them. The white ship was easily four times the size of the Grey Globes. Hundreds of red beams poured onto the lumbering ship, seemingly without effect. Steadily the huge craft moved close to a Grey Globe. When it was within a few hundred meters, a shaft would dart out of the white ship and penetrate the hull of the Grey Globe. The Grey Globe thus stung would neither move nor fire again.

Why don't the Grey Globes move away from that 'Great White Shark'?

I don't think they can; I think it holds them still while it moves closer. I wonder what's in that 'stinger'?

Shall I open a comm-link and ask?

Fun-neee!

Got enough?

Yes, let's get home.

Norma 12 System
Standard Earth Date January 5 3813

CJ's mind had left his body some time after the mutilations began; he simply could not stand the pain, so he left it. Sometimes a wave of it still crashed through to him, though, because he couldn't let go completely, he couldn't die. He had to see Phyll again. He had to live to see...

A baby? I'm a father? ...AHH! STOP IT!...I need my angel...please...
CHESTER!
Admiral? SIR!
We're on our way, son. Give 'em 'ell!
Aye-aye, Admiral, Sir! ...What had Singh told me? Oh, yeah; sometimes, the right spark can make a pit of despair erupt into volcanic determination. How do I do that? How do I give them hell? I'm in hell now....
CJ, hold on! We're coming!
John? Yes! YES! JOHN!
Where are you, you motherless bastards, where are you...where...
THERE!

The alien making the sawing movement with the serrated metal blade across CJ's naked back froze in place. It began shaking, and then it died as CJ fed The Pain into its mind.

...Another, where... THERE!

Twenty of the aliens died before CJ felt his own pain subside. Then he slept for a few minutes. When he awoke, his mind began searching for more aliens.

****

LCS-1
USF W.S. Bush
Norma 12 System
Standard Earth Date January 8 3813

"ETA, fourteen minutes, Admiral" Lieutenant Commander Phyllis Jones declared. Angus looked at her across the small cockpit of the Landing Craft, Stealth. Another one of Alex's inventions, it had only completed fitting out a few days before, and had not yet had its trials.

"John, are you ready?"

"Aye-aye, Sir!" *Thank God my voice isn't squeaking anymore!*

Admiral, are you sure it's a good idea to bring him?

Phyll, something about him increases our minds, our ability to sense things, each other. I don't think we can find CJ without him.

You can't. I have to be there. John confirmed.

"John, what do you mean?"

"I don't understand it, but I had the same feeling with the LC fighting those bears; I HAD to be there, or we all would die. Just like now."

"I believe you, son. Just stay close to me." Angus said.

"I will, Sir."

You should have had Alex come. You aren't fully recovered yet; your legs are still weak. Jen thought to Angus.

And if Alex came, you would have too, Jen!

Yes.

You need to help Alex run the diversion. The Admiral reminded them of the plan.

I know. I worry about you. Jen thought.

Me too, my love. Cindy added.

OK, you two, quit badgering him and let my father save the universe!

Thanks, Alex! Angus thought.

"60 seconds, Admiral!"

"Check. Armor powered up, all indicators green! John?"

"Armor, powered up, all indicators, um, green!"

"John?"

"My comm indicator flashed yellow, then went green. I think it's OK."

"Keep an eye on it."

Jen, I should have flown that shuttle. It was wrong to send Phyllis. Jerry voiced his concern for the tenth time.

Jerry, we couldn't stop her.

She'll be hurt, Jen.

Then we'll pick her up, Jerry.

I know. I just don't want her to hurt anymore.

"There's our LZ, Sir. You'll have about two feet of space from the door to the surface. I'll be waiting for your signal, pick up within 90 seconds of it."

"Stay calm, Phyll. We'll bring him back."

"Aye-aye, Sir."

"OK, John, drop in Three, Two, One, DROP!"

Angus and John dropped onto the station silently. There was no atmosphere to conduct any sound outside of the alien space station, and their Mk III Stealth Combat Armor cushioned their landing so none would be transmitted within the station. Angus looked up briefly, and decided that not seeing anything was a good thing.

Call me, I'll drop by if I'm in the neighborhood.

Roger that, Phyll!

Angus turned and looked down, picking a likely spot, *this looks as good as any,* he applied the molecular acid to the hull of the station. He had to go through six layers before atmosphere vented and they were able to drop through.

Left, and three decks down, John directed. *Um, Sir!*

Skip it. Stay near the walls, just in case. Follow me.

Twenty feet later they encountered the first alien.

****

USF Fortiter
Task Force Flying Tigers
Circinus X-1 System
Standard Earth Date January 8 3813

"Contact, dead ahead, Sir!" Lieutenant Holloway announced.

"Commodore MacAlister to Task Force Flying Tigers; Execute Plan Solar Storm. Good shooting!" Jen turned to the ship's captain; "Mr. Shin, fight your ship!"

"Aye-aye, Sir! You heard the woman, look sharp!"

Similar orders of purpose and encouragement echoed in each of the twenty Fortiter class battleships that made up the task force. Formed into four lines of five ships each, the coal black ships sped in full stealth mode at zero-point-nine-eight C towards the rear of the battle line of two hundred Grey Globes. Fighting at that speed was strictly the realm of computers, and these ships had the most advanced quatinary computing systems ever designed.

The plan was very simple; flash by the Grey Globes and hit as many as possible, then keep going; avoid a prolonged slugfest. Turn after thirty light minutes, and repeat. Then head home. As the last pass was made, the twenty ships would shed their stealth mode, revealing the huge versions of the painted on shark mouths used by their namesakes eighteen centuries before.

"Firing position in Three, Two, One! Weapons fired!"

Eighty plasma cannon and forty red beams struck out at the points in space where the quatinary computers predicted the Grey Globes would be.

"Miss Holloway, damage reports?"

154

"Captain, our ships were not fired upon! Grey Globes show....twelve,....sixteen ships drifting, out of action, debris fields in the positions of eighteen more!"

"Commodore MacAlister to Tigers! Good shooting! Stay in formation for one more pass, sync your stealth shields to me!"

Affirmatives came in from the other nineteen Fortiters. This was the hard part; moving in a fast, straight line away from an enemy you had just hit and hit hard. It was so tempting to slam on the brakes, turn around and hit them again...but the professionals commanding these ships knew better. They stayed focused on the battleplan.

****

LCS-1
USF W.S. Bush
Norma 12 System
Standard Earth Date January 8 3813

"I'll go nuts if I have to wait much longer!" Phyllis Jones drummed her fingers on the cockpit glare shield just a little harder. She was always the one diving in when something needed to be done; this sitting and waiting was unbearable! She had to see him! He had to see his daughter!

CJ?
Phyll! My angel, you've come to save me again!
Come to me, CJ, I need you! I don't know anything about raising kids!

****

Norma 12 System
Standard Earth Date January 5 3813

Angus and John stopped outside the door.
He's in this room, Admiral.
Angus opened the door, and looked inside the room.
There he is! Good Lord, what have they done to him!
I'll be OK, Admiral.
Admiral, these are dead, too. Just like all the others.
They are all dead Admiral.
CJ?
Phyll, you need to promise me something.
No, I can't! Don't ask me that, CJ!

Just stay in the cockpit, do not come back to see me. Wait until....tomorrow. Turn on your thought screen now, dearest. The screen blocked outgoing thoughts, allowing a little measure of privacy; however, the other developed symbiots could sense the loss of contact.

CJ! I can't stay away!

Shh....just a little while. I'll tell you about it, I promise. I had to, to do things.

Rest, CJ. I'll be here.

Admiral, can you carry him by yourself?

No, but my armor can. John, lead the way back. Phyll, stay in the cockpit. That's an order.

Aye.......

Phyll, he'll be OK. He's thinking of someone else, not you.

...aye, sniff, Sir!

****

USF Fortiter
Task Force Flying Tigers
Circinus X-1 System
Standard Earth Date January 8 3813

"Second firing pass approaching, Sir!" Shin announced.

"Admiral to Tigers; destealth in Three, Two, One, MARK!"

"Firing position in Three, Two, One! Weapons fired!"

Again the one hundred and twenty fingers of destructive energy reached out and grabbed many of the Grey Globes.

"Damage Report!"

"No shots fired at us, Sir. Twenty-six Globes destroyed, another twelve......no, eighteen heavily damaged, likely destroyed. Remaining Grey Globes have......have stopped moving and firing, Sir! They're all dead in space!"

"Commodore MacAlister to Tigers; good shooting! Let's head for home. First round is on me." *Alex, Angus, we did it!*

****

LCS-1
USF W.S. Bush
Norma 12 System
Standard Earth Date January 8 3813

"CJ, it's OK. You're in a medi-stat unit. We'll have you home in no time."

"Thanks, Sir. You shouldn't have come. Too much to risk for..." *for one dead pilot.*

Nonsense! CJ, no single one of us is indispensable. Every single one of us is important. It's what you taught your pilots, remember? They told me.

It's what you taught us all, Sir.

CJ, we hit them again. Hard. At Circinus.

How'd we do?

We knocked out almost eighty of their Globes.

Us?

Not a scratch.

Excellent! They wont be a problem now, Sir! Chester coughed twice, a small amount of pink foam flying from his mouth. *Admiral, I need to see Phyllis now.*

Are you sure, Chester?

Angus, let her go. He needs her. Now. Cindy was very stern when she needed to be.

I know, my love. He wants to spare her the pain.

You know, her pain grows each second that she can't wrap her arms around him.

So you've told me.

"Admiral, it was an honor to serve under you, Sir!"

Angus' eyes widened at the sound.

"Oh, Chester, the honor and privilege have always been mine!" *I'll get her, CJ. Stay put! That's an order.*

John, would you like a lesson on flying a shuttle?

I'm on my way, Sir!

"Phyllis, I'm coming up. John wants a flying lesson."

"Sir?"

"I need you back here, LC."

"Aye-aye, Sir" Phyllis' whisper was barely audible over the comm.

Angus was met by Phyllis' tear streaked face as he moved into the cockpit. She stood up and Angus saw the dread and fear in her brilliant green eyes. She quickly stood, but stopped after taking one step towards the passenger compartment. Angus started to reach out......

Angus, this is for CJ and her. Let it be.

I wish I could say something, do something....

So do I.

So do we all. The chorus of thoughts from Cindy, Alex, Jen, Jerry, and John surprised Angus.

I'll handle it, Skip. Angus heard Jerry's thoughts to Alex.

Whatever it takes, Jerry.

This is hitting my son hard. Phyll means a lot to his crew, Angus thought.

You know how those pilots, how we all feel about her. Jerry struggled to stay calm. *And I know how CJ's pilots felt about him. Everyone wanted to fly off the Excalibur! It was the plum assignment of the fleet, because of him.*

Go to it.

"John, come up here, have a seat. This will be your first lesson.

"Yes, Admiral. What do I do?"

John passed Phyllis, who ran to the passenger compartment and went to CJ's medi-stat unit. She couldn't see him until she was almost on top of him.

"Phyll, turn your thought screen off," Angus' powerful, quiet voice came over the comm, "so you can talk to CJ!"

"Thanks, Sir!"

She looked down to turn the screen off as she walked to CJ. When she lifted her chin up and gazed down into the medi-stat, she nearly screamed in horror;

Chester lay on his right side, a faint mist wafting over him to keep him warm, relieve some of his pain, and fight infection. His left eye was gone, a baseball-sized crater gouged out of his face. Broken teeth showed through the splits in his lips. His face was sliced in several directions, as was his back and his chest, most down to the bones. His right arm had all of the skin removed, except for the FORTITER tattoo on his shoulder. His other arm and his legs were gone. There was not a square inch of his body untouched by the horrible, ragged edged cuts, except for the tattoo.

Phyllis knelt by the side of the medi-stat and reached in to touch Chester's face. She worried that it may hurt him, but couldn't stop what her broken heart commanded her to do. Ever so gently, Phyll touched a fingertip to a spot of undamaged skin on CJ's cheek. The corner of his mouth twitched up in a slight grin.

Oh! My love, what have they done to you!

"Phyllis!" *My Angel!* Chester opened his eye and stared into hers. *Those eyes are like green flames warming my soul! If only I could gaze into them forever!* CJ's eye closed.

I wish I could hold you, make you feel better, comfort you some how!

You are my love! Soon, I will be without pain. Something.....I changed, Phyll. I could see more, do more........Phyll, I've done something.......something.......something evil, horrible.

Shhh, my love. You couldn't ever do anything evil! It's just not a part of you! Phyllis' jaw quivered and her throat tightened with the pain of

158

seeing him like this.

They were hurting me...they fed on my pain. I saw them doing it with the others, Phyll; hundreds of those pilots, they didn't die in the beams, they moved them somehow, onto ships like I was on, and did things to them to cause pain. Not just the pilots, the people, the people of Earth, and every other planet they have ever destroyed!

Oh, Chester!

When the Admiral told me to hold on, to give them Hell, Phyll, that's what I did. I reached into their minds and gave them the pain they had given to others. All of the pain, Phyll, from trillions of souls! I gave the total pain to each of them, one at a time. They died, Phyll. But they didn't stop! So I reached out and gave the pain to all of them, everyone I could reach! I, ...I killed them all, Phyll, I killed them all, every one of them in this system. Then I killed every one of them. Everywhere. All of them! I made sure they felt it before they died, felt all the pain their kind had caused others.

Phyllis took CJ's head in her hands and kissed him on the lips. She pulled back just a little and stared into his guilt clouded eye.

"Chester Jones, you are not evil!" Phyllis was talking loud enough that Angus and John could hear her with the comm off, her tough, commanding words betrayed by the tears streaming down her cheeks. "You just saved me the of trouble killing every last one of those abominations myself! Now, you just worry about getting better, because……………"

Phyllis, CJ's eye opened again, searching the room for hers. *Phyll! Let me touch....* CJ reached up with his skinless hand and gently placed it upon Phyllis' belly, all the while keeping her green eyes locked in his view.

Oh, Chester! No! You'll get better!

He is already strong, very strong. Strong enough. Thank you.

She's a girl, Chester!

He will be strong enough to protect his little sister. She will remember.

CJ! Don't go! I need you!

I want to stay with you so much....I...I will always love you. That will never die, I promise.

Phyllis watched his gaze grow dim as the first life she had ever loved more than her own faded away.

"CJ! NO!" Her scream echoed through the shuttle as she fell over him, her grief pouring out as her tears.

Angus slumped in the hatchway, bringing a hand up to cover his face.

Alex, Jen, Jerry, Cindy; CJ. He's gone!

"Admiral, contact dead ahead."

"What is it, John?"

"I, it's ships, Sir! An awful lot of ships!"

Angus rushed up into the cockpit and stopped when the vision on the comm screen registered in his brain.

"Phyll, I've activated the comm screen back there. You need to look at this. Can you see it?"

"Oh, my!"

"Phyll,…. um, LC, they've all come here. They're here for you!" John's voice croaked out. *Admiral, why are they doing this?*

John, they recognize how special what CJ and Phyllis have is, and are just trying to show they care a lot about them.

Phyllis stared at the screen through a torrent of tears; for on each side of the flight path, in perfect formation, was a line of Corsairs that stretched as far as she could see. As the LCS passed, each Corsair peeled around behind, forming two trailing lines behind her. The next thing she saw took her breath away; a huge, shimmering coal-black ship, aglow with multiple running lights ablaze, slid silently in front of the shuttle from above. As the prow of the great battleship passed her, she saw the painted form of a red, gaping mouth, rimmed with sharp, white teeth, painted upon it, with two small eyes painted above. As the giant ship's stern cleared the shuttle, it dropped down in front of the small craft, maintaining perfect formation just twenty feet ahead! Phyllis read the ship's name: U.S.S. FORTITER. Instinctively, Phyll's eyes scanned the overhead sensor readout; there was another tiger-mouthed battleship twenty meters behind the shuttle, and the Corsairs had spread out into four lines spaced evenly above, below, port, and starboard of her ship. They had to move to make room for the four battle cruisers now forming up on her, one on each side, one above and one below!

Then, as Phyllis watched, a group of three Corsairs and one old, battered Wildcat flew up off the starboard flank of the Fortiter; after thirty seconds, the Wildcat peeled away, leaving an obvious hole in their formation.

"Phyllis, you have to come up here. I can't fly in this!" Angus choked out over the comm.

"Understood." Her training took over. *Maybe getting back to flying was best.*

"John, go back and stay with CJ, call me if anything changes."

"Yes, Admiral."

"NO! Admiral, you go back. John, this will be a good lesson in concentration for you."

He's gone, Sir. The boy's seen enough death.

I, Phyllis, I thought we could talk about...

"I know, LC. He said goodbye to me as I came up here. He just wanted to see you again. He was my, my......" *he was my best friend, my big brother, and my father. I've lost them all twice now!*

Phyllis came over and wrapped her arms around the young man. "I know, John. Did CJ ever tell you what we had talked about, about you?"

"Plans? No, Ma'am. He just asked if I wanted to come live with you guys while I studied for the academy."

"John, we were going to adopt you, if you agreed. Chester wanted to ask you today, but the mission...."

John' smile shone through his wet eyes as he asked, "Mom, can I go and say goodbye to Dad now?"

"Yes, Son." She looked after him as he walked back, and thought about all he had been through, and how grown up he seemed. "He's a very strong boy. No, a very strong young man."

"Strong enough to protect his little sister." Angus replied. "Almost as strong as his adopted father. Are you OK, Phyll?"

Admiral, I really need to concentrate here! There's no margin for error.

"Phyllis, let it go."

We'll crash!

Phyllis, the computers are linked. That was the lesson I gave John. He's already learned the important things. From you and Chester. And I don't mean Calculus.

Lieutenant Commander Phyllis Jones kept her eyes fixed on the comm screen as she moved her hands a half-inch off of the flight controls, then an inch, then put her hands down at her sides. After thirty seconds, she began shaking. A little at first, but soon the sobs were racking her body. She found herself in the comforting arms of the Admiral before she fell out of the pilot's seat.

Phyllis, let it go. Let it out.

CHESTER! Oh!

John stood next to the medi-stat unit that held Chester Jones' body, but he didn't look down at the torn flesh; CJ wasn't there, after all. John just stood with his eyes closed.

...

I'm sorry I had to let you think that you killed them all. I did it so they wouldn't know when you told them. They aren't ready to understand, not yet.

...

*Your company meant a lot to me. I'll miss that very much. I promise you, I will protect them. All of them. But these two above all others, except, well, these **three** I will protect above all others. I have to include her.*

...

Thank you for understanding. You always did. John smiled as his last conversation with CJ ended.

...

By the time the shuttle and it's escort arrived back at Cygnus 78, Phyllis had regained her composure and insisted on landing the ship herself, on fully manual control. As she exited the shuttle, she saw the pilots from the Fortiter air wing lined up at attention. When her foot hit the floor of the hanger, their arms snapped up in a salute as one. They held the salute until CJ's body was carried off the shuttle and was out of sight.

****

The Hounds of Heaven
Cygnus 78 Perimeter Patrol
Standard Earth Date January 8 3813

"Wow, what a show THAT was!" Captain Fred Yeager was amazed at the formation flying into Cygnus 78. "A nice break to boring patrols!"

"That CAG must have been something special, for those lugs to go all out like that." Captain Arleta Simulak agreed.

"I've heard he was, but then again, he was The Admiral's FFC, and every Navy pilot wanted into his group. The way they tell it, he was a real special guy. And, his widow, the FFC for The Admiral's son, was just as well liked by her pilots. I hear she's expecting their first. He won't get to see his daughter; she'll have to raise the kid alone. The kid will never really know the kind of guy he was." *Damn tough break for, from what I've heard, is one first class lady. If her subords think that much of her....it's almost like The Admiral.*

"A little different from Old Man Bong, eh?"

"Yeah, like you've forgotten that time he bailed you out...."

"Bailed US out, you mean!"

"Well, I'd still follow that SOB into..."

"OK, you two clowns! Cut the chatter and get scanning!"

"Yes, SIR! Heh-he!"

"Arleta, Sector A-4. See it?"

"Got it, Fred. It's huge, with a capitol H!"

"I think we'd better report this..."

****

"Commodore, comm channel priority Alpha. Line 12."

Commodore Jenitka MacAlister hit the indicated line on her comm panel; "Commodore MacAlister. Go."

"Commodore, Captain Arleta Simulak, 524th on patrol. We have a contact, Sir. Huge, white, oval, just sitting here. Visual now."

The command vid screen on Jen's console lit up with the image.

"Main view screen, Comm."

Jen expected a gasp from the bridge crew, instead, she heard a resigned sigh, as if they all said, "not again!". The unexpected response gave her a slight grin, for it took quite a crew to have that attitude! They *knew* they could handle anything, they were just tired.

"Maintain patrol schedule, Captain. We'll handle this one. Comm, get me Major Bong. Captain Shin, set a course to rendezvous with the intruder, not too fast. Perhaps this is a 'get-to-know-you' visit."

"Aye-aye, Sir. Helm, set course for sector...A-4, 0.005 C."

"Course laid in, Sir!"

"Then let's get moving."

"ETA 45 minutes, Captain."

"Commodore, I have Major Bong, Sir."

"Major, we have an intruder in Sector A-4. Intentions are unknown. I would like some discrete back up available."

"Understood, Commodore. I have 30 Intruders on alert, and 22 Havocs as back up. I'll add 44 Mustangs as escorts. They will be very, very quiet."

"Very good, Major."

Jen wore a sour look on her face. She wanted to be comforting her friend more than anything else. *Phyll, I'll see you as soon as I can. I have something I have to take care of first.*

Jen, when you can. This is so amazing, but it's overwhelming, too. I need to just sit with you. Alone.

Soon, Phyll, I promise. Admiral, Alex.

Jen. What's wrong?

I have the feed, love.

Angus, it's the ship from Circinus, or one just like it. It's here.

I'm on my way.

Angus, take care of Phyll; Alex and I have this.

I've got it, Dad. She needs you more than we do now. When Mom gets there, then come to my office.

OK. Be careful.

"Captain, we're here. Distance 100,000 Km."

"Sensors, what have you got?"

"Nothing out of the ordinary, other than the size of it, Sir. The exterior seems to be completely smooth, almost no variation in texture, no projections or depressions. No emissions at all, Sir."

"Comm, open broadcast on standard comm channel 6."

"Channel open, Commodore."

"This is Commodore Jenitka MacAlister of the United Space Force, representing the, um, United Starclan of Humankind. Welcome. How may we address you?"

Jen, I love you, but you can write these things out in advance, you know!

Alex, you aren't helping!

Sorry. But, 'United Starclan'?

I don't know. I needed something "U.S." It just came out. Now, let me concentrate!

"Comm, anything?"

"Nothing, Sir."

"Open a broad channel comm."

"Channels open, Sir."

"This is Commodore Jenitka MacAlister of the United Space Force, representing the United Starclan of..."

"We heard you the first time."

The entire bridge crew looked at each other.

"We are sorry, that was rather rude. Eh-hem. Greetings, Starclan. We are the explorer vessel Chortlaesys of the Galactic Inner Republic. We come to ascertain if peaceful and profitable relations between our civilizations are acceptable to you. If this is so, negotiations on rights of passage, trade routes and policies, and acceptable conduct should begin at your earliest convenience."

"We would like to open peaceful and profitable relations. Please excuse us if we make mistakes along the way; you are the first peaceful beings we have encountered." Jen was dumbfounded; this was totally unexpected! *Cindy, I need you in on this ASAP!* "Please allow me a short time to contact those who are skilled in such matters for the formal negotiations. While we wait, may I invite you to our ship to share a meal, assuming your kind does eat?"

Good move, Jen. Relax, you're doing fine.

"We would welcome such an event. A shuttle will bring us to you in…twelve of your minutes."

"We welcome you! See you soon, then." *Sure, real eloquent, that last part!*

You did fine, Jen.

Alex, I wish Angus was here!

Jen, you'll do as well as I would, trust me.

I agree with my father, Jen. Just be yourself and go with the flow.

Sure, easy for you two to say! Mrs. M, how soon can you get here?

Angus, you stay with Phyllis. Jen, I'll be there in twenty minutes. Jerry, I need you.

Yes, Ma'am. Be right there.

"Captain Shin, please have the Admiral's Mess prepared. And, we'll need a suitable reception in the hanger bay."

"Aye-aye, Commodore."

Jen turned and walked briskly off of the bridge. She headed for the Admiral's quarters, for she was the Flag Staff on this mission. *What am I going to wear?*

Captain Shin stared after Jen as she strode away. "Does anyone have any idea what a "suitable reception" for an alien looks like?" He looked around the bridge, but the entire crew seemed to be very busy with something on their consoles.

"Sure, leave your Captain hanging out to dry!" he muttered as he left for his quarters. *There has to be something in the library on this. I hope.*

****

USF Fortiter
Sector A-4
Cygnus 78
Standard Earth Date January 8 3813

"Greetings, um, Ambassador?" Jen realized halfway through her greeting that she had no idea how to address the beings about to walk out of the white, egg shaped shuttle. She stood smartly in her dress whites, and watched as a section of the craft's side folded down to form an exit ramp. *That's sort of disappointing; no spiral iris opening, or something else more impressive?*

Hah-ha! You expect too much of us, Commodore Jenitka! We are more like you than you think!

Jen's eyes opened very wide as she received the thoughts from the alien. *What should I call you?*

Hmm. Trine will do, for now. When referring to my kind, you may call us Tril. A being appeared in the opening of the shuttle, then two more behind the first, one offset to each side slightly. They each wore a white jacket, rather conventionally cut, with light grey shirts and white trousers. A modest flat hat, looking like an ancient Earth style called a Panama, covered each being's head.

The lead Tril was close to seven feet tall, and stood half a foot taller than the trailing two. Each had two arms and legs, arraigned much like humans, but proportionally longer in the torso and arms, and shorter in the legs.

The faces reminded Jen of a cartoon bear that was popular when she was a child, but covered with a short, fuzzy white fur. The three walked down the ramp, and Jen noted that they walked as if they were one being.

"Trine, welcome to the USF Fortiter. This is the ship's Captain, Mr. Shin."

"Thank you, Commodore. Captain Shin. We are pleased to be here." The three answered as one while they gave a slight bow in Jen's direction. "This is a very impressive ship. To do what you did to the Arkenst vessels was most impressive to see."

Hearing three speak as one is just a little strange.

Forgive us, for not explaining. It is our way. We three are bonded for life, mated in your terms. We are truly living as one.

We also bond…Phyllis!

One close to you has lost a bond-mate. That is a tragedy we understand all too well. Do you wish to postpone our meeting, so you may comfort your…..friend?

"Your words are kind, Trine. You are perceptive and kind hearted. My friend will be comforted by others until I have completed my duties here. Come, our meal awaits." The five began walking to the Admiral's Mess.

"We sense you are stressed about being as polite as possible. While this does flatter us, please relax, please be yourself. We are not as easily offended as you fear."

"You are perceptive and kind hearted. I am beginning to like you. I will try, Trine. We will be having the favorite of my mentor, unless you have any food taboos?"

"We are mostly open to anything that does not move on the way down! What is our meal called?"

"Haggis with Neeps and Tatties."

"The best tasting dishes of every world usually are those born of the need to survive on 'less than optimal' foods."

"The beverages…are your kind able to metabolize alcohol?"

"Many forms are produced for their unique, mm, flavors on our worlds."

"We will be having a fine single malt Scotch with dinner. I suggest you sip it at room temperature." *Mrs. M, don't be late, or you could find us all under the table! I wish Angus was here.*

****

Admiral's Office
Cygnus 78
Standard Earth Date January 9 3813

"Angus, there is something going on that you need to know about."

"What, don't tell me you've been having an affair?" Angus smiled at his wife.

"You're my husband, until I find some one better. Just remember, I'm still looking!" She stepped to her husband, draped her arms about his neck, and kissed him passionately on the lips.

"Hmm. Well, now that you have my total and undivided attention, what's come up?" He gave his wife *that* smile.

"You are incorrigible! Don't ever change. But something has been going on here, it has to do with tattoos."

"That? That went around the fleet on word of my retirement. I think Will," Angus swallowed hard at the thought of his friends on the Excalibur he missed terribly, "Will passed the story of that around the fleet. It seems there was a backlog of requests. I tried to discourage it, but couldn't without hurting a lot of feelings. So, they're still getting the tattoos?"

"The military personnel finished their tattoos three weeks ago. It's the civilians who are getting them. The same tattoo."

"Civilians? Why?"

"They heard the story of CJ, somehow it got back here before you got back. They knew the only part of CJ that wasn't..." Cindy stopped for a moment, and Angus wiped a tear from her cheek. "They heard the tattoo was untouched. Angus, it has become an object of Patriotic fervor. The people don't have Earth to identify with anymore; they've embraced the Clan to replace it. Here, look at this news feed.

Cindy hit some controls on the comm screen, and a reporter was on camera talking about a school opening on one of the habitat stations. 'Habtations' were large space stations or habitats on moons and asteroids used to house and provide services for the population. Many were designed to mimic an Earth-like environment, and featured adjusted gravity, simulated buildings and streets with a blue sky, complete with clouds above. The reporter was talking, but Angus kept the sound muted on his feeds by default.

"Turn the sound, up, Hon."

"We don't need to hear him, Angus. Look at the school, the flagpole behind him!"

As if on cue, the reporter turned and pointed to the flag flying in the manufactured breeze.

Angus looked and gasped. "No, really?"

The reporter turned back to the camera with a grin on his face, the flag behind still visible on the screen; a field of MacAlister Tartan with a large yellow snake stretched from the lower left to the upper right, mouth open to show venom dripping fangs. Across the bottom of the flag something was printed. Again, as if on cue, the screen showed a close up of the wording; DON'T TREAD ON ME!

"I understand the warning, but not the relevance of the snake."

"Cin, it's an ancient symbol from the American Revolution. It's a two thousand year old symbol of defiance to tyranny. The Tartan!"

"Angus, they've started calling you the Clan Chief. The Clan is providing them an all-inclusive identity; they are teaching the children that we aren't Earthmen, we're Starclan."

Angus walked over to the sofa and sank into it, looking off into the distance. Cindy sat next to him.

"There's more, Angus. A lot of children came out with the civilians, all ages. Every one, Angus, every one over twelve has the tattoo. It started with the Mayflower children; I think Janice was the first. Angus, it's become a right of passage. Even the adolescent fashions have changed so the right shoulder is bare to display the tattoo."

"We can't let this go on. It's well, silly."

"Angus, there are over six million civilians who have the tattoo! Those who don't have the tattoo, have an appointment to get it. That goes for the children too. Angus, stopping this would insult all of them. Besides, they need this as an identity they can be proud of. Angus, it is what *they* chose."

Angus took a big breath and let it out in a long sigh. "I never liked being an object of hero worship. I used it, to improve the fleet, but I never liked it. It ended up turning my friends against me. I don't want that to happen again."

"You did what needed to be done. There was no other way to get those things done except to cultivate that image and use the public's good will to pressure the politicians into improving the Fleet. If you hadn't, we would all be dead now. Every one of us. Those people who couldn't handle your success did not deserve to be your friends. They made their own choices; you can't beat yourself up for the choices others make.

"Angus, our best choice is to let this go; not ban it, not discourage it, not endorse it. We can appreciate the gesture, but we should not comment on it through public channels. Let the people decide if it is going to continue past the next generation."

"I can't be a dictator, king, whatever you want to call it. I have no talent or interest in ruling civilians. All I want to do is lead the Fleet."

"You have more talent for leading than you think, my love. But they don't want a king; you leading the Fleet is what they want. I've almost finished the election structure for the civilian government. There will not be a king."

"I suppose you're right. You always are on things like this. Now, where were we?"

Cindy slapped Angus' arm playfully. "You beast! There's something else you need to know. The girl from the Mayflower that John is fond of, Janice."

"The tattooed girl?"

"Oh, stop! Yes, that Janice. Alex and Jen have adopted her."

"Really! Why? I mean, it's their decision, but…is there a problem?"

"No, they are both perfectly healthy. Jen saw the way she and John connected. She said it reminded her of Phyllis and CJ." Cindy paused a moment. "She and Alex knew CJ and Phyll were planning on adopting John. Jen couldn't think of separating them. Alex couldn't refuse her."

"Well, I know that feeling!"

Cindy punched Angus's right arm. "You beast!"

Angus turned and looked at his wife while he reached down and clicked on his thought screen. He put on his best 'puppy-dog' look, smiling as Cindy pulled him to her.

It was some time later that Angus noticed the new tattoo on Cindy's right arm.

****

Command Officer's Quarters
Cygnus 78
Standard Earth Date January 9 3813

"Jen, I still can't believe he's gone. It's like he's going to walk in that door, or I'm going to go to his hospital room, and he'll wake up, and hold me, tell me how beautiful my eyes are, and make all my troubles melt away like last year's snow."

"I miss him too, Phyll. He had the world's worst sense of humor…"

"Tell me about it! No pun too corny for CJ! I miss that, too. Mostly I feel sad, that she'll never know how great her dad was."

"Make sure she knows, Phyll. Tell her. Show her. The vids of the service will tell part of the story. Alex and I, Angus and Cindy and Jerry will tell some of it too. The pilots that knew him, that worked with him, flew with him, will tell some of it. And John and Janice will tell it, too. She'll know, Phyllis. Have you thought of a name yet?"

"I was going with Lorraine, my mom's name. Now, I think it will be Cynthia Jenitka. That way she will carry CJ with her, always."

"I don't know what to say. I'm so honored, Phyll."

"I can't believe that formation coming in. I don't think I'll ever forget that sight. I just wish Chester had seen it."

"I believe he did, Phyll. He knew their feelings about him, anyway. Did he ever tell you about your engagement ring?"

"No. Jen. When he asked me, I never saw the ring! I jumped over the table and wrapped him in my arms, and planted a big one on his lips! I honestly never looked closely at it until about two hours later. Then I couldn't believe how big it was! Did he rob the purser, or is it a fake? Do they even have jewelers here?"

"Oh, it's real, all right. One of the nurses here in the Sick Bay was to be married to a pilot in CJ's command on Excalibur, the day after the Admiral's retirement. The pilot had always had a problem holding on to money; nothing bad, he just wasted it. The pilots in CJ's command were more like a family than a combat unit when they weren't flying. When the pilot said he wanted to propose before they shipped out, but he had no money for a ring, the pilots all chipped in. He had enough for a nice ring, then, after everyone left, CJ stuffed a wad of bills into the pilot's hand. CJ told him that he had checked out the girl, and that they had a chance for something really special, for what they all fought for, and he wanted him to get off to a good start with a special ring. When we first got here, the nurse heard CJ made it. Her fiancé didn't. CJ was in sick bay a long time; the nurse came to visit him several times, just to say thanks, but every time she came, you were there. She read your eyes, Phyll. The day after CJ woke up, she met with him, and insisted he take her engagement ring. For you."

"And her name was Alice! I need to meet her soon, Jen. That sounds so like him." *Just hold me a while.*

As long as you need me, Phyll.

****

170

Office of the Chancellor
Cygnus 78
Standard Earth Date January 12 3813

"Trine, this agreement means a lot to us. You know our home, our colonies were destroyed" Chancellor Cindy MacAlister stated. She had stopped using her maiden name after the Battle for Earth; political imagery seemed so unimportant after that. Her husband, Angus, sat in the easy chair next to the Chancellor's, across the coffee table from the sofa occupied by the trio of aliens. Cindy had decided on an informal approach after meeting the Tril; it seemed appropriate to their personalities.

"Destroyed by the Arkenst, the Grey Globes as you say. They were pure evil. They could not be reasoned with, and they were hard to stop. The things they did went far beyond destroying planets, ending civilizations. The tactics you used to destroy them…"

Chester destroyed them. Angus inserted.

He is the one who passed on, who you all mourn so deeply. He destroyed the Arkenst? You are new to the symbiots.

Yes. Cindy continued. *We got them just before the attacks. There were ten of us, but two have not developed the telepathy, and two were killed before any of us developed it. Chester was the only one we have lost who had developed. He and the Admiral were severely injured, but healed more completely and quickly than is possible.*

So, you know the route the symbiots took to you. The symbiots become part of you, part of your DNA. When you die, they die. When you are injured, their programming repairs you. Please, Admiral, tell me; have any others developed without direct exposure to the symbiots?

There is one. A young man, one of some children we rescued for a ship in distress just before the attacks. We cannot explain his development.

May we meet this young one?

I don't see why not. He should be studying. I will get him.

Angus walked to Cindy's desk and activated the comm; "John, can you come to the Chancellor's office, please? There is some one here you should meet."

"Yes, Sir, Admiral. I'll be right there!" *What's up?*

Just get here ASAP, please.

Five minutes, Sir. Oh. Hmm.

What, John.

The Tril are with you.

They want to meet you.

I suppose it is time. I'll be there soon, Admiral.

"The young one knows we are here. He is apprehensive."

"Yes, he is. It is not his usual character."

He is more than a human youngster, Chancellor. Yet, he is still a human youngster; his body, his mind, or his powers have not yet fully developed.

That is what I thought.

You see some of what is coming.

Yes, but not all. I seem to see what I need to when I need to, and I see outcomes of situations that present to me.

If you did, you would not make the necessary decisions.

I see that. What does all this mean?

It means that you of Starclan are The Guardians. It means we will serve you at your will.

Serve?

You will protect us, and the other civilized races, from those like the Arkenst. We will support you as you direct.

We have barely survived here! How can we...

You were chosen. It is what you will do. The tools you need will be made available to you. Our screens against the Red Beams, and our grasping field that holds them, will be a part of that support, and a part of our normalized trade and cultural interactions. We will provide what you direct us to do, but the decisions will be yours.

I am not comfortable ordering you around, Trine.

Nor am I.

Admiral, Chancellor, that is precisely why your Starclan has been chosen!

"Mr. John Jones at the door, Chancellor." The computer chimed.

"Enter."

"Chancellor, Admiral. Trine." John walked into the office proud and tall, wearing a light grey shorts and a dark blue shirt, which bared his right shoulder. Angus glanced at his wife as he noted the fresh FORTITER tattoo there, the area still a little red from the needles. The three Tril stood and bowed in unison at John's approach.

"You eliminated the Arkenst. We are grateful, Protector."

"I am not ready yet, Trine. My training is not complete, and the primaries still need protection. You should have waited."

"Forgive me, Protector, but it is what we have been instructed to do. If it is too soon, then there is an urgent need."

"Excuse me, but what the bloody hell are you two talking about?"

Angus, please!

Sorry.

"I am sorry, Chancellor, Admiral." John apologized for leaving the Admiral and Chancellor out of the conversation. "The Tril are, well, caretakers of the galaxy. They are a resource, but are not soldiers. They

172

are wise, and deserve an ear. They are here to mentor and guide us, support us."

"John, what, who are you?"

"Admiral, I am a fifteen year old boy. I only found out about these powers after the battle in the Delta Mess. There was a reason the ship I was on had trouble. Something came and…changed me. I can see things; but only as the situations come up. I can make some things happen, under certain circumstances, and with the help of you and your symbiots. But, Admiral, I'm still a young man. I still need to grow up, to learn, to love; my life will be normal until the times I am needed. But I will protect you, all of you. *If it comes down to it, I will protect three above all others.*

"John, what does this mean?"

"Chancellor, the young one needs to grow normally. He has to. He is a Protector; he is not The Galloglaigh."

"Trine, what are you saying?"

"His purpose is to protect the ones who will produce The Galloglaigh.

He is to protect the ones who will produce…………CJ and Phyll's child will be one. Who will the other be?

"Admiral, the time is not right for knowing that now. We do not know, The Protector does not know. Admiral, you are The First Galloglaigh."

Angus stared at the Tril for several seconds.

"Trine, you are right. I can't pretend to understand it all. But I do believe you." Angus stood up and offered his hand to the tallest of the three known as Trine.

"Thank you for your patience, and your trust." Cindy stood and shook hands with the tallest Tril after Angus.

"Admiral, thank you for your vision. It has played no small part in your being chosen. You may contact us as needed. For now, we wish to see home. It has been too long since we have." Trine turned to John, and gave a respectful bow.

"How long have you been away from home?"

"Thirteen of your centuries."

"What have you been doing for so long?"

"Fighting the Arkenst, and waiting. For The Starclan."

Angus watched the three Tril leave. When the door to his office once again closed, Cindy turned to John and said, "John, how can…."

ANGUS!!!!CINDY! Um, I mean, um Dad, SIR! Mom, Ma'am, Oh, damn it! I screwed it up! Grandpa, Sir! Grandma, Ma'am!

Jen?

Admiral! Grandpa Admiral, Sir! Chancellor, Grandma Chancellor, Ma'am!

What are you…oh. OH! OH, MY!

Honestly, Angus, you can be so damned dense at times; I wonder why I married you!

Dad, we're pregnant! I mean, Jen's pregnant!

Let me guess, it's a boy?

Yes, how did you know?

MacAlisters only have girls every other millennium. Angus looked at John and tilted his head to one side. "So, now there are four you must protect?"

"My Primary is only one."

"There is another Protector?"

"No comment."

Angus shook his head. "I won't tell anyone. It must happen naturally."

"You won't. And it will."

Chapter Ten

Camp Caruso
New Kintyre
Altair 66 Gamma
Standard Earth Date September 21 3828

Angus MacAlister looked over the large lake, listening as the waves lightly lapped at the shore a few feet from the back porch he stood upon. The small rowboat pulled up on shore reminded him he had to put a dock in. Sometime.

Perfect!

"I'm glad you like it, Angus. Dinner is ready." Cindy called from the doorway.

A bitter-sweet smile flashed on his face as Angus turned and walked into the cabin. *Every time I feel this good, something…*

Stop it!

Yes, dear.

"The terra-forming is even better than we had hoped. With the help of some Tril technology, the GravGens are providing extra gravity to hold the atmosphere, which keeps the planet's temperature more even. And the bio-cached flora and fauna make it seem like Earth. Hmm. This steak is amazing."

"Of course! I can still cook! Angus, are you ready for this? Can you retire?"

"I think so. How about you?"

"Angus, I went into politics to help *you* fix the fleet. I became the Chancellor because there was no one else to do it. I never did *any* of it for myself."

"But you enjoyed it."

"Yes, some of it. But I don't have a need to fill up my day while you are with me. You going fishing after dinner?"

"I was thinking of planning a cook out. Maybe have Phyllis, CJ, and John; Jerry; Alex, Jen, Janice and Artair. Maybe Trine. The beef here is very good."

"You need to wait; you can't have them here the first week of your retirement! Make it in six months. That gives them time to plan things."

"OK. I think I'll take a nap after dinner. This steak is really amazing!"

"Wait 'till you taste dessert, birthday boy!"

"I'm looking at quite a dish right now!"

Somerled High School
Freshman Biology Class
Cygnus 78
Standard Earth Date September 23 3828

Artair MacAlister looked around the classroom. Everyone else was absorbed in the teacher's explanation of the cell walls of plants vs. the cell walls of bacteria. Artair already knew this material, having read it a few years ago. His sister only left him her old textbooks to read when mom and dad were off with the fleet. He focused on one of his classmates, Cindy Jones. She was very pretty, with amazing green eyes and brown hair that almost looked red when the pseudo-sunlight hit it a certain way.

Artair! Get your mind on the subject!

Geeze, sis, give a guy a break, will you? I know this stuff already!

I know, but you can't get caught staring at girls in class, you'll get a reputation.

OK, ok. There's only a minute or so left in class. Hey, sis?

Um, one second. Yes, Art?

How do I, I mean, uh, what is the best, how, um...

How do you talk to her?

Yeah.

Just like you talk to me, when you are not being a brat.

Aw, c'mon, sis!

Think to her.

I've tried that to other people. Only Grandpa and Grandma, you, Mom and Dad, and Uncle Jerry can hear me.

I can hear you, squirt.

John? Janice, your boyfriend can hear me?

So can his mom and his sister, Art. And, as long as we're on the subject, so can Commodore Shin and Vice Admiral Perry.

All the time? That sucks!

As the class bell rang, Art stood up and began walking out of the room. Lunch was next, and he hoped they had something good. He looked at Cindy Jones, and she turned and smiled at him.

Oh, God!

Art, control yourself, little brother!

Cin-Cindy?

Yes, Artair?

Oh, God!

He-he! You're funny!
Would you, um, like to, ah…
Sit with you at lunch? I'd love to.

****

Camp Caruso
New Kintyre
Altair 66 Gamma
Standard Earth Date June 21 3829

"Angus, that was an amazing meal!" Vice Admiral of Training Command Jerry Kowalski sat back, a satisfied look on his face.

"Angus, we are very honored to be included here. We know it is a special gathering. And, the building on this world is progressing very well." Trine thanked the host.

"Admiral, very nice!" Commodore Phyllis Jones echoed.

"Angus, Phyll. I'm retired. Now, do you really mean that, Phyll, or are you just agreeing with your boss?"

Phyllis blushed and glanced quickly at Jerry. "No, Sir! The Vice Admiral will tell you that I have never had a problem expressing my disagreements with him."

"Well, it's very nice you all could come." Cindy MacAlister smiled as she brought out the drams of single malt.

Angus stood up, and raised his glass. Alex and Jen, Phyllis and Jerry stood with Trine and him. "To good friends, no, to family!"

The others looked at each other, and in unison said, "To Starclan!" Glasses touched, and all sipped the golden whiskey.

As they all sat back down, Alex said, "I'm sorry that Janice and Artair couldn't make it. Janice's fighter group is assigned security patrol, and Art has a dance at school."

"John's group is also on patrol, and CJ is going to the dance with Art!" Phyllis beamed. She again shot a glance at Jerry, too quick for him to notice.

"Those two seem to have hit it off pretty well. What are John and Janice's plans, Jen?"

"I think John is just about ready to ask her, Angus."

"We've, um, had some discussions about that, Dad. I think John feels it's time."

He will know best. He will have the vision to see the best timing, We will not.

Already? Don't Art and CJ need more development?

John says it's time.

So does Janice.

"Well, who am I to question the orders from Father time!"

"Cindy, can I help you clean up?" Jen and Phyllis chorused.

"Hah-ha, sure, you two! A ladies hour sounds nice! You boys, off to sea! Go fish! Just, get out of our way!"

"Come on, guys. Let's get the boat in the water!" Alex said as the men walked towards the dock.

Angus stopped after a few steps, turning to face the three Tril.

"I'm so sorry, Trine. I don't know if you can split up that way!"

"We can, Angus. The two will go with you. I will remain here. This best approximates your arrangement."

The five walked down to the boat.

Once the boat was moving out onto the lake, Jen and Cindy turned to face Phyllis as Trine watched.

"Well? What are you waiting for!" Jen shot at her friend.

"Wh-what do you…"

"Don't give me that crap." Cindy said as she brought out a plate of sugar cookies.

"Phyll, we both saw you. You can't keep your eyes off of him! Spill it, girl!"

"I'm not a girl anymore! I'm, well, too old for these kinds of feelings. And he's my commanding officer. And, well…"

"CJ."

"Yeah." Phyllis whispered as she stared at her shoes.

"Phyll, I knew CJ for his entire career, and longer. He was three years behind me at the academy. What he wanted, more than anything, was for you to be happy."

"Phyll, Jerry will never replace CJ, and loving Jerry won't mean you love CJ any less. What does your heart tell you?" Cindy loved Phyllis, and since CJ's death, saw her as the daughter she never had, taking the roll Jen had filled until her marriage to Alex.

"What about little CJ? She'll think I'm abandoning her father!"

"You wish to bond with another, since your first bond mate has passed. It is common to feel much anxiety in that situation, especially when a young one is involved. My experience is that you should bond again. It is an important part of your health. Your young one will surprise you; she will put your happiness foremost. You should speak of it with her directly." The advice from Trine surprised the women. Jen brought them back to the task at had.

"She'll think no such thing! Abandoning Chester indeed." *She worries about you. Ask her yourself how she feels about this.*

Mom!

CJ?

What is it, mom? You're upset!

CJ, your mom thinks she likes some one, but is worried about how you feel about that.

Mom, you want to go out with a guy? Cool!

Yes, dear. How do you feel about that?

I think you're stupid for waiting. You should have asked Uncle Jerry out like five or ten years ago!

Oh, CJ!

Mom, do it. He won't, guys are dumb that way, at least the good ones. And Uncle Jerry is a good one. I have to go, John is taking me to pick up my dress. You'll be back for the dance tomorrow?

I wouldn't miss it, CJ. I love you!

I love you too, mom. Jerry is cool. Do it! Bye!

Phyllis looked at her two best friends. "You set me up!"

Jen and Cindy looked at each other and shrugged.

Sometimes, the right spark can make despair erupt into celebration! The three women turned and stared at Trine. Then they all smiled at the Tril's observation.

"So, any idea what they're planning?" Alex asked as he cast his line out.

"No idea, son. Jerry, do you have a clue?" Angus asked as his line hit the water.

"No, Angus. What makes you think they're plotting something! Uh, what kind of fish do you catch here?"

"Catch? None. It hasn't been stocked yet."

Alex and Jerry turned and stared at Angus.

"What is a 'fish'?" the two Tril asked in unison.

The three men laughed a little.

"Fish are vertebrates that live in water. Many are good to eat, and many are fun to catch."

"Oh" the Trill pair said, then each tossed a line over the side.

The three men laughed again, then Angus and Alex turned and stared at Jerry.

"What?"

"Jerry, you have been my friend for as long as I've known you. Spill it." Alex commanded.

"I think I need to retire."

"What?" *Dad, this was not the answer I expected!*

Let him finish, Alex.

"What do you mean, Jerry? Why? I know you love running the

Academy, and the quality of officers you graduate is the best I've ever seen."

"The man wishes to bond with a female, but is afraid his superior rank will cause trouble with the bonding. He is also unsure of the female's acceptance." The tree men stared at the two Tril again, then Angus and Alex turned back to Jerry.

"I want...I, um. OK, here goes. I love Phyllis. I can't do anything about it as long as I am her commanding officer. I can't ask her to transfer, she loves flight instruction, and she's damn good at it."

"Have you talked to her about this?"

"No, I can't."

"Jerry, neither of you have any further promotions in the career paths you are on. The only thing Phyll can move up into is your job, and you have to retire for that to happen. Ask her."

"Jerry, I've seen how you've been a father to little CJ. You can bet that Phyllis has, too. She's very sharp. Ask her."

"You both think it's OK?"

"YES!" the father and son chorused.

"OK. So, how long do we stay out here fishing in an empty lake?"

The three men laughed for quite a while at the Tril's question.

****

Somerled High School
Wells Hall
Freshman Semi-Formal Dance
Cygnus 78
Standard Earth Date June 22 3829

"Are you sure?" Phyllis Jones was not happy. Not happy at all.

"You try it. I can't find them." John Jones was nervous as he scanned the dance floor; this was not supposed to happen! His purpose was to protect her, and now he's lost her!

"I can't find her!" *Jen, can you find Artair?*

Phyllis? What's wrong!

John and I can't find CJ! She and Artair went onto the dance floor, and then we just lost them, like they had a thought screen. I can't see them, the floor is too crowded.

I can't find Artair! Janice?

I'm shut out as well.

OK, lets all sweep the dance floor.

The four adults spread out and began walking across the dance floor. About halfway across he spotted them, lost in each other's arms even in the fast paced dances.

"Eh-hem! Artair! CJ!"

Oh, shit!

"Eh, hi, Janice."

The two teens reluctantly broke their embrace and stepped back from each other.

Phyllis broke the uncomfortable silence on the loud dance floor. *We need to talk, you two.*

The six walked over to a relatively empty area of the gym. Jen looked at Art, Phyllis at CJ.

Art, where did you get the thought screen? You KNOW you are not to have one until you are 21!

I don't have a thought screen.

CJ, where did you get a thought screen?

I don't have one, either.

Well, Ito and Peter's kids aren't here, and no one else would have a reason to have one. How did we lose your thoughts?

Well, um, I, eh, I blocked you.

Me too.

You what?!

We can block out everyone except each other.

But only when we're together.

Great!

Don't you trust us?

It's not you two we're worried about.

You know better than that! And, you know why your older siblings are here!

To protect us.

We don't need to be protected anymore.

John and Janice looked at each other. After about twenty seconds, they smiled.

They are almost correct. Soon, there will be little that can harm them, especially when they are together. But right now, there is still some risk.

OK, you two; back to the dance.

Be good.

Thanks mom!

Thanks, mom!

****

Somerled High School

The final buzzer was lost in the cheers of the happy crowd. Somerled had played hard and earned a comfortable win behind the powerful inside play of power forward Artair MacAlister. Art left the locker room, smiling at CJ, who waited patiently for him.

You look so hot in that cheerleader's outfit!

Well, cool down lover-boy! You're pretty hot in those short-shorts yourself, but you changed out of them!

You told me you didn't like me all sweaty and smelly!

So you showered just for little ol' me?

Just like you kept that outfit on for me, because you know I love the way you look in it!

Art bent down, placing his hands on CJ's hips as she reached up to drape her arms about his neck. They gazed into each other's eyes for several moments before the kiss began.

All of the others had gone home by the time they broke the kiss, so no one saw where the gas came from.

****

"NO!"

Angus sat up in bed, eyes open wide in shock.

"Angus, what is it?"

Art and CJ. Something's wrong. They are in danger.

I don't like your tone.

JOHN! JANICE!

Angus. What…

Where are they?

We've lost them. Um, what…they block us sometimes, when they are together. Not very often, but it's not unusual. Fuzzy. Something happened.

John, this is different. I see danger; they need you and Janice. Now.

Angus, something…gas? Yes. We were gassed…we did not see it. How?

****

"We have not heard anything from them, nor have we received any ransom or any other demands." Alex paced around his office. The big man was not in a pleasant mood, but his training kept him focused.

"We need to find them." Jenitka was angry.

That is how she looked on Excalibur, in Delta Mess John thought.

They get stronger at times like this; that's how you were able to help CJ kill the Arkenst.

Yes. I told him about the girl. His powers grew to save her, to save Phyll, and to avenge his pilots. He supplied the raw power. I focused it for him.

Angus is almost here. They will be complete.

Then we can save them. I hope.

****

Galactic Energetics Warehouse 44
Cygnus 78
Standard Earth Date November 29 3829

"We were supposed to kill them. If they find out you're asking a ransom, we'll be spaced for sure!"

"Do you really think they won't space us anyway? They can't have us around. Our only chance is to get a big pay off so we have enough cash to hide from them."

"I don't know. I shouldn't have gotten into this."

"You should have thought of that before you lost so much at the casino!"

"Shuddup! Hey, what was that?"

"I don't know. Is that thought screen still on?"

"It looks like it. How do we know if it works?"

"Moron; because no marines are busting down the door."

"There, again! Over by the…"

The first marine into the warehouse found the two teens bound and gagged in their chairs. The two kidnappers lay lifeless, face down, nearby, a reddish grey liquid oozing out of their ears.

****

"We never saw anything coming. We were outside the gym, then we woke up in that warehouse."

"They used a thought screen to hide the danger. We could not see it either."

It won't work again. On any of us.

The symbiots. They've modified us again.

Great! What happens when…

CJ and I will teach you how to block that.

Will that work when we're…you know, not concentrating on it?

I was recently an adolescent male, remember?

Oh, right.

Art, I don't need to be reminded of what you mean by that!

Sorry, mom.

****

Theresa Chapel
The Cygnus Shipyards
Standard Earth Date July 4 3834

Cling-cling-cling-cling! Admiral Of The Fleet Alex MacAlister stretched up to his 6'8" height as he tapped his Champaign glass for the reception guests' attention.

"Today, we celebrate the wedding of Phyllis Mor Jones and Jerome Kowalski Junior. I can not think of two kinder people, or of two people who belong together more. Phyll, Jerry, may your days be filled with joy and laughter."

That was a lovely toast, Alex.

Well, Jen wrote it.

"Alex, thank you. You have been my friend since we were Navy brats terrorizing the grade school teachers at Hampton Roads Naval Base. My future will be a happy one because of you.

"Phyllis, you are the most amazing woman I have ever met. I am truly complete with your love. Words fail to describe my happiness on this day. Thank you so much."

"OOH-RAH!" boomed from the Marines' table as the guests' lifted their glasses to the toast.

"Nineteen years ago, my brother called me to say he had given my number to a love-stricken young woman. He'd done that before, but something in his voice said this was different, more than just a CAG looking out for his pilot. That young woman kept me on the comm for three hours; before we said goodbye, she had became my best friend.

"Today she has become my sister. And I couldn't be happier!" Jen wiped the tears from her cheeks as Phyllis stood up and gave her a hug.

"Growing up without meeting your father can be very difficult. Graduations, proms, dances, tennis meets could all seem to have something missing. These two we honor today, along with John, the world's best big brother, never let me feel there was anything missing from my life. And they all made sure I knew…who my father was…" CJ stopped for a moment, bringing her hand to her nose, then continued; "Jerry, Mom, you have always been there for me. I love you both so much! I am so happy you have finally come together. Some things are just meant to be."

Phyllis stood and hugged her daughter for a moment before turning to look at the guests.

"My life has been truly blessed. All of you here today, Alex, Jen, Cindy, who was my mom when I needed it the most, Little CJ; CJ; and now Jerry.

"Little CJ, you scared me. I had no idea how to raise a baby. I look at you today, and I can see the wonderful woman you are becoming. Babygirl, I am so proud of you! Little CJ, you start at the Academy this fall! My baby girl is all grown up!

"Jerry, you mentored me when I was a clueless rookie. You made sure I was always on the correct heading. You looked out for me when I was too preoccupied to take care of myself. You supported me when I lost my foundation. You reminded me what love is. I am truly blessed to be with you.

"And I have to thank one more. Chester, you made me understand what true love is. You gave me CJ. And, along the way, managed to save the universe. I can never forget you."

Why, Angus, you're crying. You big softy!
Just too much spice in the dinner.
We haven't eaten yet!
I love you, Cindy.
I know, Handsome. I love you too.
Hey, gorgeous, do you have any plans for after the shindig?
I do now!

****

Sims Chapel
New Kintyre
Standard Earth Date August 2 3838

Cindy and Angus MacAlister looked around the chapel. Many of their friends were there, Admiral Perry, Admiral Shin, Jodi and Bill Campbell; even Trine had come. All wore full formal dress kilts, even though the vast majority was much younger, two generations younger. These were friends of Alex and Jen, Phyllis, CJ and Jerry, John and Janice, and, since it was their wedding, of Little CJ and Artair.

Angus held his wife's hand as they stood and watched the bride walk down the aisle on Jerry's arm. Angus thought she was really glowing, but Cindy would later pooh-pooh that. Artair stood, tall and handsome in his dress kilt, on the altar, totally absorbed in the vision of his bride. *Life is good,* Angus thought. *The life they have ahead of them will be some adventure!*

Angus looked over at Alex and Jen, and then moved his gaze to Phyllis, then to John and Janice. *All of us are here,* Angus thought, *every one of the symbiots, and the two Protectors, and the parents of The Galloglaigh…*

The hair on Angus' neck stood up. He saw John and Janice straighten too. Cindy grabbed his arm.

Every damn time I think life is good…

Angus, stop it!

Yes, Dear. Alex, Jen, Phyll, Jerry, Ito, Pete, John, Janice, CJ, Artair; do you see it? We are all here, one big, fat and happy target.

"Dearly beloved, We are gathered here today in the presence of God to join this man and this woman in holy marriage,"

Yes. We have an hour; let's finish the wedding.

John, are you sure?

"Who gives this woman to be married to this man?"

I have twenty BBs in system, Dad.

"We, her Mother, her Father, and I do"

It's a group of two hundred projectiles, 80 thousand tons, headed here at zero-point-nine-nine C.

The projectiles are a diversion.

"I, Artair MacAlister, take you, Cynthia Jenitka Jones, to be my wedded wife, to have and to hold, from this day forward, for the better, as for the worse, for richness, as for poverty, in sickness, as in health, to love, to nurture, and to cherish, till death do us part"

Everyone relax. We have it under control. Trine, please have your ships ready to accelerate the planet zero-point-zero-zero-three percent. CJ's and

Artair's thoughts surprised everyone.

"I, Cynthia Jenitka Jones, take you, Artair MacAlister, to be my wedded husband, to have and to hold, from this day forward, for the better, as for the worse, for richness, as for poverty, in sickness, as in health, to love, to nurture, and to cherish, till death do us part"

Angus, there are two of our ships orbiting New Kintyre. They aren't for defense. They're for propulsion. With our tractor beams, we could move the planet enough to cause the projectiles to miss.

Thank you, Trine.

"This ring I give to you in token and pledge of our constant faith and abiding love. With this ring, I wed you, and pledge my everlasting faithful love"

Angus and Cindy watched their grandson's wedding with nerves on edge. *I wonder what the real attack will be?*

It is outside the chapel. There are four heavy rail guns and six plasma cannon circling the church at ranges of eight to twelve hundred meters. They plan to open fire when we leave.

"Cynthia Jenitka, and Artair, I now pronounce you husband and wife. What God has created and so joined, let nothing and no man put asunder."

There are no ground forces here to take them out. We need air strikes from the BBs.

"Flotilla reports, 'targets acquired and locked', Captain."

"Flotilla Alpha, activate Red Beams, *FIRE!*, *FIRE!*, *FIRE!*" Captain Alimonte watched as the two hundred planet-killer projectiles were vaporized in the twenty Red Beams.

The BBs won't launch; there will be an Air Control 'malfunction'. Airstrikes will take them out though.

"General Marx, we are in position."

"All units, execute Operation Trash Day."

Across the twenty Fortiter Class battleships that made up Flotilla Alpha, marines moved into place and arrested Air Control officers and hangar bay maintenance staff identified as traitors and co-conspirators. On every ship, the loyal sailors, officers and marines couldn't help but notice the lack of tattoos on the right shoulders of the traitors.

The wedding ceremony ended as the music began playing. Twenty-four SF-12 Mustangs from the 524th flew past at high subsonic speed. The homing missiles had been released from over the horizon, so the explosions happened as the fighters' contrails arched with the crossed Claymores over the bride and groom leaving the chapel. To the guests showering them with rice, it all looked like one big fireworks show.

Angus looked over at John and Janice. His gaze was just in time to see them turn and offer a slight nod to each other.

John, Janice; good work.

Angus, we did not do this. CJ and Artair did.

They don't need your protection anymore, do they?

No, they do not.

So, when is your wedding?

John and Janice stared into each other's eyes as smiles blossomed on their faces.

The grandfather of the bride smiled the rest of the day.

****

General Aerospace Building
55th Floor
New Manhattan
New Kintyre
Standard Earth Date August 3 3838

"Again, we have failed. Who planned this, this disaster?"

"I did."

The laser was not visible to those around the huge mahogany conference table. The hole it made in the man's forehead was.

"We need to find some more subtle avenues of attack. Perhaps something less…hurried."

"It's not just him we must target now."

We can ignore him. The young ones are whom we must destroy.

"They are well protected. It will be hard to get close."

They will be able to see everything. We will be exposed.

"That can not happen."

We need a new approach.

About James W. McAllister

I am a Registered Respiratory Therapist living near Syracuse in Central New York State. Currently I am employed in Healthcare Accreditation. I founded Fortiter Publishing LLC in November 2013 as a vehicle to get all these great Science Fiction and Fantasy stories out of my head.

"FORTITER" is inscribed on the MacAlister Clan Crest. The word means "to go forward, boldly." I am grateful for the Clan Chief's permission to use the Crest and Tartan in my company's logo, and to use "FORTITER" in my company's name.

I have been interested in science fiction since reading the Lensmen Series of books by E. E. "Doc" Smith in Junior High School. TV shows like Star Trek and Battlestar Galactica, as well as movies such as Robinson Crusoe on Mars and Star Wars further peaked my interest in the genre.

See my Amazon Author's page here:

http://amazon.com/author/jwmcallister

If you enjoyed my story, please leave a review.

Other James W. McAllister Books

STARCLAN Book I
THE TURRET
Starclan Foundation

STARCLAN Book II
THE BEST LAID PLANS
Birth of the Starclan

STARCLAN Book III
A MATTER OF HONOR
Starclan Chrysalis 2015

RODS
A John Martin Story

THE PAGE
The Year of the Dragons

THE UNIVERSE, While You Wait
28 short stories to read while you wait

.